"Look out!" shouted one of the Pangbars, his hand coming up as if to ward off a blow.

The freed huge show beast began to sweep about with its front legs, its long, pointed hooves making impressive gouges in the furniture where it struck. The other animals became angry and restive.

The senior officer of the Guard rushed toward the enormous animal, bringing up his ceremonial flail to strike. The creature beat him to the blow, its enormous reach giving it fatal advantage. In a single, savage knock with its massive foreleg it smashed the officer's skull and shoulder before the rest of the company was able to move.

As the officer collapsed, more of the Guards came at a run, and moved to protect the Comes Riton. While the Guard faltered, shaken by what they had seen, from the audience Haakogard, commander of the Harriers, drew his stunner from the concealed pocket in his sleeve and fired, hoping that the charge would be enough to slow the animal.

There were screams in the room now as the animals, freed from the bondage of their trainers, went after the sudden bounty around them, snagging for arms and legs with pointed hooves and claws.

"Harriers!" Haakogard shouted, hoping some of the crew could hear over the sudden outburst of noise. "Stunners on!"

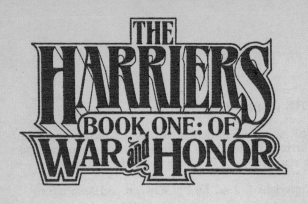

# THE HARRIERS
## BOOK ONE: OF
## WAR and HONOR

# Created by

# GORDON R. DICKSON

BAEN BOOKS

THE HARRIERS

This is a work of fiction. All the characters and events portrayed in this book are fictional, and any resemblance to real people or incidents is purely coincidental.

Copyright © 1991 by Bill Fawcett and Associates

A Baen Books Original

Baen Publishing Enterprises
P.O. Box 1403
Riverdale, N.Y. 10471

ISBN: 0-671-72048-1

Cover art by Studio H

First printing, April 1991

Distributed by
SIMON & SCHUSTER
1230 Avenue of the Americas
New York, N.Y. 10020

Printed in the United States of America

# Contents

# OF WAR AND CODES AND HONOR

## Gordon R. Dickson and Chelsea Quinn Yarbro

## 1

Four *Katana*-class Skimmers came slicing down out of the clouds in diamond formation at over twice the speed of sound, their very profiles lethal; bright sunlight glinted on their vanes and the red horse-head symbol of the Petit Harriers—not that any of them had ever seen a horse.

In the lead ship, Line Commander Goren Haakogard watched the surveill screens display the terrain underneath the clouds. It was a rocky, forbidding place, this Neo Biscay, inhospitable: all he was seeing was canyons, gullies and occasional high, arid plateaus. Of the five main land masses, most were rugged, jagged upthrusts and abrupt defiles showing the struggles and pressures deep in the core of the place. The two colonies that had settled three of the small continents eighteen and sixteen generations back, respectively, had scratched and scrambled their way from barest survival to a civilization of sorts.

"We got something coming in to port," said Line Commander Haakogard's Executive Officer, Mawson

Tallis, a tall, angular kid from Buttress with an aristocratic accent and a threadbare uniform. "Coming very slow. Subsound speeds, in fact."

"That slow?" Haakogard asked, still watching the surveills for signs of the capital city of the second-largest continent. They were expected to arrive there within the hour.

"Subsound," Tallis confirmed as he read over the calculations. "No chance of being overtaken, but they could fire on us. Shells or lasers could catch us."

"Why would they do that?" asked Haakogard. His eyebrows went up. "The Comes poMoend invited us here. This is his territory according to the documents at the Hub." The fretwork of lines at the corners of his eyes deepened in a quick, cynical smile. "They sent for us, didn't they? Maybe they're an escort?"

"Doesn't act like an escort," said the navigator, a soft-spoken woman from the junior branch of the most ancient family on Xiaoqing. She brushed her dark-blue hair back from her brow. "No hailing, no sign of welcome or formal acknowledgment, and I don't think the heading we've been given will get us to Civuto poMoend."

The youngest of the eight human crew members, she was going out of her way to show herself a real professional.

"And the device on the wings doesn't match the one for poMoend," she added. "In fact, we don't have it on file anywhere."

"How much doesn't match poMoend?" asked Haakogard, catching sight of a wide road on the ground. It was promising, very promising. He tapped his hailer. "Follow to starboard," he ordered the other three Katanas in the formation. "Dachnor, drop back five lengths, just in case." This last was to the ship directly behind him. "Check out the company."

"Done," said Group Chief Eben Dachnor, who

had been in the Petit Harriers for sixteen years, all of them active, and would sound just as laconic if they were under heavy fire from a superior foe and going down.

"The device for poMoend is a four-leafed stem. That ship . . ." Navigator Zim looked toward the screen and revised her figure. "Those ships. There are six of them, Line Commander. They have five leaves on the stem."

"Relatives!" It was an expletive and a question all at once. It always came down to relatives. Haakogard looked to his protocol officer. "Well? What now?"

"Put on the poMoend hail. It can't hurt," she answered, not bothering to look at the screens. "If they have any questions about us, the hail will reassure them; they'll probably leave us alone. We're newcomers. Could be they don't recognize the Petits. But they know their own hailings. Everything we know about the place says they'll respect the hail. If they don't, then we're free to leave."

"We return fire?" asked Tallis, not hiding his anticipation. He had been hankering for a battle since he came aboard the *Yngmoto*.

"It's up to them to make the first move," said Haakogard, trying to curb Tallis' eagerness. "At the speed they're going we can outrun them; no contest."

"What if they're faster than they've shown us? It could be a ploy, their coming up slowly to catch us off-guard," Tallis said.

"We'll find out," Haakogard answered.

He signed to the navigator to start the poMoend hailing on all frequencies. "Zim, keep an eye on them!"

"Done," said Zim, concentrating on her screens. "How are we doing down below? Do you know where we are?"

"No break in the cloud cover, but there's signs of

civilization down there—I've got three roads now, and there's a town of sorts up ahead." Haakogard did not like to divide his attention between the unknown ships following them and the job of finding Civuto poMoend. Technically he didn't have to, but he did not like to delegate his command in tight situations.

"I think we're on track," he said.

"About time," said Section Leader Jarrick Riven. "I've got the other three Katanas in my screen. Group Chief Dachnor's holding further to the rear, as ordered. Fennin, number two, has more company. Three ships, by the look of it."

"Same as the others?" Haakogard asked, glancing at his own screen to try to pick up the new ship.

"A dozen of them now," said Zim, then added, "Straight poMoend devices on the newcomers; four leaves." Haakogard's hand hesitated over the alert button. If the new ships were a second part of an attack force . . .

He looked toward the oddest member of his crew, the squat, eight-limbed, single-eyed Mromrosi. The only of the crew who was not a Petit Harrier, he represented the Emerging Planet Fairness Court and was supposed to be an impartial observer. None of the humans knew and the Mromrosi would not accurately explain which of his species' six sexes he was; everyone referred to him as "he" for convenience. Luckily—and unlike the other nine species of the Emerging Planet Fairness Court—the Mromrosi thought humans and human descendents were quaint, while humans tended to regard the Mromrosi as cute.

"What do you think, Advisor?" The Mromrosi tossed his enormous mop of curly pink hair. From time to time the Mromrosi changed color, though the reasons were not always apparent.

"Things done in haste are definitionally unconsidered acts," he replied.

"That they are," said Zim, who always got a kick out of the things the Mromrosi said, which she insisted were aphorisms.

"The guys behind us are going home," reported the voice of Group Chief Dachnor from the rear Katana. "I don't know if it was the hail or the other guys showing up that did it."

"We'll find out," said Haakogard, hoping he would. He moved his hand from the alert button. He could not afford to let himself be pressured into a defensive position unless it absolutely could not be avoided.

"So, no fight today," said Tallis, not entirely pleased it was so. He lifted his hand to the others; two answered his gesture and a couple others whispered a cheer.

"Life's always interesting in the Petits," said Riven, grinning at the relief on the faces of the crews of the other three Katanas. "You can say that about the service."

"Better than the Grands." Zim knew mockery in Riven's words when she heard it. "You can have your parades and pomp and titles and gold braid; I'd rather be in the Petits any day. You do something worthwhile when you're a Petit."

She shot a single, angry look at Riven.

"And unlike you, I could qualify for the Grands, but I didn't want to."

Riven leaned back and chuckled. "That's right; you're the forty-third cousin of some old First Fifty-Six Colonist, isn't that it? Just because we can't authenticate our patent of arms—" Zim said nothing. He knew she would not dignify his slight with an answer. "Say, look; those new guys are trying to form some kind of an escort. What do you know?"

"They're sending out the poMoend hail," said Group Leader Viridis Perzda, the protocol officer, her very ordinary face showing no reaction at all; people often thought that meant she was not paying attention or did not care about what was going on, which was their first mistake.

"Assessments are in order," said the Mromrosi, uncharacteristically direct.

"We'd better slow down so they don't think we're trying to outrun them," said Haakogard, and thumbed the deceleration toggle. "And cancel the poMoend hail in case they have something they want to tell us." He signaled the fourth Katana at his rear. "Dachnor, close up as we slow down. I want diamond formation when we land."

"Done," said Dachnor. "These guys are okay, you think?"

"Apparently. They've got the password and the hail," said Haakogard, feeling the tension between his shoulders begin to ease; a decade ago the strain would not have bothered him. And a decade ago, he reminded himself, he was only a Minor Group Chief and did not have assignments like this one.

He leaned back in his command couch and reviewed all the surveill screens.

"There's a city down there, up ahead a little way," he said. "It's got to be Civuto poMoend. It fits the description. There's nothing else that big between here and the coast." He looked at the screen and did the calculations in his head. "Ten Standard Minutes out, I make it, fifteen to twenty if we go slow."

Communications Leader Alrou Malise straightened up his own stiff back, at his station. So different from Gascoygne, the Harriers, he thought. He had fled the rigid, nightmarish society of his birth-world for the freedom of this, three years before he was technically permitted to join the force. But the habits of youth die hard—he knew most of the crew thought him sullen.

"This is the *Katana*-class Skimmer *Yngmoto* of the

Petit Harriers of the Magnicate Alliance, Line Commander Goren Haakogard commanding, and accompanied by the three *Katana*-class Skimmers *Freyama*, *Sigjima*, and *Ubehoff*. We are here at the behest of the Comes Riton poMoend and the orders of the Alliance."

The response came quickly, heard in all four Alliance ships. "Welcome, ships of the Magnicate Alliance. We will guide you to the Most Excellent Comes Riton. Be certain you always address him as 'Most Excellent.' All others are to be spoken of in his presence as Mere: as the True First, only he deserves the Most Excellent title."

"What was that all about?" asked Haakogard when Group Leader Perzda had finished all the proper formalities. "That thing about being the True First?"

"I don't know, but you can bet they do. They'll expect us to, as well. Be sure you pay attention when they talk about it." Perzda put her six-fingered hands together. "Well, I suppose you'll want me to figure it out as soon as possible."

"Yes," said Haakogard. "And find out what the story is on those ships that moved in on us. Everything you can."

"Done," said Perzda. She was amused, but she hid that in back of her ordinary brownish eyes; for in addition to being the protocol officer for the ship, she was also their spy.

Civuto poMoend was an uneasy hybrid of a very new and advanced engineering and architecture, the kind that was found throughout the Alliance, and an ancient, convoluted series of hodge-podge, interconnected buildings dating back to the founding of the city.

On the ride to the headquarters of the Most Excellent Comes Riton, Line Commander Haakogard observed the abrupt transition of styles. This puzzled him. Had there been fighting or a natural disaster that had destroyed part of the center of the city? Or was it simply result of the desires of the Comes Riton himself?

"How did all this happen?" he asked, waving at the stylistic jungle to the leader of the delegation that met them at the travelport.

"A war. There is always a war," answered Pangbar Thunghalis poTorMoend, a massive individual whose Pangbar rank had translated roughly as "gate breaker." "Of late, it has been worse."

"Nuh-huh," said Haakogard. With any luck that remark would be interpreted as positive or negative, depending upon which Thunghalis found appropriate.

"The last phase of the Most Excellent Comes was heartbroken by the tragedy that brought the war inside the gates. There are those who said it hurried his death. It is a dreadful thing when honor is forgotten," said Thunghalis. Haakogard heard strong emotion in his voice. "It would never have happened if Syclicis had not stolen the clone when she did."

There had been something in their mission briefing about clones, but at the moment Haakogard could not call it to mind. It looked now as if his earlier lack of attention to this could be serious oversight. What else had he overlooked—or not been told?

Clones, he said to himself, hoping that the word would jar the rest of the information loose. Clones. Clones. No luck.

"How long ago was that? The theft, I mean," he asked Thunghalis.

"Thirty-four years. Consider the omen in that!" Thunghalis rolled his eyes upward to acknowledge the enormity of the portent in the figure. "Thirty-four years."

"Nuh-huh," said Haakogard again, keeping to safe ground.

"You can hardly blame the Most Excellent Comes Riton for his fears, and with the conduct of the clone, he has reason for his actions." Thunghalis did something with his hands that Haakogard suspected was intended to counteract bad fortune.

"It's that serious?" Haakogard probed blindly. He had to discover what he and his Harriers had got into. "After all, a clone—"

"Exactly! Of the True First!" Thunghalis fairly pounced on the word. "We had to send for you, of course. You can see that. We cannot act honorably without your presence. What else would be acceptable? No matter which clone we oppose, we commit treason against the True First."

Haakogard was still confused, but a little less so than when their conversation began.

"Forgive the fact I don't quite follow you, Pangbar Thunghalis. Perhaps my briefing was incomplete."

He was really getting angry at the lack of information he had been given.

"As if such delicate questions could be explained in a briefing," scoffed Thunghalis, his expression dour. "No wonder you did not know the proper address for the Most Excellent Comes. I am disappointed in the Magnicate Alliance."

"You have every right to be," said Haakogard. Time to start smoothing over relations now. "I share your disappointment. But knowing how vast the Alliance is, I'm not surprised that we didn't get full information concerning Neo Biscay."

Thunghalis pouted, still unappeased.

"I'm sure you are aware of the difficulty in obtaining accurate translations, even with the Series 81Vs. Often there's a slight shift in meaning between one language and another. This may be such a case, considering the differing status clones have throughout the Alliance. Many of the Alliance worlds do not permit cloning of humans. I come from such a planet myself. On Grunhavn all we're permitted to clone is trees."

"Fools, then, if you trust to open breeding," said Thunghalis with scorn. "To disallow so natural and sensible a thing as a clone, and give favor to the caprice of the genetic code. When one being has proven satisfactory in every way, isn't it wiser to renew that being rather than take chances on another genetic shuffle?"

He laughed at his own joke, though the sound was more of a honk than a laugh.

"Is that your usual way of . . . reproducing? You don't appear to have the facilities for so ambitious—" Inwardly Haakogard was cursing the Commodore and administrators of the Petit Harriers for being so lax in their preparations for this mission. He had always suspected that the head of Alliance Intelligence Operations was more political than patriotic in his devotion to the Magnicate Alliance, but rarely had Knapp so blatantly revealed himself.

"Not for most people, no. As you observe, the process is complex and requires more support than we are in a position to give. It is the aim of the Most Excellent Comes to make such a project possible, but that is still many phases away. Of course, our leaders are clones."

He gestured toward the enormous building ahead of them, a collection of huge, jewel-like bubbles and shining curlicues. "The Comes' palace."

As the vehicle stopped, Thunghalis gave Haakogard a quizzical look. "Well?"

"Well?" Haakogard stared hard at it. "It's a very impressive palace." Especially, he added to himself, out in this desolate stretch of land on this remote planet.

But Thunghalis was not appeased. He made an exasperated gesture. "Isn't it proof that it is best for leaders to continue as the being you know?" he said. "Beings who have proven themselves? Don't you think that cloning prevents all manner of conflicts and difficulties?"

"I must say it sounds sensible," said Haakogard carefully. Inwardly, he was only further convinced it was idiotic. He followed Thunghalis down a wide corridor, thinking he would have preferred his crew to be with him. But he remembered that this was forbidden.

"My people are being taken care of?" he asked.

"Of course!" said Thunghalis, stiffly. "You will meet them later. They are being properly entertained; you need not fear. The Most Excellent Comes Riton knows the correct way to receive guests and is always ready to make their stay memorable."

Haakogard hated ceremony, display and courtly functions. It had been one of the reasons he had joined the Petits instead of the Grands—over strong family objections. Now, it seemed, he was having to endure them anyway.

"No doubt," he said, reminding himself that "memorable" was not necessarily the same as "hideous." He attempted to appear respectful but nonchalant; a combination he had been working on for the last seventeen years and had yet to perfect.

"It isn't fitting for them to come into his presence until you have been established as a First. Otherwise, who can say which among you might assume the position for himself?"

Thunghalis made a sign, and two very tall, gold-studded doors swung open, revealing a reception room that would comfortably hold all four Katana

Skimmers and a traveling circus besides without crowding.

"Very impressive," said Haakogard, his admiration the first honest response he had been able to make since Thunghalis had picked him up. This time it was not an effort to put a better face on his response.

"It is a tribute to the Most Excellent Comes Riton. He caused it to be built in his second phase and, naturally, it has suited him ever since." Thunghalis continued across the room, motioning for Haakogard to follow.

"And was that long ago?" Haakogard asked as he tagged after the long-legged Thunghalis.

"Well, the Most Excellent Comes Riton is in his eighth phase now, so it was over three hundred Standard Years since his second phase. Let me see . . . 348 Standard Years. But that is nothing to a True First." He clapped his tremendous hands twice, making a point definitely, and indicated a place on the patterned floor where he wanted Haakogard to stand. "He will be here very shortly."

"Fine," said Haakogard, wondering what it was proper for him to do while he waited. Should he talk about something? Whistle? He needed Perzda here to work out the protocol. Well, there was still Thunghalis. "Before he gets here, would you help me out?" he improvised. "Can you fill me in about the current war? I don't think I know as much as I need to."

"Small wonder you should say so. It is a terrible tale," he began with such enthusiasm that Haakogard stared at him. "The Comes Riton, being the True First, has many potential phases waiting for vivification, for all True Firsts come from a single budding of clones, so there will be no genetic drift possible. The proto-embryonic clones are kept viable and are vivified at the order of the current phase. The immediately previous phase of the Comes Riton ordered his next-phase clone vivified, all in accord with our scientific traditions, and ordered an alternate vivified at the same time, as is the practice. Of course, the alternate is—"

"Wait a minute," said Haakogard. "An alternate? What do you mean? What alternate?"

"I was about to explain. Every Comes has an alternate to take over the phase should anything befall him before he is given the flail and the reins. The alternate is trained as the Comes himself is, and in every way is like the Comes, except he is the alternate. Once the Comes is authenticated and is in possession of the flail and the reins, the alternate is devivified. As should have been the case for this phase—all perfectly proper, you see. But then!"

He threw up his hands.

"There was a rebellion?" Haakogard ventured, for that was what he had been told. Some of the earlier colonists had mounted a revolution and attempted to overthrow the later colonists.

"Hardly anything so significant," said Thunghalis contemptuously. "But a group of malcontents from the Other Colonization managed to infiltrate the Comes' clonery. We believe they were trying to destroy all the clones, for they rely solely on open breeding—they make a religion of it, almost. You can imagine the chaos of their society, with no continuing leadership."

He looked at Haakogard, expecting to see his horror shared. Haakogard did his best to comply.

"But I gather they didn't succeed?" he asked. Since Civuto poMoend was still the headquarters of the Comes Riton, it seemed a safe bet.

"They made off with the alternate. We were all outraged, as you may well imagine. With the current phase of the Most Excellent Comes Riton ruling now, there are hints that the Other Colonists will bring forth the alternate to challenge his authenticity. It is a dreadful predicament for all of us." Pangbar Thunghalis made a movement with his shoulders to indicate his perplexity. "The alternate is a True First, a viable clone of the Comes Riton, and he can be authenticated just as the Comes himself can. Those of us who are in the service of the Comes Riton have all taken a blood oath to defend the Comes Riton unto death, and to oppose all who come against him. Where does our duty lie, with *two* Comes Ritons? We cannot attack the Comes Riton in any phase, and we cannot attack his alternate: both are perfidious treason and would disgrace our families. If the men with the alternate attack us, we cannot act, for the alternate is . . ."

He made a sound like a cough that Haakogard suspected was a sigh. "We cannot take any actions whatever." He slapped his hand to his wide forehead. "What else could we do but send for you? You, at least, can act."

"Aha," said Haakogard, still baffled but now with a better notion of the stakes of the game, and its rule. "Are we to recover this alternate . . . uh, phase?" Was that the right way to discuss this other clone?

"Of course, of course," said Thunghalis impatiently, but with every sign that he had something else in mind. "He must surely be recovered. That is necessary. But we must not betray honor in making the recovery."

Haakogard was about to ask why such a recovery would compromise honor when a four-man escort entered the chamber to the sound of huge bells, so deep in tone that the room trembled at their sound. Another man in a gaudier version of what the others were wearing came forward and bowed to Thunghalis.

Haakogard doubted this was the Comes Riton; and he turned out to be right. The man was some kind of herald, who in a high, loud voice began to rattle off the titles and virtues of the Comes Riton from the first phase until that very afternoon. The entire recitation required about ten Standard Minutes and Haakogard did his best to listen politely.

Finally the Most Excellent Comes Riton himself came forward.

Haakogard looked at him with real curiosity: he was a man just turning from youth to maturity; he was not much more than average height, but he had a massive chest and broad shoulders that more than made up for it. His hair was bronze and his eyes were the color of sand. When he spoke, his voice was soft and resonant, the kind that would carry without being raised, that would provide the illusion of profundity by its nature; a beautiful voice. Haakogard realized that the voice more than any other asset made the Comes Riton a leader.

"They tell me your rank is Mere Line Commander," were his first words to Haakogard. He raised his hand to his shoulder to enable Haakogard to press his palm with his own.

"That's correct, Most Excellent Comes," said Haakogard. He was cautious but did not want to appear hesitant. He used a standard greeting, knowing that it might not be entirely right, but it was also not entirely wrong. "It is an honor to meet you."

"Most surely; one rarely granted to those not of poMoend," said the Comes Riton. "How worthy of you to acknowledge it." He gestured toward Thunghalis. "I trust my faithful Mere Pangbar has seen to your needs?"

"He has brought me to you, Most Excellent Comes. It is my mission to see to *your* needs, I believe."

Haakogard thought he handled that rather neatly and was pleased when Thunghalis smiled an approval.

"If such a thing is possible." The Comes Riton scowled and spoke at a deeper, more mesmerizing pitch. "For what are my needs? Who can answer that, with the alternate clone still vivified and in the hands of the Other Colonists?"

He stared at some point about six meters behind Haakogard's head.

"I ought to sense him, because we are the same," he went on. "But I don't, not that I am aware. But it may be that I sense him so naturally that I give no attention to it and do not recognize it for what it is."

He shifted his eyes back to Haakogard.

"What do you think?"

"I haven't been here long enough to have an opinion, Most Excellent Comes," said Haakogard, carefully.

Comes Riton considered the answer and made the spread-palm gesture of approval. "You are astute, Mere Line Commander. You give me a little hope. Hope! After so long a time and so many disappointments. My alternate must be rescued. How can I remain authenticated while the alternate continues to act against me? It must be resolved. That much is certain. My former phase demanded it of me, which, as he and I are one and the same, more than father and son, and the alternate and I are one and the same, more than twin brothers, I can do no less. Blood and gene call out, and blood and gene will answer."

The ringing tones of his last words made them a battle cry. He looked expectantly toward Haakogard.

It was tempting to applaud, but Haakogard only said, "We'll do what we can, Most Excellent Comes." He saw the fervid light come into Thunghalis' eyes. "As soon as you can present us with all the pertinent information, we'll set about . . . finding this alternate and working out a peace settlement."

"Good. Good. A wonderful beginning. What a relief your coming here is, Mere Line Commander." The Comes Riton stood back but in no way gave ground. "I have asked for the pleasure of the company of your crew tonight. There will be a banquet for you where you will sit in places of favor. Does that please you?"

Haakogard, seeing another endless official function before him, bowed in his best court form. "We're not used to such courtesy, Most Excellent Comes."

"I know," said the Comes Riton complacently. "I understand it is left to the Grand Harriers, not the Petits; but under the circumstances there is no reason not to host you properly. We are not quite a backwater here."

If Neo Biscay were not a backwater, thought Haakogard, the Grands would be here, not the Petits. As it was, the Commodore had not ruled out the possibility that the Grands might be needed on Neo Biscay if the poMoend succession were not straightened out.

"We'll appreciate that, I'm sure," he said, now making a slightly different, complicated ritual bow he had just remembered was the one the Most Excellent Comes preferred, according to Haakogard's briefing. "You show us more favor than we deserve. Perhaps you should wait until we have done something before you honor us."

The Comes Riton smiled a little. "A bit old-fashioned but well done, Mere Line Commander." His smile deepened. "But I am something of an old-fashioned fellow myself—it's in the genes." His chuckle was dutifully echoed by Haakogard and Thunghalis. "We are prepared to offer you some entertainment, of course. We do not expect you to dine with us and protect us without any acknowledgement of your service."

"That would be dishonorable?" Haakogard guessed.

"Very," said Thunghalis softly.

"We have arranged for animal trainers to come with their beasts. On such short notice it is the best we can manage." The Comes Riton made a gesture that was as close to an apology as he could come. "They are reputed to be the best that can be had."

"Your men?" asked Haakogard, anticipating the answer.

"We do not sully ourselves with the training of wild beasts," said the Comes Riton, as if such sentiments were universal. "We leave that to the degenerates who came here earlier."

Haakogard clenched his jaw. When he spoke, he made an effort not to sound upset. "What security measures are you taking?"

"Security?" echoed the Comes Riton. "What do we need of security? If we were to mount a guard beyond those appointed to the honor of guarding this phase, we would show ourselves to be cowards, afraid that we could suffer at the hands of the Other Colonists. What man of honor would do that?"

This announcement did not surprise Haakogard; he gave a fatalistic shrug. "You asked for the Petit Harriers to assist you, Most Excellent Comes. We can't do a very good job of it if you do nothing yourself."

"We will do all that is necessary," said the Comes Riton. "It is *not* necessary to bring in our fighting men because a few of the Other Colonists come here with animals. Only cravens take such action, and no craven is entitled to rule when demonstrably without honor. We will not dishonor poMoend by arming ourselves against animal trainers. We are not wretches."

"Certainly not," said Haakogard, thinking that the Comes Riton was an arrogant, pigheaded fool.

"Well, then, we are in agreement," said the Comes Riton.

"We understand each other," corrected Haakogard.

The Comes Riton paid no attention to Haakogard's implication. "I will leave you to make your arrangements. You are welcome in Civuto poMoend, Mere Line Commander Petit Harrier."

"You're most gracious, Most Excellent Comes," said Haakogard, convinced that there were other words he would rather use.

Thunghalis motioned his approval once more as he turned to follow the Most Excellent Comes from his reception hall.

In the end, all thirty-five Petit Harriers had to attend the banquet. The Mromrosi went along out of curiosity.

The protocol officer was chewing on a Kleestick— one of her few indulgences—and leafing through a huge stack of documents just zapped in from the Magnicate Alliance Hub. "How'd it go?" she asked without formality as Haakogard stepped into the central cabin of the *Yngmoto*.

"You tell me." He reached for the red horse-head insignia on his wide, shiny collar and removed it, handing the tiny spool concealed in it to her. "As required, O Protocol Officer. Where is everyone?"

"Zim's asleep. She stood five watches straight, and so I told her to rest up." She leaned farther back in her chair, putting the documents aside. "Sometimes I wish you'd leave Riven in charge while you're gone, just for variety. It's beginning to pall on me. On the rest of us, too, I suspect."

"You're Protocol, Perzda. It's your job and you know it." Haakogard no longer argued with her about this, but went through a ritual of affectionate bickering on every new mission.

She took a deep breath, sighed, and took a second deep breath. "Tallis is working out again. He won't accept that he's always going to be skinny as a hoe-handle. Who knows what the Mromrosi is up to; he's in his quarters. The rest are out on local escort, taking in the sights of Civuto poMoend." The slight wrinkling of her nose expressed her opinion of the sightseeing opportunities on this desolate planet. "Dachnor's being leader on that." She reached out for the documents, but hesitated. "Goren, do you have any idea why this is so important?"

He did not answer her promptly. "I thought you knew. You're Alliance Intelligence Operations; I thought you'd be better briefed than I am. Or is this some kind of test? Something the Grands have dreamed up?"

"No test," she said with a single, decisive gesture. "It's just that, well . . . I don't know. I can't get rid of the nagging suspicion that something isn't . . . There's a piece missing, and it's missing on purpose. I always get nervous when that happens. I'm worried that the other piece is the Grands and they're up to something." She did her best to sound amused, then thought better of it. "I don't like it when I don't know the truth."

"Neither do I, Viridis," said Haakogard, and left her to continue with her documents. "None of us do."

In his quarters, he bathed and donned the most impressive uniform he had with him, the glistening one with the Petits' horse-head and the insignia of his rank picked out in jewels: the Senior Bunter had set it out for him, and Haakogard knew better than to argue with a Bunter. He studied himself in the mirror, thinking that age was starting—just starting, mind—to sink its claws into him. His dark-blond hair seemed lighter now that there were occasional strands of white through it. The lines around his eyes that used to show only when he laughed or squinted were there all the time now, and his cheeks were a bit more hollow than they had been at this stage of his last mission. There was no cure for it but dying young, Haakogard reminded himself, and smiled at his own vanity.

"Oh, no," exclaimed Jarrick Riven as he met Haakogard coming out of his quarters. "Not top dress."

"It's formal, it's court, and it's only third-class top, no capes or swords." He made a what-can-you-do shrug.

"And no stunners," said Riven, disgusted.

"Technically we shouldn't," said Haakogard. "But we'd better carry them."

"For effect?" Riven asked, startled.

A frown flicked Haakogard's brow. "If that's what they want to think, fine. But make sure they're charged."

Riven looked surprised. "Are you expecting trouble?"

Haakogard shook his head slowly. "No. That's what's bothering me. Given the lax state of their security and their unconscionable pride, I ought to be." He took a step away. "I'll make sure the Bunters are on notice."

But Riven wasn't quite through. "Is it true we all have to go?"

"Every last one of us, with the Mromrosi as well." He gave Riven a quick, ironic salute. "We've been through worse than this together. You survived the collapse of Feddalsi Oasis Station. You can survive a banquet on Neo Biscay."

"I could fight back at Feddalsi Oasis." Riven's snarl was not quite as humorous as he intended it to be, but he would not protest again.

All the Petits were assembling, gathering for their briefing for the banquet. Most of them took advantage of their dress uniforms to poke fun at one another.

In the full glory of her third-class top dress uniform, Group Leader Viridis Perzda still looked ordinary. Her hair was smartly arranged, her Bunter had applied the correct cosmetics for Neo Biscay, but she still looked unremarkable, which suited her very well.

In contrast, Navigator Nola Zim was spectacular, her jeweled uniform dyed to match her dark-blue hair; from her shoes to the last coil of her coiffure, she was an example of what was most splendid about the Magnicate Alliance. Perzda and Zim smiled at each other, enjoying their private joke.

"If you don't distract them," Perzda said wryly, "I can't think what will, short of the walls caving in." She looked at Communications Officer Alrou Malise. "You'll do for the rest." There was nothing in her expression to suggest that she was looking over each of the crew, but everything about them was etched into her mind. "Keep your translators handy and visible."

"And keep the stunners hidden," said Haakogard, who had joined them. He felt a familiar twinge of pride at the sight of his Petit Harriers.

Perzda shook her head. "I hope you know what you're doing, Goren."

"So do I," said Haakogard. "Go on."

She gave a little shake to her head and addressed the others again. "The spools in your insignias will give us a lot of information, so don't worry if you can't get everyone to open up. You can admit to known difficulties within the Alliance, but dismiss anything else as rumor, no matter how correct. You all know the drill. You've done it before. Keep your wits about you and don't get distracted. If there is something you don't understand, ask them to explain, no matter what it's about. We're more in the dark about this place than we thought and we've got to make up for that as quickly as possible, before we do something stupid. I want your reports before tomorrow morning." She glanced toward Haakogard. "Is there anything else, Line Commander?"

Haakogard considered. "Not really. I agree with everything our Protocol Officer has said. Don't stay together. Circulate. Be available. Pretend to be Grands"—he ignored the groan of protest from three of his crew—"and smile. Encourage them to talk. We don't know nearly enough about this place. Don't get dragged into any arguments. These people are very touchy about their honor, and we can't afford to get on their bad sides. And whatever else you do, no game and no gambling. This isn't Standby: this is Neo Biscay, and right now it's a cipher."

Since Jarrick Riven was the only member of the crew to have gambled on Standby, he was indignant. "That was a mistake! How long do I have to keep telling you that? How was I supposed to know about cutting off fingers? Besides, those guys have four arms and twenty-four fingers. They had an unfair advantage!" He laughed suddenly, and so did everyone else in the cabin.

"You took quite a chance," said Zim, grinning.

"Well, what else do you do out in the middle of nowhere?" he asked with tremendous innocence.

Hoots and hollers met his protestation, and Tallis shouted, "Nothing like a friendly wager, is there?"

"I'll wager you, you Buttress-bred—" Riven challenged in a comic threat.

More cries and chortles errupted. This time it was Haakogard who brought them to order.

"All right, all right. Save it for after. We're going to need straight faces for Civuto poMoend. Be good," said Haakogard as he put on his jeweled cap with the iridescent tassel. He hoped he did not look as foolish as he felt. "Let's go to work."

\* \* \*

As soon as the thirty-five Harriers and the Mromrosi were escorted into the banqueting hall, the Most Excellent Comes Riton exclaimed over the beautiful Navigator Zim, his magnificent voice sweet as warm syrup. He made the most banal observations seem like poetry. Navigator Zim seemed at once bemused and doubtful of the purpose for his singling her out.

From his vantage point at the next table over, Haakogard watched the Most Excellent Comes offer Navigator Zim the place beside him. "Does the Comes Riton have . . . how to put this? . . . many women in his life?"

"No. No, he does not." Thunghalis was troubled as he saw how the Comes danced attendance on Navigator Zim. He went on, slightly embarrassed. "He is a True First. It is not appropriate."

"Ah. Free breeding can be—" Whatever the rest of Haakogard's comments might be, they were shattered by a loud consort of brass instruments braying out to announce the meal and to signal the night closing of Civuto poMoend's gates.

"Is the closure necessary?" asked Haakogard, who did not like being away from the *Yngmoto*, no matter how well the Skimmer was secured. "Since you refused to post guards for this reception, I wouldn't have thought—"

"It's because of the Other Colonists. They attack the city at night. We make sure they cannot get in, and that way we do not dishonor ourselves with battle against those who are not our equals." He made a gesture of condemnation. "You know, it is because they came here first that they have forgotten civilization. We never were wholly lost. But they had over seven generations when they had no contact at all. There were N'djowul here part of the time, on the southernmost continent, and they had to abandon everything they had built there and take refuge here. It turned them into barbarians." Thunghalis shook his head. "So they come at night, as if we were N'djowul, too, and if they can get inside they do all manner of heinous things. They burn and kill and steal."

"That's very unfortunate," said Haakogard as he followed Thunghalis' example and took his place. "Are you sure you will be safe with the doors locked?"

"What harm can they do us, if they cannot get in?" Thunghalis asked.

For the time being Haakogard thought it wisest not to speculate.

There were over a hundred small L-shaped tables set around the room, each with a setting for five. Aside from the table of the Comes Riton himself, there appeared to be no obvious social order to where people sat, or with whom, though Haakogard suspected that such an order did exist. Thunghalis was careful to explain to Haakogard about the food they were served, once or twice warning him away from a questionable dish: "That merlle is an acquired taste, Mere Line Commander. You might like to try some of the s'was; we find most off-worlders prefer it." He made certain that Haakogard learned the names of everyone in attendance, and at the conclusion of the meal, while a troupe of animal-trainers demonstrated the skills of their charges, he did his best to explain the complicated relationships that were inherent in Second Colonization Neo Biscay families. "More attention is paid to lineage in the capital, of course, but we do our best to maintain the standards."

"Then let me see if I have this straight so far," said Haakogard when the evening was almost over and the animal trainers, dressed in bright, engulfing costumes, were being kept busy by over twenty dissimilar beasts, at least four of which had impressive, tusk-like fangs. "Because each phase of the Comes is a clone of the original Comes . . . would you call it original?"

"True First," corrected Thunghalis. He was more relaxed now than he had been earlier, mellowed with food and a strange concoction called Sand Juice, which apparently was mildly hallucinogenic. "The actual True First died long ago, but almost all his clones have lived long."

The animal trainers were building to a climax, creating an unlikely pyramid of very carnivorous-looking beasts, each of which seemed to dislike and distrust the others. "Come Riton was a True First, one of the Second Colonists, the group that was sent because it was believed the First Colony had been lost. You know already what had happened to the Other Colonists. In fact, they regarded the Second Colonists as a return of the gods, or some such thing, and for some time they behaved very sensibly toward us. We were able to establish our Colony with honor. But the Other Colonists did not remain as reasonable as they had been at first. They gradually came to resent our superior civilization and accomplishments, and rather than emulate us, they decided to plunder us instead." He nodded toward the Comes Riton. "To all intents and purposes, the Most Excellent Comes has been present since the conflict began."

"But not this phase," said Haakogard. He would have liked to enjoy a Kleestick but was told that the Comes Riton disapproved of the mildly intoxicating root, though he drank a fair share of Sand Juice.

"This phase, any phase, is precisely the same Comes Riton as he was at the beginning." Thunghalis looked around as the deep bells rang and rumbled again. "We rise," he whispered, tugging at Haakogard's sleeve.

Haakogard did as Thunghalis told him, and was

surprised to see the Comes Riton coming toward him, carrying a metallic gauntlet. His wonderful voice was as gripping as the echo of the bells. "We thank the Magnicate Alliance and the Most Distant Gods for aiding us in this time of need through these Petit Harriers. They can, without dishonor, attack our rivals and recover my alternate. We will then be in a position to restore civilization here, and to enter into a greater participation in the Alliance, which is a very dear wish to me, and has been since my first phase." He offered the gauntlet to Haakogard.

"Touch it but do not take it," Thunghalis said softly. "On the fingers only, not the palm."

Haakogard did as he was ordered. "We are pleased to assist all those who are friends of the Magnicate Alliance, for that is the task of the Petit Harriers," said Haakogard, trusting that he was close enough to court form to satisfy these aristocrats of Civuto poMoend.

"We have great hope," said the Comes Riton, making the air ring gloriously, "that none of our misfortune will dishonor you; your presence alone should serve to bring about a rapid settlement to the disruption. We anticipate the day when my authentication is assured and all hostilities cease."

"Good of you," said Haakogard. He wondered if he should say something about the hospitality he and his crew had been ordered to receive. The Mromrosi, near the kitchen door, was no help.

One of the animal trainers made a signal and the largest of the beasts lumbered onto its hind legs, making it almost three times the height of its trainer. Many of the guests stared at the creature, some of them showing anxiety, for it appeared that the trainers were having some difficulty with their enormous charge.

"Look out!" shouted one of the Pangbars, his hand coming up as if to ward off a blow.

The huge beast began to sweep about with its front legs, its long, pointed hooves making impressive gouges in the furniture where it struck. The other animals became angry and restive.

"Most Excellent Comes!" yelled the senior officer of his Guard as he rushed toward the enormous animal, bringing his ceremonial flail up to strike at it. The creature beat him to the blow, its enormous reach giving it fatal advantage before the Tydbar could get close enough to damage the animal. In a single, savage knock with its massive foreleg it smashed the Tydbar's skull and shoulder before the rest of the company was able to move.

As the Tydbar collapsed, more of the Guards came at a run, and Thunghalis moved to protect the Comes Riton.

The enormous metal gauntlet Haakogard had touched dropped onto the floor; a dozen of the poMoend soldiers cried out in horror.

While the poMoend Guard faltered, shaken by what they had seen, Haakogard drew his stunner from the concealed pocket in his sleeve and fired, hoping that the charge would be enough to slow the animal down. He was not certain where to aim, so he chose the neck, reckoning a stun on the spine would work best.

One of the trainers was being mauled by two of the other, smaller carnivores, but the rest of the entertainers had vanished, leaving their ferocious animals behind.

There were screams in the room now as the animals, freed from the bondage of their trainers, went after the sudden bounty around them, snagging for arms and legs with pointed hooves and claws.

"Harriers!" Haakogard shouted, hoping some of

the crew could hear over the sudden outburst of noise. "Stunners on!" He fired again, standing much too close to the huge creature to feel secure, but afraid to step back, in case he might endanger one of the others. There ought to be one or two more charges in his stunner, and then he would be without a working weapon.

The largest creature had dropped back onto its front legs and was beginning to wobble as it walked. It craned its neck and made a growling cough before it toppled forward.

Group Chief Eben Dachnor had already stunned two of the smaller animals into unconsciousness and was stalking a third; Executive Officer Mawson Tallis was grinning merrily as he aimed at an animal with imposing fangs and a long prehensile tail; Communications Leader Alrou Malise just avoided being knocked off his feet by the sudden rush of one of the midsized beasts; Section Leader Jarrick Riven had managed to stun three of the smallest creatures and was now giving his attention to protecting a group of unarmed courtiers.

Five men lay on the floor, dead or broken, and the beasts were starting to fight over them.

Thunghalis was no longer defending the Comes Riton by himself; Navigator Nola Zim stood between the Comes and the beasts, her stunner leveled at a low-slung animal with a broad head and a double row of triangular teeth. The Comes was staring at her as if she were the most amazing sight he had ever seen. Haakogard sheathed his stunner, its charges exhausted, and glanced toward Zim one more time.

The Guards had drawn their ceremonial flails and were now making their way from one half-conscious beast to another, bludgeoning them to death. The Petit Harriers moved out of their way, a few trying to conceal their disgust, one sorry to miss the fun.

From his place near the door the Mromrosi bounced on six of his eight limbs and made a sound like the patter of hail on glass. His tremendous mass of curls was candy-pink.

When the last of the animals had been dispatched, the Comes Riton raised his splendid voice. Even frightened and nervous he sounded as if he were singing. "I thank you deeply. If your action had not been swift and your weapons sure, my next phase would have had to begin his rule long before he is prepared to do so, and the alternate would claim to have the right to serve in my place. You have shown yourselves honorable and dependable, and I will hold you always in high regard, and have each of my phases to come do so as well."

Pangbar Thunghalis dropped flat on his face in front of the Comes Riton. "O Most Excellent Comes, give me permission, I beg you, to expiate my disgrace for not acting more swiftly. In your need I failed you. The dishonor is intolerable." He half-rose; his shining uniform was mired with blood and other things. "I do not deserve to continue as your Pangbar. I do not deserve to live."

The Guards were beginning to drag the animals away, leaving bright bloody smears to mark their departure.

The Comes Riton sighed. "Yes. You ought to be permitted to kill yourself; I know. But it is not convenient for you to kill yourself just now, Pangbar Thunghalis. I would rather you delay your death until the alternate is found and devivified."

As he lowered himself to the floor again, Thunghalis moaned as he knocked his forehead against the bloody stones. "How can I bear the shame of what I have done?" he pleaded. "Let me end it."

Navigator Zim, who was watching this aghast, turned to the Comes Riton. "You can't seriously intend to give up a good soldier because we moved a little faster. It makes no sense."

"It is a matter of honor," said the Comes Riton unhappily. "I know how keenly he feels his error, how the magnitude of his betrayal poisons his vitals. But just now it does not please me to give him up. Yet how can I refuse when he has disgraced his oaths to me?"

"But death—isn't that a bit extreme, given your present situation? You're in no position to give up good fighting men, Comes"—though she had not called him Most Excellent, no one seemed to notice—"and Thunghalis is supposed to be one of your best. Isn't there anything else he could do?" She put one hand on her hip, trying to present an attitude of nonconcern. "Suicide is so . . . impractical."

"I am nothing," said Pangbar Thunghalis miserably, countering Zim's attempts at pragmatism. "Let me become nothing. It is all that is fitting."

The Comes Riton was staring at Navigator Zim. "What else could he do? What else would be right?"

She gestured impatiently. "I don't know. He doesn't have to die, though, does he? Isn't there something you could demand of him that would clear his honor other than taking his own life? Set him a task, a very difficult task, to accomplish."

"I am not worthy to perform a task for the Most Excellent Comes," protested Thunghalis, shocked at the notion. "It is not our way to usurp the honor of others when ours is gone."

"But it's a—" She gave an exasperated toss of her dark-blue hair.

Haakogard interrupted, hoping he was doing the right thing. "Would it be possible for Pangbar Thunghalis to be put under my supervision while we try to recover the missing clone? My honor is not at stake here as his is, and he would not compromise what the crew does. In fact, he might very well help. We need the advice of someone who knows this world, understands your ways, who can guide us." He took care not to look at the prostrate figure. "I was going to make the request in any case, but given the circumstances I think it might be best if you will agree to this."

Thunghalis howled as if branded.

"It is not an honorable thing to serve foreigners," said the Comes Riton, his tone as much speculative as condemning.

"All the more reason to loan him to us, then," said Haakogard at his most unperturbed. "It would make his dishonor known as much as his suicide would."

The Comes Riton strode about the room, pondering. He looked at the dead animals and gestured toward them. Then he looked at Thunghalis. "It is not honorable to serve foreigners, and you are now without honor. The foreigners have shown worth that has made you valueless." He came to stand over the prone figure, then looked directly at Navigator Zim. "I gave him to you, foreigners. I make a worthless present of him to you." This time his gesture was different, but it caused one of the Guards to stare in dismay.

"What?" Zim asked, as if she had not understood the words through her translator. "What are you talking about?" She was too astonished to stick to procedure. "You can't give him away like . . . like a goblet."

"I am providing what you seek," said the Comes Riton. "Since you do not want this disgraced man to die, he will be my gift to you." He stared down at Thunghalis again. "You are hers. You are worse than a masterless beast." He turned on his heel and strode away. "Most Excellent Comes," Haakogard called after him, and had the satisfaction of seeing the Comes falter. "Tell me, who would make such an attempt on your life?"

He came back a few steps to face Haakogard, his expression polite and closed. "Attempt on my— Surely you do not assume that—"

"The only trainer left is dead," Haakogard said, deliberately blunt. "He was killed by a knife-thrust, not by the animals."

The Comes Riton shrugged. "Most animal trainers are Other Colonists, free-breeders without honor, who go from city to city and live off the leavings from civilized tables."

"And plot insurrection?" Haakogard inquired.

This time the Comes Riton denied it more forcefully, "That would require a plan, and many men to carry it out over a long time. The Other Colonists are not capable of such action. They have no aptitude for such plans."

"But some of them kidnapped your clone," Haakogard reminded him, and continued sarcastically. "Well, you may be correct, and the Other Colonists have no reason to come against you now. Still, it seems to me that their performance was very convenient." He looked from the Comes Riton to the last two dead animals. "Tell me: do most animal trainers use such formidable beasts?"

"This troupe certainly does. They are famous for their work with the most dangerous animals," said the Comes Riton as if that settled the question. "They have been summoned here many times before, and they have performed honorably. I do not want minor skills around when there are major ones to be had." He looked toward Navigator Zim again. "I never thought they would lose control of their animals, and I apologize for putting you into danger, no matter how inadvertent it was."

"Who is to say that they lost control?" Haakogard

asked, his voice just loud enough to be heard by everyone in the room. "What if this was intended from the first, and they waited for the opportunity your summons provided?"

The Comes Riton glowered; there was a short, hostile silence. "You are new here, and for that reason I will not take offense at what you say. But I warn you that you are not to question me in this manner again. If you do not accept my truth, you must pose your disbelief as a question relating to known facts. Anything less would impugn my honor, and there would be trouble between us. Do you comprehend what I am saying, Mere Line Commander?" His reprimand seemed less insulting because of the sound of the voice delivering it. "Do you comprehend?"

"I hear what you say," said Haakogard.

"I remind you that you are here because I petitioned the Magnicate Alliance for support. You are here at my behest and to do my bidding." His face was rigid with fury, but still his voice held them with its resonant beauty.

'That's a thought over-simple, Most Excellent," said Group Line Chief Dachnor. "We are here to do the bidding of the Magnicate Alliance: the Alliance has ordered us to work for you, as they ordered us to work for Samblahrazi on Kousrau two years ago and Ngomai-yn on Drought Central the year before that." He watched as the next-to-the-last animal was hauled away by five soldiers. "We answer to the Alliance, not to you." He smiled a little. "No offense intended, Most Excellent Comes."

The Comes Riton glared at Dachnor and then transferred his baleful gaze to Haakogard. "I will inform the Magnicate Alliance of your statements and your actions. I will praise where it is deserved and I will upbraid where such is merited. It is clear to me that your understanding is imperfect, and so I will not hold you entirely accountable for what has been said here." His voice was as icy as it was possible for it to be.

"You must do as you think best, Most Excellent Comes," said Haakogard, deliberately making himself relax. "You have your duty and you must do it. Just as we must." He signaled to Navigator Zim. "Come on. All of you. We need to confer. We have reports that must be sent." He held out his hand to Zim and was pleased when she took it. His bow to the Comes Riton was so perfect it bordered on insolence.

In a surge of speed unexpected in so absurd-looking a being, the Mromrosi shot across the room on six of his eight limbs, his masses of curls a shade of yellow none of the crew had ever seen before. He stopped beside Haakogard and said, "The Emerging Planet Fairness Court will want to know about this."

"Emerging Planet Fairness—" began the Comes Riton, his sand-colored eyes filled with mockery. "What ridiculous—" Haakogard held up his hand. "It's not part of the Magnicate Alliance, Most Excellent Comes. The Mromrosi is an observer only."

"That? An observer?" Watching angrily, the Comes Riton was about to leave when he rounded on Haakogard one last time, pointing toward Thunghalis. "Take that offal with you, then." He turned away and was gone before the Petit Harriers could leave ahead of him and bring him further disgrace.

2

"It would be better if you would let me die," said Thunghalis; he steadfastly refused to answer to his civinymic or his rank. "That I should live and see the gauntlet fall!" He had lamented these two things for the last several hours. It was very late; on Neo Biscay the days were a little more than twenty-nine Standard Hours long, and the Harriers were feeling the difference. The Adjusted Hour clocks all seemed to mock them, claiming it was only two-twenty. In the staff room of the *Yngmoto* most of those questioning Thunghalis were finding it increasingly difficult to stay awake.

"No, it wouldn't be better for you to die," said Group Leader Perzda in her levelheaded way. "Unless you want to leave your Comes exposed to his enemies—and I promise you he is exposed. Your system exposes him." She leaned back in her chair. "Tonight's entertainment was just a warning, you realize? Something to put you on notice. You were made to see how easily the enemy can reach you and how little you can do to stop them. Next time the danger will be greater for the Comes and for everyone around him. Without your help, he might as well surrender now and save his—"

"Surrender? He is the Most Excellent Comes. To whom would the Comes Riton surrender?" Thunghalis scoffed desperately.

"Why, to his alternate, of course. They are both Comes Riton, and their claims are of equal merit. They are both authenticable clones. From what you have said, the alternate exists to take the place of the Comes should any misfortune befall him in his youth." Perzda sounded more bored than tired.

"But that is unacceptable. It has never happened. All alternates have been devivified when the Comes Riton inherits." Thunghalis stared from one of the Harriers to another. "What you suggest is . . . absurd."

"And how would you know for certain? The clones are indistinguishable one from another. Though this clone was kidnapped when he was very young, he is still legitimately the Comes Riton as much as your leader is." Jarrick Riven looked once at the Mromrosi and shook his head. "How would you handle this mess?"

"It is for you to handle it, not I: I am an observer," said the Mromrosi.

Perzda took up the argument again. "No man sworn to follow the Comes Riton could touch his clone without dishonoring himself—that's what you've said, isn't it? It would be treason to defend the Comes Riton against any clone of the Comes Riton. So who is to stand between the Most Excellent Comes and his alternate? We Petit Harriers? Is that why we were sent for?"

"Of course," said Thunghalis, turning sullen. "We are sworn to protect the Comes Riton." He frowned. "The alternate must be devivified. That should have been arranged years ago.

"The Comes Riton . . ." He hesitated. "But it wasn't settled properly when the alternate was taken."

"And the alternate is still out there, with the same personality and leadership as your current Comes," said Riven. "You have two Comes Ritons, haven't you?"

"In point of fact," said Perzda thoughtfully, "they probably do not have the same personalities, not quite. The alternate was not raised and educated with the current phase, and what he has been taught and the life he has led is still unknown to us. We need to establish contact with these Other Colonists to find out what became of the alternate clone. That's first. Then we can figure out how to go from there." She glanced over at the Mromrosi.

"Anything you want to add?"

"What you are saying is fair," the Mromrosi replied, and was rewarded with a shocked stare from Thunghalis. "Permit me to observe that your meth-

ods of selecting your leader, Gate Breaker, by failing
to anticipate a time when two clones might be rivals
for the position of Comes, have created the current
dangerous impasse. I advise against such arrangements."

"Why do you listen to . . . *that*?" Thunghalis demanded, pointing at the Mromrosi, his voice rising.

"Because he is here to observe, and the Magnicate
Alliance often works in conjunction with the Emerging Planet Fairness Court," said Haakogard, not wanting to have to explain anything more.

"What could something like that observe?" Thunghalis
attempted to hide his shock but was not wholly successful. "It—"

"He, or so he says," Haakogard interjected.

"He. How can something like that comprehend
what humans do?" Thunghalis set his jaw.

"We comprehend many things, many interesting
things, things done by those much odder than humans are," answered the Mromrosi with a faint show
of what Haakogard now recognized as amusement.
He changed from candy-pink to anticamouflage orange. "Surely you did not think that everyone in the
galaxy came from Old Earth, did you? Or was human?"

"No," Thunghalis lied; he watched the Harriers for
some hint on how to behave toward this peculiar
being.

The Mromrosi went silent but continued bright
orange; Haakogard suspected the Mromrosi was
laughing.

"All right then; we'll have to make contact with
these Other Colonists," Haakogard said to Thunghalis.
"We have to know what the stakes are if we support
you. We'll have to decide if we *ought* to support you.
The Alliance has guidelines, and we have to hold to
them." It was not entirely true: the Grand Harriers
were bound by convention and protocol, politics,

glory and diplomatic ritual. The Petits had less pres-
tige, fewer restraints, and much more interesting
assignments than their exalted upper regiment.

"I suppose I will have to accept that," said Thunghalis,
not seeming very pleased with what Haakogard said.

"So where do we start?" Haakogard made a point
of asking Communications Leader Alrou Malise. He
wanted to encourage Thunghalis to speak without
overtly questioning him; if Thunghalis would only
correct him, he could learn a great deal. "I assume
both sides are armed."

Thunghalis coughed. "The Other Colonists have
sticks and stones and bows and arrows. There is little
they can do to harm us."

"Well," said Haakogard carefully, "they managed
quite well with animals. They must have other skills
as well. We'll accept that both sides are prepared to
fight. Do you think we can make contact without
combat?" He did not wait for Thunghalis to claim
this was ridiculous; his attention was directly on
Malise.

"I think maybe the Mromrosi's right," Malise said.
"This whole system is eating its tail. I don't think we
can assume anything until we learn something about
the Other Colonists directly. If we can speak to the
alternate clone, so much the better. We shouldn't
accept the Comes Riton's explanations without question." He pinched the bridge of his long nose. "Tomorrow I'll think more clearly."

"What a subtle hint!" Navigator Zim marveled.
She had had little to say since they returned from
the disastrous banquet. "Not that I don't agree. I'm
exhausted."

Haakogard leaned back, trying hard not to yawn.
They were right, it was very late and they were all
tired. "All right; that's it for now," he said. "Thunghalis
will have Guest Cabin number two; make sure he

has a Bunter. No after-watch games tonight. I'll expect to see you at nine S. A. Any objections?"

"Everyone? All four ships?" asked Group Line Chief Dachnor.

"Yes, everyone," said Haakogard.

Group Line Chief Fennin made a disapproving noise.

Dachnor was about to join this protest, then he grinned. "We'll be here. We'll be asleep, but we'll be here." He rose, stretching without apology. "Fennin will, too. I'll have all the sentry stands operational by then."

"How many did you deploy?" asked Group Leader Perzda, who knew how many there were because she had ordered them.

"Fourteen," said Dachnor at once. "We'll have them running by eight S. H." He regarded Thunghalis carefully. "What happens if this alternate Comes Riton attacks Civuto poMoend?"

Thunghalis made a gesture of hopelessness. "If we know that it is the alternate, there is nothing we will be able to do in honor. We are sworn never to attack the Comes Riton in any of his phases, and that must include the alternate. To oppose him is unthinkable."

The Mromrosi went from orange to a pale, straw-like yellow.

"Nuh-huh," said Haakogard.

By ten S. A. it was agreed that Communications Leader Malise and Navigator Zim would be the ones to approach the Other Colonists. They were closeted at once with Thunghalis to be filled in on the immediate past of Neo Biscay, especially what little was known about the kidnapping of the alternate clone.

"You have to remember it was Syclicis," Thunghalis was saying, "who caused all the trouble, stealing the clone to be her child. If she had not taken the alternate, none of this would have happened. At the time she announced what she had done she was already safely into the hills. Forces were sent out to try to recover the alternate, but in those crags, the Other Colonists have the advantage over us, and they escaped with Syclicis at their head. She claimed that she was descended from the leaders of the Other Colonization and would be a ruler herself if the first phase of the Comes Riton had not destroyed the strongholds of her clan when the Second Colony arrived. But what else can you expect of one of the Other Colonists? To hear them speak, all of them are the children of rulers and high-ranking officials. You would think that there was never a peasant or a farmer among them. They claim we forced them to become what they are, but how could we?" He slapped his enormous hands down flat on the conference table. "She stole the alternate because she said she was entitled to him."

"You mentioned they have no cities, only scattered towns and moving camps," said Zim. "Is it because your Colony wiped out their cities as the Other Colonists have claimed in the past?"

"Of course not. Any cities they may have had were on the Low Continent and we had nothing to do with their destruction. Don't be obtuse. These people are not capable of building a city, let alone defending it and maintaining it." Thunghalis' patience was growing thin. "They live in small camps. They move around as their whim suits them. They are as wild as the beasts they tame. They've always been like this, and if you ask me, they were this way from the start."

"And that makes them hard to catch?" Zim suggested, expecting no answer.

"They are not being hunted; there is no reason for them to live as they do but that it is their wish to be vagabonds." He was growing uncomfortable. "We offered to assist them at first, but all our overtures were rejected."

Zim appeared not to notice as she pressed on, a speculative light in her dark eyes. "And yet last night I heard three different references to the great lost city of the Other Colony. Why is that, if they have no cities?"

"There are always myths," said Thunghalis, and attempted to change the subject. "Do you think it was Other Colonists who tried to attack you as you arrived yesterday afternoon? It was not—"

"I think," said Malise, giving Zim the opportunity to muster her questions again, "that legends and myths are often based on fact. I think that for the First Colony to survive at all they had to find ways to protect themselves, and that probably means a city or a town, or more than one city or town. Your group of colonists did that when they arrived, didn't they? The history we were zapped said that there were seven thousand colonists in the First Colonization, enough for one or two fortress towns. They had supplies enough for one." He cocked his head. "My home world is a lot like Neo Biscay, and we've got many hill fortresses. You're a soldier; you understand these things. And your Second Colonization started out with twelve thousand colonists and four walled cities. Isn't poMoend the smallest of them?"

Thunghalis was not willing to concede the point. "Only seven thousand people would vanish amid these crags. All they are is feuding clans, consumed with internal rivalries. All the clans practice free-breeding, and there's no record kept of consanguinity. They live in chaos."

"Chaos protects them, though, doesn't it, by making them hard to identify." Malise smiled with false sympathy.

"Speaking of identity," said Zim, "is there anything known about Syclicis, other than that she kidnapped the alternate? Is she alive or dead?"

"Who knows?" asked Thunghalis as if bored. "There are rumors that she had died; she would be very old if she has not. Occasionally there are rumors she is still alive, but no proof. Since the Other Colonists have no clones, we have thought she must be dead."

"Unfortunate," said Navigator Zim. She stood up. Her uniform was utilitarian and austere but that in no way diminished her beauty. "Is there someone who it would be helpful to seek out, if not Syclicis?"

"Well," said Thunghalis shortly, no longer cooperative, "you might speak to the alternate."

She gave him the full benefit of her smile. "Yes. That is what we intend to do."

As soon as the scooter was set down and secured, a dozen men surrounded it, each one armed with primitive weapons; they were somewhat taller than their Civuto poMoend equivalents and were certainly much poorer. Most of them had long hair clubbed at the backs of their necks, and all wore beards. Their clothes were made of homespun cloth and ground-cured leather.

"We're officers of the Magnicate Alliance Second Harriers, called the Petits," said Navigator Zim, adjusting her translator so that the announcement would carry. "We have been sent here by the Magnicate Alliance to answer a complaint. We want to talk to you. Are you willing to speak with us?"

The men surrounding her kept her under close guard, three of them moving near enough to make their pikes a threat. They listened intently to the mechanical voice, and made signs to one another as Navigator Zim continued to explain the purpose of their presence on Neo Biscay.

"We need your help to locate this missing clone. We guarantee your protection, and we will not judge anyone until all the facts are known. We cannot finish here until the clone has been located and the entire dispute resolved. That is what our leader has promised to do. If this clone is making a claim on the Comes, we will do what we can to settle the question. If he is not interested in the title, then we will make sure the Second Colonists understand; so that there will be no further conflicts between you, and neither group will have to suffer."

A steel-haired man with scarred hands stepped forward, raising his mace-and-chain. He swung the weapon suggestively, smiling at the crinkling sound it made. "Prove it," he said via the translator.

"Fight to prove our good and peaceful intent?" Zim asked, although she had already palmed her stunner. "Isn't that at cross-purposes?"

"You are soldiers in a regiment: you fight," said the man with happy anticipation.

"You should meet our Executive Officer Tallis; you're of a piece," whispered Malise.

Nola Zim sighed as she turned to face him. "The two of us, then, no matter which way it goes?"

"On my honor," said the man, and swung his mace-and-chain, enjoying the deadly sound it made as it cleaved the air. "I am an honorable man. I fight for my leader as he requires me to fight, to uphold his honor. You need not fear; I understand the conduct of honorable combat. I will not offend you by unfair fighting."

"You won't object if we take a few precautions?" Malise drew a more impressive and obvious weapon, a shoulder-cannon; he rested it in firing position but did not aim it at anyone.

"It isn't necessary; you will see it is not." He held out his weapon. "Let us engage." The man with the mace-and-chain was clearly an experienced fighter. He moved carefully, never letting himself get off-balance. He shuffled rather than strode, he crouched and kept his upper body weaving as he waited for an opportunity. He presented as small a target as he could and still fight, giving himself a better chance at her. He swiped out with the mace-and-chain again, this time coming close enough to Zim that she was forced to jump back.

She held her stunner carefully, aiming for the legs. All she needed to do was knock him off his feet and she would be all right. The last thing in the world she wanted to do was kill or maim him, though with a stunner that would be ridiculously easy. Her jaw ached with tension.

He changed his tactics suddenly, bringing the mace-and-chain down, then rising up, his weapon striking upward, nearly clipping her shoulder. He took care not to aim for her head.

"All right," she said, and before he could lower his arm, she aimed her stunner at the arm holding the mace-and-chain. As she thumbed the charge button, the man shrieked, his weapon falling from unresponsive fingers. "Enough?" she asked.

For an answer he rushed at her, his undamaged arm upraised and his face dark with rage.

She thumbed the charge again—the man bucked at the impact of stun, and this time he collapsed unconscious.

"Anyone else?" Zim asked, the stunner still in her hand. She was trying to bring her breathing back to normal but without much success.

One of the men stepped forward, a figure somewhat taller than the Comes Riton; with a full-sunbleached beard and skin roughened by living in the open, he did not appear much like the Comes Riton, but when he spoke, the voice was unmistakably beautiful. "You have great courage, and you have shown honor as well as restraint. What do you want to know of me?" he asked, his sand-colored eyes intent on her.

Navigator Zim motioned to Malise to let her deal with the man. "The Comes Riton?" she asked, realizing she was on very uncertain ground.

"Syclicis' son," he corrected her. "I suppose Riton doesn't see it that way, though?" He permitted those with him to laugh a little before he continued. "I have nothing against my clone. How could I? It would mean I have something against myself."

"You haven't discovered any reason to resent him?" Communications Leader Malise asked dubiously.

"Not the way you mean. We're clones, each is the other. He is as much my clone as I am his, since we are buds of the same source. We were vivified at the same time. It was never decided that I had fulfilled my purpose; I was gone long before then. Until we were almost four, he and I, we lived in the palace of poMoend. He still lives there, but I have been more fortunate." He shouldered his pike and indicated that his men should do the same. "I have lived for myself and not for where the cloning began. I am not the Comes Riton, master of poMoend, I am a trainer of animals and I live where camp is made. But I am a man of honor. I uphold the honor of my line."

"How do you mean that?" Zim asked.

"I would not dishonor myself and my lines with unworthy conduct." He indicated his fallen fighter. "You saw yourself that he served me honorably."

"He lost," said Zim.

"Of course he lost. To win would have dishonored me, and he would never do that." The Comes Riton's clone stared at Zim as if she were ignoring the obvious.

"You had him fight in order to lose," she said,

taking care to keep her tone of voice level. "It was your intention to have him lose."

"What else could he do in honor? He could not refuse to fight, for that would dishonor you and me. He could not win, for that would be a greater disgrace." The Comes Riton's clone made an imperious gesture that was very like his other self. "How could you think I would be so lost to honor that I would countenance his winning against you? I am no savage or barbarian."

Malise nodded as if it all made sense to him. "Not fighting was dishonorable but winning was more dishonorable." He shrugged. "Makes sense to me."

"Malise," Zim warned, hearing the sarcasm in his voice.

"The same kind of sense as not having guards at the banquet because it would mean that the poMoend fighters assumed that the animal trainers were capable of fighting them. It's all the same screwy logic."

At the mention of that encounter the Comes Riton's clone's expression changed slightly. "Yes. The banquet. I saw you at the banquet. You were the most fascinating woman there, and the loveliest." He all but devoured Zim with his sand-colored eyes.

"'How could you see me at—" She cut herself short. "You were with the animal trainers."

"That is my trade, and I am one of the finest," said Syclicis' son without false modesty, sounding a great deal like the Comes Riton version of himself. "Ask anyone: I have an enviable reputation; I have more success than most."

"But not the other êvening?" Zim suggested.

"It was a misfortune. Quite lamentable. Very nearly a disgrace. We did not intend it to happen." There was no indication that he was lying, but the sudden flatness of his tone was disturbing.

"A coincidence?" Malise said incredulously.

The man who had fought Zim stirred and moaned.

"Would you call your performance at the banquet successful?" Zim challenged the Comes Riton's clone.

He stared at a distant point over her left shoulder. "I am distressed that I did not keep control of my animals," he said, not quite able to conceal a glimmer of satisfaction. "As a trainer, I take pride in the behavior of my animals." He laughed once. "Perhaps you will be able to watch another time, when you will see how adept I can be with them."

"You're confident of that?" Malise asked, then indicated the men with Syclicis' son. "Were you looking for animals to replace the ones you have lost? Or were you hunting?"

"No," said the clone, unperturbed. "We were watching for the soldiers from poMoend."

"What soldiers?" asked Malise. "I thought soldiers were dishonorable. We have been informed that—"

"You don't think that they tell those over-bred curs who serve at court what the army is doing, do you?" The clone's smile bordered on a snarl. "They're as remote from us as the Comes Riton is." He turned toward Zim again, as if she were north and he a magnet. "Not my clone, and not his close associates; they are puppets. But there are many just below them, the second rank of the court, who hold the real power. They use it without honor. The rest is nothing more than posing and tradition. That was one of the first truths I discovered when Syclicis brought me into these mountains." He took a few steps back, then came up to Zim once more. "Among these people . . . they call me Tenre."

"Not Riton?" she asked, deliberately making the question light.

"No. Never Riton." He made a sign to the others but spoke directly to her. "Go about your work, then, but if any soldiers follow after you, dishonor-ably seeking to kill us, I will not die and I will hold you and all the Harriers responsible for any deaths."

"Oh, not all the Harriers," said Zim. "Just the Petits."

Haakogard read the latest zaps for the third time and then stared up at the ceiling of the small parlor. Why did they never tell him how complicated things were until he got there? He remembered the benign smile on Fleet Commondore Herd's wizened features as the crafty old man gave him his orders and assured him that this venture would be a simple task, done quickly and without undue risk. "Would you like something to relax you, Mister Haakogard?" his Bunter inquired.

He glanced over his shoulder at the cyborg, trying to stifle the annoyance he felt at the interruption, though he knew the Bunter was responding to his monitored requirements. "Did you know there was a time when Bunters were called Butlers? I recall reading that when I was a boy."

"Butler is a perjorative for Bunter," said his Bunter without inflection. "It comes from Old Earth."

"No offense intended," said Haakogard quickly, knowing that the delicate tuning on these machines often made them touchy. "Just something I came across once, and the clerk sending the zaps signed off as Butler. Jogged my brain." He tossed the pages into the low table. "Don't recycle those yet; I need to review them, and I don't want them put into the system—we don't want Thunghalis or anyone else here retrieving them by accident." He stretched his long legs and got to his feet.

The Bunter tried again. "Would you like something to—"

"Relax me? I don't think so," he said, then changed

his mind. "On second thought, bring me a small glass of that Standby Hooch. Warmed."

"A small glass of warmed Standby Hooch," the Bunter confirmed. It left the room at once, looking almost human in size and proportion—except for the four telescoping arms. By the time it returned, Haakogard was in his study, a stack of tutorials by his terminal. He looked up at the Bunter's discreet low two-note signal and motioned it to approach.

"Your Standby Hooch, sir; and the Mromrosi wishes to see you," said the Bunter as he held out the glass on an antique silver tray that had come from the stuffiest of the First Fifty-Six Colonies Victoria Station.

"Thank you," said Haakogard, and the words appeared on the opposite wall. "Erase that," he told the wall.

"What shall I tell the Mromrosi?" the Bunter inquired politely. Bunters did everything politely.

Haakogard sighed and shut down the terminal. "Send him in. I need to talk to him anyway." He leaned back in his chair as the Bunter left and contemplated the ceiling with a supreme blankness of expression until the Mromrosi toddled through the door. "Have a seat if you want one," Haakogard offered.

The Mromrosi selected one of the chairs to lean against. He was a very pale beige and his single eye, enormous, green as sunlight coming through new leaves, appeared brighter by contrast. "What have you decided?" he asked without preamble.

"I haven't decided anything," said Haakogard. "Except that we haven't enough information about this place. The response from the Hub was premature, at least in my estimation. Commodore Herd gave his assurances to the Comes Riton, but I don't think he knew what was at stake here." He pinched the bridge of his nose. "For that matter, neither do we."

"A very exact thing," said the Mromrosi, a little blush suffusing his massive ringlets.

"How the devil did these people get it into their heads that cloning was the answer to leadership? And the elaborate codes they have regarding the clones, and all honor tied up in it." He slapped his hands down on the arms of his chair. "Maybe the first Comes Riton thought it was a good idea that his entire armed forces take an oath never to attack him in any form, but look at the mess it's causing now. And it's lucky that it's only happened once. What if rival factions at court got hold of one clone apiece and each side insisted that theirs was the true clone? They couldn't actually fight about it, could they? That would mean dishonor, wouldn't it. So they would have to resort to covert actions." He glanced toward the Mromrosi. "For all we know, that's going on right now, and there are people in this government who are working on the sly."

"I do not think so," said the Mromrosi. "Why would they bother to contact the Hub and ask the Petits to assist them if that were the case?" He gestured with three of his legs, making a complicated, invisible pattern that Haakogard did not understand. "They did not bother to contact the capital, but came directly to the Magnicate Alliance. Surely that is significant."

'It means they don't trust anyone in Bilau," said Haakogard. "Nothing new in that. The provinces often distrust the capitals."

"But for what cause?" asked the Mromrosi. "Why would that be a factor in what seems a fairly simple case of a family dispute? Surely the courts of Bilau are more prepared to appreciate the difficulties than the Petits are." He bounced several times. "Yes, there are factors here that are hidden."

Haakogard bit back a sharp retort. "What about

the Emerging Planet Fairness Court? Is this a case
where you would . . . advise them?"

"It is not the issue. This is a strictly planetary
crisis, and we have no mandate in these cases. Our
interests lie elsewhere." He made a low, rough sound,
not quite a growl, not quite a hum. He did not
change color.

"Well, whether it's in your jurisdiction or not, if
you get any good ideas, I hope you'll pass them on to
me," said Haakogard, feeling rather weary. "I haven't
got a clue about it yet."

"There is time still. More information is needed,"
said the Mromrosi, shaking himself. "If the Wammgalloz
were with you, instead of me, they might perceive
the solution more quickly."

Haakogard shuddered at the thought. "No, thank
you." He had never become used to the sight of the
Wammgalloz, enormously tall aliens, known for their
tremendous intellects and solid judgment. To Haakogard—and to most humans—the Wammgalloz looked
too much like tremendous predatory insects; to the
Wammgalloz, humans appeared undeveloped and de-
formed, and they smelled atrocious. Both humans
and Wammgalloz avoided each other except when
the congresses of the Emerging Planet Fairness Court
required they meet.

"That is what the Wammgalloz think, too," said
the Mromrosi with a trace of amusement.

"Most of the EPFC are pretty hard to take, for
us," Haakogard added. "You're different."

"Fortunately," said the Mromrosi, and skibbled
toward the door. "By the way, I have received word
that a small unit of Grands are scheduled to stop in
Bilau very soon."

This caught all Haakogard's attention. "What?" he
asked, sitting upright.

"That is what I have been informed, through the

Court." He faded to a soft peach shade. "I thought it strange that you have not been notified. Unless you have been?"

"No," said Haakogard, his eyes darkening. He cursed inwardly. Had the Commodore decided to intervene after all?

"Perhaps it has nothing to do with your mission," the Mromrosi suggested.

"And perhaps Spica's going nova tomorrow," said Haakogard. Reluctantly he added, "Thanks for letting me know."

"It is part of my task here," said the Mromrosi, and slipped out the door.

A small unit of Grands were coming to Bilau: Haakogard turned this over in his thoughts but could discern no reason for it, which made him more apprehensive than ever. The Grands never did anything by chance. Commodore Herd had hinted it might be necessary to send the Grands, but he had not said why. Haakogard wanted to know more about it, but knew he could not zap the Hub for information, since he had not officially been told of the event. "And who's to say they'd tell me the truth?" he asked the air. Better to concentrate on his immediate problems here, he told himself. Maybe the Mromrosi would be able to keep him informed about the Grands.

He took the tutorial cassette out of the feeder and slipped in another one: the history of the settlement of Neo Biscay. The most nagging piece of information which had been repeated in three of the four tutorials he had examined was that the First colonization would have numbered among the First Fifty-Six if they had been able to establish and maintain contact with any of the other Colonies. As it was, they were occasionally able to reach Old Earth, but by that time the planet was little more than a museum and a tourist attraction, and Neo Biscay was officially forgotten. The arrival of the N'djowul had ended the isolation, but not for the better. And by the time the N'djowul were gone, the Second Colonization arrived. Was the First Colonization truly part of the First Fifty-Six, as the records of Old Earth suggested? "Support for this theory?" Haakogard asked when he had reviewed all the tutorials.

"The names of the two ships were recorded when the Ninety went out," the screen answered, words appearing on its surface as it spoke. "Of the five artifacts brought here for identification in case the colony did not survive, four are still in the hands of the Other Colonists."

"So, strictly speaking, we ought to be the representatives of the First colony and not the Second," Haakogard mused. "I wonder if Fleet Commodore Herd knows this? Would the arrival of the Grands support the First or Second Colonization?"

"This tutorial is not equipped to advise you," said the wall screen as Haakogard took a long, slow swig of his Standby Hooch.


Trumpets and gongs announced the arrival of the Comes Riton at the four *Katana*-class Skimmers, and three men demanded that the Most Excellent Comes be admitted to the company of Mere Line Commander Haakogard.

"They'll keep up the noise until you see them," Group Leader Perzda warned him. "And the longer you take, the louder they'll get, at least that's what my tutorials say." She hesitated. "You could deputize one of us—perhaps Zim?"

There were hoots of approval at that suggestion.

Haakogard looked at her across the conference table, his hand lifted in admonition. "No-no-no, Viridis. She's got them riled up already." He sig-

naled to his Bunter, which waited on the far side of
the conference room. "I need one of my parade
uniforms, but not a full dress one. Ask the Senior
Bunter to make the selection. He'll know which one
is right."

"You're going outside, then?" Group Leader Perzda
inquired critically. "Don't you think that might be a
bit dangerous?"

"It's more dangerous staying inside. These Neo
Biscayans, or whatever you call them, have hot fuses."
He reached for the all-deck announcer. "This is Line
Commander Haakogard. I want Dachnor, Fennin,
and Chanliz to meet me in proper parade dress in
half one Standard Hour in the center of the formation. Other members of the crew stand by, parade
dress optional. Pangbar Thunghalis, please remain in
your quarters unless the Senior Bunter advises you
otherwise. Observer Mromrosi is welcome to come
with us."

A voice came from the outlet beside him. "I will
venture this," the Mromrosi informed him.

"Good," said Haakogard, knowing that the alien
would serve to distract the Comes Riton and his
men.

"Clever. They're still trying to figure out what the
Mromrosi is," said Perzda.

"Aren't we all?" Haakogard interjected.

She ignored this. "But once they get used to him,
I will wager that the Comes Riton will be looking for
Zim again. He's captivated by her. It's the blue
hair." She chuckled; her chuckle was one of the few
things about her that did not seem ordinary—she
sounded like a very large and lazy cat purring.

"Was it a mistake to use her? I didn't anticipate
this infatuation," Haakogard mused aloud.

"Who knows?" said Perzda. She saw the Bunter
returning. "I'll let you get dressed. We'll review

later." Without waiting for his dismissal, she left the conference room.

By the time Haakogard emerged from his quarters, parade-perfect, the jangle and blare of the Comes Riton's military band had become loud enough that he knew he would have to use his ship's hailer to be heard over the noise. He stood at his command couch in the bridge and watched the surveill screens.

The Comes Riton was accompanied by thirty musicians and eighty-eight soldiers. If they were going to have to fight, thought Haakogard, the odds were bad. "Tallis," he said to his Executive Officer, "I want you to keep an eye on the surveill screens at all times. Pay special attention to those monitoring the perimeters. We'll need warning if anything is happening out there."

Mawson Tallis offered a halfhearted salute. "I'd rather be out there with you, just in case."

Haakogard was familiar with the complaint. "Be glad you're not. And while you're in here, keep your fingers off the triggers. We're supposed to be *helping* these people. We've been sent to assist them." As he said it, he could not conceal the uncertainty that had been with him since his arrival on Neo Biscay.

"But if they're armed . . ." Tallis protested, his eyes growing brighter with anticipation. "I've got to protect you first of all."

"No," Haakogard corrected him patiently, "you have to protect the *mission* first of all." He watched while Tallis considered this, then went on. "We are here because the Twelve sent us here." In the Magnicate Alliance there was no higher authority, and Tallis flushed at the name.

"What do the Twelve care about Neo Biscay?" he challenged, glowering.

"I can't imagine," said Haakogard. "But I was given my orders by Fleet Commodore Herd himself, and he answers only to the Twelve. So . . ." He pressed the inter-ship hailer. "Are you ready?"

The three Group Line Chiefs responded in unison.

"Then let's get it done." Haakogard drew on his pale gray gloves. "And Tallis, remember: nothing hasty."

The Comes Riton was clearly offended by the long delay, and as he approached Haakogard, he said, "I am not used to such a reception. I have never needed to wait as you have required me to wait." His beautiful voice carried over the racket his band was making.

Haakogard and his three Group Line Chiefs stood the proper distance away from the Most Excellent Comes. "Sadly," shouted Haakogard so that he could be heard over the din, "since we were not informed you were coming, we had no opportunity to prepare ourselves for your visit, and as a result could not welcome you as you arrived."

"Ridiculous!" jeered the Comes Riton, but not as confidently as before. He paused, then signaled his musicians to stop. The silence was so abrupt that it was nearly as intrusive as the music had been. "But I will excuse your execrable behavior because you are strangers and you have upheld my honor."

"We have done as Petit Harriers do, Comes Riton," said Haakogard, deliberately leaving off Most Excellent; he was rewarded with a hard stare. "We are sworn to the Magnicate Alliance, not to you. If there is ever any dispute between you and the Alliance, we are Alliance troops, not poMoend's and—"

"That is enough!" The Comes Riton was very angry and his sand-colored eyes had an implacable yellow shine to them. "I will hear nothing more of this!" He gestured to some of his officers and weapons appeared in their hands.

Haakogard fell silent, still.

The men with the Comes Riton were restive now,

and a few of the musicians were so nervous that they could not keep quiet.

The Comes Riton paced back and forth in front of Haakogard, his expression more and more forbidding. At last he stopped and pointed directly at the Line Commander. "Where is Zim?" he demanded.

"At her work," said Haakogard mildly. "She has readings to enter in the permanent log of the mission. They must be made at specific times every day. Each member of the crew has such obligations." It was a convenient fiction used on missions, and the officers with him supported the lie now.

"That's the truth," said Section Leader Jarrick Riven mendaciously. "If these readings are not entered regularly, the Alliance ships will come to find out why they have not been made." He grinned mirthlessly. "They will assume there has been trouble and they will be prepared to fight."

"I wish to see Nola Zim," the Comes Riton said, making it a command. "She interests me."

Standing behind the Petit Harriers, Thunghalis paled and stared at the Comes Riton as if the man were suddenly a complete stranger to him.

"Oh, really," said Group Leader Perzda with feigned amazement. "You arrive with an army and then you say she interests you." She shook her head as if watching an ambitious child attempting a task beyond his skill. "She is doing her sworn duty, Most Excellent Comes Riton. It would not be honorable for her to fail in this." She nodded in the direction of Group Chief Leilah Chanliz, an angular, graceful, tall woman from Lontano, with pale, flawless skin and bright hair. "Would someone else be able to assist you?"

"No," said the Comes Riton gracelessly. "I must speak with Navigator Zim, and no other." The men around him were standing nearer to him, weapons still drawn, and their expressions were no longer bored or polite; a few reflected the astonishment on Thunghalis' features. One or two lowered their weapons. "I will speak with her or you will answer for it."

"Oh, Bleeding-root Rot!" Haakogard said under his breath, using the same mild oath his father had all those years ago on Grunhavn. This was turning into a standoff, and he hated standoffs.

"What's the matter, Line Commander?" asked Group Chief Eben Dachnor.

"Nothing," said Haakogard, speaking a little louder. "This whole impasse is ridiculous. We're supposed to be aiding them. That's what Commodore Herd ordered. We're not here to fight with them."

"Better let them know," Dachnor suggested, smiling tightly.

A poMoend officer with the shoulder points of a Tydbar came directly up to Haakogard. "The Most Excellent Comes Riton is here to speak with Navigator Nola Zim. Any attempt to prevent this will be known as a hostile act and we will respond as honor demands. We are sworn to uphold the honor of the Comes Riton."

"This isn't about honor," said Viridis Perzda, just above a whisper so that the poMoend men could not hear her, "it's about manners."

Haakogard concealed a sigh and bargained for time. "All right. I'll speak with Navigator Zim and find out what she wishes to do. If she is willing to interrupt her work to speak with you, then I'll allow it. If she isn't willing, I will have to stand by her decision." He looked directly at the Comes Riton. "And our firepower is superior to yours. I ask you to keep that in mind if you're tempted to force the issue."

"You have been sent to protect me," protested the Comes Riton. "How can you refuse what I demand of you when you are here to protect me? You are failing in your purpose, and that is not honorable."

"We are here to prevent a war. That was what you required, and that is what I am going to do. I will do nothing that will cost me one member of my crew, and if that means firing on your troops, so be it," said Haakogard. "If you will wait here? Dachnor, will you be good enough to present my compliments to Navigator Zim and ask her if she would join me and the Comes Riton at her earliest convenience, if she is agreeable?" He said it in the best form, as neatly as a Grand Harrier would have, he told himself.

"You do not order her? Why do you not order her?" the Comes Riton demanded, his sand-colored eyes looking pale with emotion. "It dishonors you to make your order a request."

"She has this time at liberty unless we are in actual combat alert. It would not uphold my honor to countermand our traditions. My authority is curtailed during liberty hours," said Haakogard, then added, "and she does not like being ordered about. I know this about her, Most Excellent Comes. She's served on the *Yngmoto* for six years. I've learned that much about her."

"So." The Comes Riton folded his arms and glared at his officers. "We will remain here until she comes. Eventually her liberty will end."

Haakogard bowed a little. "It's your planet; do as you wish. Perzda, make sure we have all the monitors operating, will you?"

"Done," she said, "already."

"I might have known," Haakogard said softly and heard Riven and Dachnor chuckle. "The Group Chiefs remain here, except Dachnor. The rest of you can return to your ships and get back to your duties." He signaled to Thunghalis. "I need a word with you, Pangbar, if you will? I must make a log entry."

"I am no longer a Pangbar. I forfeited my right to

the rank," Thunghalis corrected him as he followed Haakogard to the entry hatch of the *Yngmoto*.

"You're the closest thing I've got to one," Haakogard pointed out as they stepped inside. He drew him into the suiting alcove. "What is going on out there? Will you tell me that? I've been going over the tutorials and I didn't find anything in them about the Comes Riton's women."

"He doesn't have any," said Thunghalis miserably, looking more worried than ever. "Why should he, being a clone, have need for a woman? And if he were to have a woman, it would not be a free-breeding one. Women are for those who free-breed, or who are not entitled to the honor of clones." He folded his long hands, cracking the knuckles loudly. "I have never heard of the Comes Riton so . . . forgetting himself in this manner. It goes against all traditions. No phase has ever done—"

"But you say that any phase is still the same Comes Riton as the first," Haakogard reminded him. "How can you account for this? Is he a late developer, perhaps?" His feeble joke was not understood at all.

"He develops as all others do," said Thunghalis seriously. "He repeats himself." His frown deepened as he spoke.

"Seems that cloning doesn't cover everything, after all," Haakogard said, and in another, crisper tone, he went on. "All right, go to your quarters but keep ready. Watch the surveills in the wall; I'll have the monitors routed there. You'll know if something happens that requires we respond. If that happens, use the hailer to warn me."

"I should remain at your side," said Thunghalis with determination.

Haakogard shook his head. "I don't want to remind the Comes Riton that you're around; he's touchy enough without that. Who knows, he might decide to pass the time by having you kill yourself for his amusement if you stay with me."

"I wish he would," said Thunghalis, his eyes alight with fervor.

"Well, I don't," said Haakogard bluntly. "Let me know if you see anything—anything!—that does not seem right to you. Don't hesitate. We can't afford delay."

"Very well," said Thunghalis unhappily.

At that Haakogard relented. "We'll get this figured out, Pangbar, don't worry about it." He started to turn away but saw Navigator Zim coming down the hall, her short forest-green Petit Harriers' cape swinging around her. He motioned Thunghalis to remain where he was and stepped out of the alcove. "Nola."

"Line Commander Haakogard." She was looking annoyed, but her expression changed. "Dachnor's at my station. I just reviewed the surveills. What does the Comes Riton think he's up to?"

"He's courting you," said Haakogard, somewhere between disgust and amusement.

"Is that what he thinks it is? Really?" she asked of the air. "Courtship? I know part of my job is to be a distraction, but this time it backfired, didn't it?" Before Haakogard could answer, she flung up her hands. "What am I supposed to do now? This is impossible."

"Use your good sense," said Haakogard. "And try not to escalate the situation if you can. He wants to fight someone right now, and that would not be . . . convenient."

"What is this, a schoolyard? Fighting over girls is for children," she protested, "not some sixth or seventh or eighth generation clone." She fastened the four decorative frogs that closed her cape so that she was now enveloped to her knees in the garment.

"He might as well be a child," said Haakogard.

"Thunghalis says that the Comes Riton has never been involved with a woman before: being a clone, he has no need for women, you see." He kept his voice completely neutral.

"Lord of the Poisons!" Zim swore. "What kind of lunacy is this? How can this happen?" She tapped her foot in exasperation. "All right, I'll talk to him, but you'll have to come with me. I don't want to be by myself with him. What were they thinking of when the colonists started this cloning nonsense?" She did not wait for an answer but opened the main hatch. "You'd better be coming. Sir."

"Right behind you," said Haakogard, planning to speak with Thunghalis later about what the Pangbar had surely overheard.

As soon as Zim stepped out of the ship, the brasses and gongs set to work again, and the racket was overwhelming. She stood still, trying not to clap her hands over her ears, and watched while the Comes Riton approached her with an escort of five Tydbars.

"It is ultimate delight to see you," he said, silencing the music with a decisive gesture. His splendid voice rang more than all the brazen voices of the gongs and trumpets.

"What can I be but flattered?" Zim replied, glancing over her shoulder to be certain that Haakogard was there.

"What else is possible?" the Comes Riton concurred, wholly unaware of her sarcasm. "You have done that which has never been done before, in any phase of the Comes, from the True First until now. It is not surprising that you are from a distant planet and unlike anyone on Neo Biscay, for only a woman as remarkable as you could cause me to depart so totally from the nature of myself and the traditions of all my phases." He beamed at her.

"How kind of you to say so," said Zim expressionlessly.

"We will begin proper arrangements." He laughed, the sound deep and theatrical. "For once there are no traditions to guide us, and I have nothing to draw upon for myself, except my ingenuity and my honor. For both of us it is an experience entirely unique. I will have to hope that you will contribute your wishes to the planning and negotiations."

"What planning and negotiations?" Zim asked, for the first time showing real alarm.

"Why, to arrange for us to marry." He was startled by her question.

This announcement brought stares from the Petit Harriers, but the soldiers and officers who accompanied the Comes Riton were openly distressed at what he said. One Tydbar turned on his heel and walked away, and several men fingered their weapons.

The oldest Tydbar, who stood very near the Comes Riton, cleared his throat. "That would lead to free-breeding, and it is prohibited for all of us. You are a clone, Most Excellent Comes, and the strictures are intended to preserve you without contamination."

"This isn't free-breeding," said the Comes Riton, making a gesture to show how little the issue concerned him. "I will have no part of any female from this planet, just as has been the case before. But Navigator Zim is not from Neo Biscay. Therefore she is not part of those who are free-breeders, and therefore it is fitting and honorable that she marry me. It is because she is alien to Neo Biscay that it is permissable."

Most of his men did not seem positively impressed by the Comes Riton's reasoning, one of the Pangbars going so far as to make a short, scoffing sound.

"Navigator Nola Zim," she said of herself in the third person, as she would have done at home on Xiaoqing, "is not able to marry the Comes Riton or anyone else. As the Comes Riton is governed by the laws of his homeland, so is she governed by the laws of hers. Regretfully she must decline the generous and flattering proposal of the Comes Riton because she is not free to accept it." She bowed to him, then shot a look at Haakogard that clearly said *get me out of here*.

"Impossible!" the Comes Riton burst out.

Haakogard stepped forward. "No. What Navigator Zim tells you is the truth. In the tradition of her homeland, she is married already. She would not be allowed into the Petit Harriers if she were not."

"All the women in the Petit Harriers are married?" the oldest Tydbar asked incredulously.

"No, just all the women from Xiaoqing, which is Navigator Zim's home, which is their tradition." He rested his hand on his stunner, making sure that the Comes Riton saw him do it. "We would be failing in our duty if we permitted you to take her away from us, not only as Harriers of the Alliance, but as those answerable to her husband and family." He indicated the monitors at the perimeters of their site. "These machines are set to guard us—all of us. It isn't wise to press your case, Comes Riton."

The Comes Riton glowered at Haakogard. "We would do no harm to those who serve with Navigator Zim." He made a single, chopping gesture and his men formed into ranks of six. "We will return when I have come upon a way to deal with this. If there is any attempt at departure, we will send our ships after you and we will bring you down."

"With Navigator Zim?" Haakogard asked, pushing his luck.

"She will take no harm," said the Comes Riton a little wildly.

Haakogard knew his *Katana*-class Skimmers could easily outrun the old-fashioned flyers of Neo Biscay, but he did not mention it. "We are here at your request to help you settle the matter of your alternate clone. Or has that slipped your mind?"

Now the Comes Riton was truly furious. "It is more essential than ever that my alternate be devivified. If I am to have a wife, the alternate cannot continue to exist, for that would endanger everything. There would be too much confusion about the succession, for we will have sons to succeed me, and the clones will be for an alternate if the sons are not sufficient." This time there were shouts of anger and disapproval from his men but he ignored them.

"She cannot marry you, Comes Riton," Haakogard said carefully and patiently, thinking that everyone had gone insane except him.

"I am married, Comes Riton," said Nola Zim in much the same tone as Haakogard had used.

"A way will be found," said Comes Riton. Then he bellowed three terse words, turned and departed with his men, the band striving to make music and keep up with the fast march.

As they watched the Comes Riton's party leave, Haakogard said, "I've got to zap the Hub about this. We're up to our necks. Something's wrong." He started toward the main hatch when he paused and looked back at Zim. "We'd better arrange a story about this mythical husband of yours, so it'll stick."

"And we'd better include it on the zap to the Hub. If the Comes Riton checks up on us, I don't want him being told a different story." She seemed oddly tired, and she walked as if her feet hurt.

"What is it?" Haakogard asked as they went into the *Yngmoto* together.

She stopped, her head cocked to the side as if she sensed something following her. "It just struck me: Riton and Tenre are really the same person. What if I have another proposal to handle?"

"One crisis at a time, if you please. We'll deal with

that when and if it happens." He noticed the Senior Bunter hovering nearby and resigned himself to dealing with the cyborg for an hour.

"Oh, it'll happen. It's bound to," said Zim quietly, with certainty. "This is one of those places."

Haakogard was in the conference room attempting to get an assessment from the Mromrosi when a band of Other Colonists attacked the Katanas. It was quite late, and two of the Neo Biscay's three moons were down making the night as dark as it ever got. For the last hour the Mromrosi's conversation had wandered, going into subjects and concepts that the others could not entirely grasp. Twenty members of the crew were asleep, their Bunters serving as sentinels.

"We'll have zaps on this by morning and we'll know how they want us to handle this mess," Haakogard was saying just as a large rock thudded against the hull of the *Yngmoto*. He looked around as two klaxons began to whoop. "What was that?"

"Primitive artillery," said the Mromrosi. "There is another."

The Katana echoed with the impact, and yet another klaxon sounded. Lights came on throughout the ship, and the Bunters whirled into activity.

"Surveills on, conference room," said Haakogard, thinking he would have liked this better if the attackers had waited until morning. He was tired and grouchy, not the best frame of mind for battle, even as minor as this one might be. "Nightscreens full."

The gray panels on the walls filled with images.

"Those are . . . catapults, ballistas," he said as he recognized the weapons. Even as he watched, another large rock was lobbed at his ship. When it hit, he swore.

"The Other Colonists," said the Mromrosi, his color

fading from pink to a tawny beige. Haakogard recognized this as a sign of condemnation.

"Interior hailers, all four ships," said Haakogard, and addressed the disk near his shoulder. "This is Line Commander Haakogard. We have been attacked by the Other Colonists, who are throwing big rocks at us. Do not return fire. I repeat: do not return fire. Set personal stunners on maximum, and if any approach you, stun your attacker. Otherwise, raise the deflection shield of your ships and wait it out. Report any serious damage at once. Good morning, everyone. Haakogard out." He stood up, hearing the soft, high shriek made by the deflection shield. "I'm off to the control room. Would you like to join me?"

"Directly," said the Mromrosi. "I wish to finish reviewing the zaps first."

"Whatever you like." Haakogard left the alien alone in the conference room and hurried the short distance to the control room directly beneath the bridge, where he found Navigator Zim already waiting.

"I couldn't sleep anyway," she explained, accounting for her presence in the control room. "The others are coming. Everyone's buzzed in."

"Good. Have one of the Bunters whip up something to wake us up, would you?" he asked her as he sat down at the tactical console and began to go over the damage assessments.

"Done," she replied, and signaled for a Bunter. "I wonder how they fit this attack into their honor? Or do they plan to lose this fight, too?"

Another boulder slammed toward the *Yngmoto* but crumbled as it encountered the deflection shield.

There was a series of emphatic and creative oaths as Section Leader Jarrick Riven stumbled into the control room. "What in the name of everything round is going on out there?"

"Zim has another suitor, I think. I recognize the style," said Haakogard, then immediately softened his remarks. "Or maybe the same suitor. That's the trouble with clones—they're the same thing in the same package." He was rewarded by Zim's wan smile.

"Are all the ships getting bombarded?" asked Riven as he took his seat and gave a quick, cursory glance at all the displays.

"Looks like it," said Haakogard. He reviewed the damage reports again and was relieved to see that the worst any of the four Katanas had got out of this encounter was a dent or two. He peered at the communication frame and shook his head.

"What is it? Goren? Why that look?" asked Mawson Tallis, who had just arrived with his Bunter following him, comb upraised to put some order into the Executive Officer's fair hair. "Why the commotion?"

"The Other Colonists?" Haakogard said.

"No, I mean, what's bothering you?" He relented and stood still for his Bunter, saying to the cyborg, "We are under attack, you know."

"Class five attack," said the Bunter. "Class five attack is very low priority and does not relax uniform codes." It took one more swipe at his hair, then moved, three of its four arms neatly telescoped into its body.

"Never argue with a Bunter," said Riven. He yawned. "I'm not awake yet. Someone nudge me if we get into any real trouble."

"I think we might have some real trouble," said Haakogard as he finally brought his attention to focus on what was bothering him. "I received a zap a couple hours ago that has me worried."

"What now?" asked Zim, her voice rising.

"It was from Fleet Commodore Herd. He leaves it up to our judgment but says that the Twelve have agreements with the Comes Riton and the government in the capital. That means we can't just walk out; they want something guarded here, but I don't know what it is. I don't know why the Twelve want it guarded. I don't know what it has to do with this clone business. Has anyone here ever been to Bilau?"

"It's on the other side of the continent, almost," said Tallis. "We might as well ignore it. It's too far away to—"

"I was there a couple years ago," said Riven. "It was a layover during a transfer. Bilau's like a lot of capitals on marginal planets—it has a few sights, a few thrills, a red-light district with some kinks, and the rest is utilitarian. PoMoend is more interesting for architecture, and the Hub has better entertainment."

"Yes," said Haakogard slowly. "But there was something in code for Perzda from Knapp at the end of the zap. If Alliance Intelligence Operations is mixed up in this—"

Everyone in the control room made sounds of disgust, and Nola Zim actually shrieked.

"That is what I think. So I want to talk to Perzda, and she's probably in the bunker. She ought to be there." Haakogard looked toward the surveills again. "No one fire back. They can't do much but keep us awake, but we would wipe them all out."

"Maybe that's what they're all after," suggested Tallis.

"Why do you say that?" Haakogard asked.

"Maybe they want to go out in a blaze of glory instead of having these long battles with the Comes Riton. Look what they did with the wild animals. They could all have got killed. This is the same thing, maybe." He looked rather smug; he was pleased with his assessment.

"Maybe, but I doubt it," said Haakogard. He rose, making up his mind. "I've had enough of this. I want Dachnor and Fennin to go out and catch me one of those Other Colonists. It's time we heard their side of it. Then we can decide what we want to do, if anything."

"I've already—" Zim began.

"That's not enough," Haakogard interrupted, kindly enough. "We'll get an Other Colonist together with Thunghalis and then we'll see if the Mromrosi can make sense of it." He stared out of the control room, bound for the security bunker where he trusted Perzda was waiting.

He was right. She held half a dozen fresh zap sheets in her hands and was thumbing through them as Haakogard came into the bunker. "I expected you before now."

"Sorry; things are a little confused," he said, and found himself a place to sit on the edge of her worktable. "What's the news?" He offered her the zap he had. "The last bit's yours."

"I've already read it," she said. "Fleet Commodore Herd has had the Marshal-in-Chief of the Grands arrested for taking bribes." She shook her head. "Stupid thing to do."

"Arresting him or the bribes?" Haakogard asked as he watched her go over the zaps.

"Both, probably," she said, a little distantly. When she put the zaps aside she looked at him directly. "We'd better do what we can to keep this farce here from exploding. Knapp's given me orders to report any divergence from specific instructions. We don't want to upset any of those delicate balances at the Hub, do we? So if you change sides now, or do anything that might make it appear you're countermanding what Herd wants you to do, you could end up in trouble. We all could." She sighed, her flinty eyes softening. "I don't want anything to go wrong. Not after all the years I've put in. I want to retire to Kousrau and study those ruins. They fascinate me. Imagine an entire civilization, a whole intelligent species, vanished and gone!—and only those ruins left.

"But I don't want to do it quite yet, and not in disgrace," she amended; then she touched one of the zaps. "Speaking of retirement, that's what the old Marshal-in-Chief of the Grands is going to be made to do, according to this. It's unofficial, of course, and there will be no public announcement for months. They're arranging for him to take over a tree plantation on Hathaway. He can't get into trouble there, and everyone can pretend the scandal was minor, including the Marshal-in-Chief. All very neat, all the nasty bits covered up." Her eyes were cynical and bright. "Less embarrassing this way." She flung three of the zaps into the air.

"Viridis," said Haakogard, not certain whether he was arguing or agreeing with her. When she looked at him directly again, he said, "Thanks for the warning. Now if only we could it explain it to everyone here." He hitched his thumb in the direction of the attacking Other Colonists. "Can we activate your surveills?"

"Sure," she said after a light hesitation. "If you want to. What do you expect to see?"

"I expect to see Dachnor and Fennin get one or more of the Other Colonists. I want someone to answer questions." He would have started the surveills himself, but in this bunker only Group Leader Perzda's geneprint would start the equipment.

"Is Alrou Malise on the bridge?" she asked as she stuck her hand to the identplate.

"Yes," said Haakogard, watching the screens come alive. "Look. They're on the other side of the *Sigjima*. They're wearing nightsuits." He indicated where Dachnor and Fennin were making their way through a low outcropping of rocks, taking great care with their footing as they went.

"Fennin's a good outside man," said Perzda as she studied his progress. "Dachnor's too quick, he gets noticed that way."

Haakogard did not say anything, being caught up in what his officers were doing. He leaned forward and watched the screens, as if he could protect them with the intensity of his gaze. At last he said, "Look just the other side of that boulder."

"Three of them," Perzda said. "I wish I'd put out a few more monitors. We might have got more of them, with less risk."

"It's all right," said Haakogard while his two Group Chiefs converged on the three Other Colonists, stunners ready.

In the next instant, one of the Other Colonists started to turn, made a muffled shout, then collapsed as the stun charge felled him. The other two were a fraction of a second too late, and both of them collapsed as well.

"Now what?" asked Perzda. "Two Harriers, three Other Colonists. You can't leave one or two behind, because they'll tell the others, and that could make them heat up the attack on us, which we don't want. So what do you think they should do, Line Commander?" She was teasing him but her question was sensible.

"They'll bring them all back here, of course," said Haakogard. "In fact, we'd better get the loading hatch open and arrange for the *Freyama* to provide some kind of diversion. Get me Chanliz and tell her it's urgent." This last was to the communications nodule set in Perzda's worktable.

The nodule beeped and three seconds later, Leilah Chanliz said, "What is it? And it better be good."

There were times when Haakogard would not allow such a response to go uncorrected, but this time he did his best to chuckle. "That'll be up to you," he told her, and explained what he wanted. "Be careful, but not too careful."

"Give me four minutes and we'll do it," she said, the irate tone gone and now replaced with faint amusement. "We'll give you—what? ten minutes? —outside. But tell Dachnor and Fennin to work fast. We can't distract them forever, no matter what we do." With that she signed off, and Haakogard sat back to watch with Viridis Perzda.

True to her word, four minutes later the side hatch of the *Freyama* opened and Chanliz, splendidly out of uniform in a gauze gown from her home planet of Lontano, stepped into the night, followed by her Communications Leader, Yenne Ciomat, who was wrapped in a lounging robe. The two of them wandered from one of the monitors to the next, taking time to stop and embrace each other at every monitor. Their attention seemed to be entirely on each other, and only the thud of a boulder landing a short distance away from where they stood attracted their notice, though not for long.

"Is this what you had in mind?" Perzda asked as she watched, a smile playing at the corners of her mouth.

"No, but it works better than my plan," answered Haakogard. Chanliz had slid halfway out of the clinging layers of gauze and was reaching inside Ciomat's lounging robe. "I only hope they don't divert *our* attention as much as the Other Colonists'." Then he saw Dachnor and Fennin crouching low, bringing the first of their three captives up to the loading hatch of the *Yngmoto*. "Better get ready for the first one," he said, addressing the nodule. "Everyone stand by."

There was the sound of the loading hatch opening and the scuffle of feet, then a few hurried whispers of instructions, and then silence returned.

"Watch them," said Perzda, pointing to Dachnor and Fennin on the surveills. "They're after number two."

"Good for them," said Haakogard, preparing to leave. "I've got to go find out what we've brought on board. You want to come with me?"

"I think I'd rather watch Chanliz and Ciomat," said Perzda with a wicked grin. "They're outrageous. They give me some good ideas."

"They certainly are outrageous," said Haakogard, hurrying toward the loading hatch. Now that he had a chance to speak with one of the Other Colonists, he was excited. Finally he could start to make a correct assessment of the situation here on Neo Biscay.

Two Bunters and Jarrick Riven had brought the first captive aboard. The Bunters were in the process of waking the captive out of the stun, and Riven leaned back on the wall, watching closely. As Haakogard hurried through the door, he offered a slight wave of his hand before he pointed. "Bagged one. Two more coming."

"I saw on the surveills," said Haakogard, squatting down next to the Other Colonist. "Big man, outdoor skin." He took the fellow's jaw in his hand and tipped his head back. "Looks pretty healthy."

"In a place like this you're healthy or you're dead," Riven pointed out. "There's no room for sickly types. Notice his hands. Someone mashed his knuckles more than once."

"Fighting?" Haakogard asked, and answered for himself. "No; there's no scars on his face that say he fights, and his ears are all right. His nose hasn't been broken. He might have got his hands hurt working with animals." He rose to his feet, a tad more slowly than he had five years ago, but still quickly enough. He let the Bunters continue their work. "I want the Medical Leader from the *Ubehoff* to come over and check these Other Colonists out. And I want Thunghalis to go to the conference room. We'll do our questions and answers there."

"You want to wait for Dachnor and Fennin?" Riven asked, noticing that the Other Colonist was starting to move on his own a little.

"Yes. But I don't want these men piling up here in the loading bay." He brushed off his hands and hurried away, wondering if Chanliz and Ciomat were still astonishing the men guarding the ballistas. A faint shudder of near impact answered the question for him.

Dawn was still almost a Standard Hour away; only the tasty and stimulating drinks supplied by the Bunters kept the crew of the *Yngmoto* at their work as the long night wound down.

In the conference room, the three Other Colonists had sat in weary silence while Haakogard and the Mromrosi attempted to coax them into speaking. It was not a promising beginning, and there was nothing to suggest new avenues to explore. Thunghalis kept to his end of the table, but he stared at the Other Colonists with such outrage that Haakogard wanted to order him to look away.

"We're not asking anything impossible," Haakogard pointed out, trying another tack with the three captives. "If we had decided to punish you for trying to damage our ships, I assure you we would have done it by now. We only want to talk to you, to find out the nature of your grievances with the people of poMoend."

The one who appeared the youngest of the three

gave a single bark of contempt, then resumed his silence.

"We can do nothing to aid you if you will not inform us of what wrong needs redress." Haakogard looked over at the Mromrosi, knowing that the Other Colonists had been frightened by him. "He is here to be sure that you are treated fairly, and he cannot do that if you will not tell him what is happening here, and why poMoend is on the brink of war."

The silence continued, more ominous than ever.

"You are not helping yourselves or your people or your cause by refusing to talk with us," said Haakogard, feeling idiotic.

"You will say that we lie, whatever our answers are. We all know that you are here at the behest of the Comes Riton and will do whatever he demands of you, for his pleasure and satisfaction, not for ours." It was the youngest one again, the one with the beautiful voice.

"We're here at the behest of the Twelve of the Magnicate Alliance, and the direct orders of the Fleet Commodore of the Harriers, Grands and Petits," said Haakogard for what he felt must certainly be the hundredth time. "The Comes Riton asked for our help, but we are not his men; we are Petit Harriers of the Magnicate Alliance." He looked over at the Mromrosi again, trying to learn something from the alien, but the shaggy curls remained pink, and for all the movement he made, he might as well have been asleep.

"You will serve the Comes Riton's honor. You will kill the alternate and that will be the end of the conflict. You will discharge your obligation." He was speaking more loudly, his voice ringing with emotion. "You will consent to it because it will end the dispute and your record will be favorable."

"That's not true," said Haakogard testily. "If it

isn't fair to everyone, the Mromrosi won't allow it, and if it goes against the Alliance interests, the Twelve will forbid it." At least one of the Other Colonists was talking, he consoled himself as he took a long sip of his Bunter's concoction; the taste wasn't bad and it kept him awake.

"But by then we will be honorably dead," said the Other Colonist in gloomy satisfaction as his silent fellows gestured their agreement.

"No," said Haakogard, getting up and stretching. His shoulders were aching again, and in spite of the stimulants, he knew he needed sleep. His thoughts were turning woolly and thick. He went to the door and said softly to his Bunter, "Go get Navigator Zim, will you? Maybe they'll answer questions from her." Then he went back to his seat, and leaned over the back of it. "If you don't tell us what's going on, we will have to accept what the Comes Riton says. We don't want to do that, but we'll have to if there is no counterevidence to offer. Our hands are tied." It was a variation of the same case he had been pleading ever since the Other Colonists were brought aboard, and he did his best to make it convincing. "We do not want to make an expedient choice if that choice is wrong. Help us."

"You need nothing from us but our deaths," said the youngest one. He fixed Haakogard with his sand-colored eyes. "We are not afraid to die. Death will not dishonor us."

"Of course not," said Haakogard in exasperation. "You've made that obvious. But do you want to live, or is this a grand and tragic gesture you're making?" He could see that the Mromrosi was turning a darker pink; at least the alien observer was paying attention.

"We have more honor than that!" exclaimed the youngest Other Colonist, all but leaping to his feet.

The other two thumped the table with their hands as the youngest cried out, "You disdain us, you impugn—"

"I'm trying to make sense out of this," said Haakogard, cutting the other man's outburst short, "and you are not helping." He heard the door hiss preparatory to opening. "Zim? Sorry to get you up, but I need you."

Nola Zim had been asleep three minutes ago and had put on her simplest uniform, a single-piece coverall in matte gray with the horse-head insignia on the collar tabs. There were soft shadows under her eyes almost the same dark blue as her hair, and her voice was three notes lower than usual. "Why did you send for me, Line Commander?"

"Because I hoped you could help," said Haakogard, indicating a place at the table for her to sit. "Join us."

She went to the chair and was about to sink into it when the youngest of the Other Colonists nearly climbed onto the table, sand-colored eyes glowing. Zim stared at him, the last vestiges of sleep falling away from her like unwanted garments. "Tenre?" she whispered.

"It *is* you," he said, making a song of it.

She gazed at him, unmindful of the others in the conference room. "You were one of the men they caught?"

"To think I was so foolish that I cursed my luck," he said tenderly. "I should bow to these men for bringing me to you."

"Because they caught you?" She looked anxiously at Haakogard, but without the same tension she had shown when the Comes Riton had visited her. "How can you feel that way?"

"Because they caught me, I offer them my sublime thanks. Yes!" he exclaimed, one hand extended toward her. "I came here for you."

Haakogard nodded, satisfied at last. "The alternate, I presume?" he said, not expecting an answer.

At the far end of the table Thunghalis rose from his place, his features set in amazement. "Comes Riton. It is, it is the Comes Riton," he declared, abasing himself. "I am now doubly unworthy."

"Oh, no," Haakogard murmured, looking toward the ceiling as if he might find inspiration there.

The Other Colonist was shaken from his comtemplation of Navigator Zim; his hand went to his belt though he no longer carried his throwing star there. "Do not speak of the Comes Riton, not to me. I want no part of him," said his alternate in the same mellifluous tones as the Comes Riton used.

"But—" Thunghalis began.

"I am Tenre, son of Syclicis," he stated in tones so firm no one could dispute them. "The Comes Riton is my clone, but I am not his alternate." He pounded the table and the two Other Colonists thumped along with him.

Thunghalis remained bent over. "I am stripped of all honor. Give me permission, O Most Excellent Comes, to expiate my wrongs before I compound them further. Allow me the comfort of an honorable death." He looked up at Tenre, his eyes eager for the chance to kill himself.

"Stop it," Haakogard interrupted. "There's no reason for any of this. Thunghalis, get up. You, Tenre, you sit down. We have a great deal left to discuss now that you're talking."

"While this woman stands, I cannot sit," said Tenre with feeling. "I would not offer her such an insult."

"Then sit down, Zim, so the rest of us can." Haakogard thought that under other circumstances he might find this amusing, like a festival game, but not at this hour of the night after his ships had been attacked. He studied Zim as he dropped into his seat, wondering if she were merely tired or something about the clone Tenre had actually captivated her. He hoped it was the former and not the latter.

Thunghalis was the last to obey Haakogard's suggestion, and he was obviously ill-at-ease complying. He sat hunkered down so that his head was lower than Tenre's, and he never took his eyes off the Comes Riton's clone.

"Why did you attack us?" Haakogard asked Tenre. He discovered that his warm and stimulating drink had gone cold, and he signaled to his Bunter to refill it as he waited for the answer. His head was starting to feel as if it were wrapped in pillows. *Maybe*, he thought, *I should ask for a stronger stimulant*, though he knew it was a bad idea.

Tenre did not answer at once, but directed his adoring gaze toward Zim. He spoke to her as if offering her an apology. "We weren't attacking you, not directly. You must believe this. We wanted it to be plain that we would not accept anything done by the Comes Riton, no matter what it was. He brought his men here, and his musicians, and that could only mean one thing. We realized that a truce was going to be signed and we were determined to show that we would resist you, no matter what the Comes Riton promised you, or what assurances he gave you." He folded his arms and regarded Thunghalis steadily for more than a minute before turning back to Zim again.

Haakogard felt like someone or something left over from a celebration, but he told himself not to regard his emotions. He cleared his throat, more for attention than because he was worn out. "Why would the men and musicians make you think we were signing a truce?"

For once Tenre looked directly at him as he answered. "How else is a truce declared, but with trumpets and gongs? That is the way it has been since the First Colony arrived and so it is now."

"But there is no question of a truce," said Zim, using this as an excuse to reach out and take his hand. "We have no power to enforce one even if we had been asked to negotiate one. That was not the purpose." To Haakogard's astonishment, she blushed.

"How do you mean, not the purpose?" Tenre demanded impulsively. "For what other reason would the Comes Riton bring musicians as well as soldiers if not to—"

Thunghalis answered, very unhappy to provide the answer. "The Comes Riton has experienced a departure from himself, away from his nature and his understanding," he said heavily. "He is now like one made or failed in his thoughts. Never has a phase of the Comes Riton been so lax or . . . He came here to . . . seek that woman." He pointed to Zim. "He has declared he will claim her, and use her as men use free-breeding women."

"No! *Never!*" shouted Tenre, coming half out of his chair. "No."

"Exactly," said Haakogard, who had to suppress a sudden irrational impulse to laugh. "That was more or less the response he was given."

"It is shameful that the Comes Riton should sully himself in this way," said Thunghalis, who was not amused by any part of the situation. "He is a dupe of this alien woman. He has forgot everything that is right and moral and traditional to Neo Biscay and his rank. He is insane. It will surely ruin him."

Zim's eyes glittered. "I do not wish to accept the offer of the Comes Riton. I have informed him of my decision, and he has heard me out. I do not have to listen to you speak of me this way." She pulled her hand away from Tenre and moved a little closer to Haakogard. "Do I have to remain here?"

"I'd prefer you do, but I don't absolutely require it," said Haakogard quietly. "I know it isn't pleasant for you; I'm sorry about that. But I need your help, you can see why. This is the first real talking we've got out of these Other Colonists. If you remain, perhaps we can keep them going?"

He folded his hands and made himself more comfortable. "She has a point," he remarked to the company around the table. "If you want to express your outrage, Thunghalis, go ahead, but don't blame Zim. She did not seek out the Comes Riton, he came here, and she has told him she is not willing."

Thunghalis shook his head, his eyes still on Navigator Zim. "She has done something to him. No phase of the Comes Riton has ever behaved so senselessly as this phase has since he met her. The Comes Riton is a clone and cannot—must not—deviate from what he was before. But now he is no longer himself, so it must be that she has influenced him. There is no other reason he should conduct himself as he has, in a manner that borders on dishonor." He gathered his large hands into fists and ground his knuckles together. "It is that woman. She has power."

"You must not say these dreadful things of her," protested Tenre, glaring at Thunghalis, his arms in the posture for direct attack. He was ready to forget his own honor to battle the disgraced Pangbar, and only a warning cry from his own men stopped him. In compromise, he moved so that he was between Thunghalis and Zim, saying, "Speak one more word against her now and I will make you account for it in blood."

"You are in her thrall as well," said Thunghalis, awed.

"No. Those who are in thrall are thus against their desires, and I can want nothing more than the honor of her presence and the grace of her affection. It is a privilege to be in her presence, not an imposition. And you do her and yourself no honor by making such a statement." Tenre lowered his arms, no longer pugnacious. "Zim would captivate any man who saw her, and she would be his ultimate treasure, as dear as his honor. The only thing I have heard of the Comes Riton which I can endorse is his devotion to her."

He hesitated, looking first at Haakogard, then Thunghalis, then he spoke to Zim. "If I were the Comes Riton and not his alternate, I would not permit honest officers to kill themselves to regain honor. My honor would be in their loyalty and service. I would not ask my men to seek ruin in order to prove themselves. I would praise them for all they have done and ask that they continue to serve me in honor, as I serve you."

The two Other Colonists who had been captured with Tenre echoed Thunghalis' laughter, and one of them growled an oath that made the Pangbar sit more rigidly.

"I'll check the monitors," said Zim, glad of a reason to leave the room.

"Come back," said Haakogard to her. "Soon."

She looked away from him. "All right. All right. Soon."

## 3

"Anything?" Haakogard asked Perzda as she came from the bunker. Afternoon had faded into evening, the monitors posted around the perimeter of their zone had been doubled, and so far they had no trouble. The Other Colonists had withdrawn into the mountains, though their scouts appeared near the Katanas frequently. For the time being, things were quiet.

"More of the same," she said with an eloquent lift to her shoulders. "Until the Twelve are satisfied that the Grands are cleaned up, we'd better keep our heads down. We don't want to give them any excuses to drag us into their mess. Just remember what we're supposed to be doing here and leave the rest for later." She faltered, and continued awkwardly, "There's something I probably shouldn't tell you. It came in double code. Without the brain implants it can't be read."

"What did it say?" Haakogard asked, feeling the beginnings of real apprehension; information sent in codes only brain-implanted spies could read always worried him. "Why do you think I ought to know?"

"Well, it's completely secret, but I can talk about it, so there wasn't a brain block in the code." She looked down at her feet. "Apparently a company of Grands are being sent to the capital here."

"Here?" Haakogard felt his innards go cold. "Already? Neo Biscay?"

"Neo Biscay; Bilau," she said, in case there was any doubt.

"But . . . Why?" He stared at her as if she might show him the answer in a single, encompassing gesture. "We can't do what we're supposed to be doing here as it is," said Haakogard. "And now they're bringing the Grands in on the other side of the continent. I'd heard they might come here, but I didn't think they'd arrive yet. Why? What do they need the Grands for? We're confused enough as it is. If they put their men in . . . It doesn't make any sense, not at this time." He was rested now and he no longer felt as if he were moving about a step behind himself.

"It's pressure," said Perzda. "The Grands putting it on the Petits. They probably want a way to throw attention off what happened with their Marshal-in-

Chief. What better way than to show up here a little early, before everything's settled? If we bungle the mission, the Grands can point at us while their Marshal slips off to Hathaway without fuss." She looked directly at Haakogard. "They're making us a target."

Little as he wanted to, he realized she was right. "There's got to be a way," he said, speaking as much to himself as to her. "There's got to be a way to change it around so that it doesn't blow up with us in the middle of it." He locked his hands together, then gave her a quick, quirky smile. "I'm open to suggestions."

"I wish I had some to give," he said. "If I think of anything . . ."

"No matter how zany," he said.

"Yeah. Just like the rest of the mission," said Perzda fatalistically. "Is there anything you want to do, Line Commander? Right now?"

He considered, then shook his head. "What can I do? I'm not supposed to know about the Grands. We were told to support the Comes Riton, but it's anyone's guess which of the clones is entitled to the position. If we could figure that out, maybe we'd have the answer to it all." He took a deep breath; somehow, he thought, there had to be a way. There had to be a solution that did not end in war and did not make his mission scapegoats for the Grands. He was damned if he would sacrifice his mission and poMoend to a Grand diversionary tactic. "Any other observations you want to make?"

"Not yet," she said. "It's too . . . confused."

"Meaning crazy," he suggested.

"That, too."

By midnight the soldiers and officers of the Comes Riton were back and camped around the four Katanas. Their signal fires blazed at the top of every hillock and outcropping while the army drilled long into the night, gongs and trumpets sounding at unfamiliar intervals, and drums rolling incessantly.

"How many?" Haakogard asked as he came into the control room. He had spent the last hour with the Mromrosi and was eager to catch up on any changes in the poMoend camp.

"Two thousand four hundred seventy six," said Communications Leader Alrou Malise. "According to the monitors."

"Close enough estimate," said Haakogard, his humor forced. He was at his seat but remained standing, restless. "The Mromrosi says that our position here is crucial. He doesn't elaborate." Another complicated fanfare blared.

"I don't know that I don't prefer the ballistas—they're quieter and less continuous. At least the First Colonists didn't have the bagpipe. How many hours of this do we have to put up with? Are they trying to wear us down?"

"What do you reckon? Are they going to attack?" asked Executive Officer Tallis, his youthful features bright with the promise of conflict.

"I don't know," said Haakogard as he watched the surveills. "We're ready to repel them, but the Comes Riton won't like it. We have no business standing against them, that's the trouble. We ought to be prepared to fight beside them, not . . . this." He turned away from his seat and paced the length of the conference room. He never liked waiting, and waiting for someone to fight was worst of all.

"We could take off, go make a dozen passes over Civuto poMoend, nice and low. We could drop something harmless so they'd figure out we could hurt them if we wanted to. They can't keep the Katanas grounded with their flyers, so why not?" suggested Section Leader Jarrick Riven. "That would give them something to think about. Make them aware of how exposed they are."

"We're not supposed to strike first, and we're not supposed to provoke attack, especially not from the Comes Riton. Taunting them won't work. We're here to defend him. He asked for our help, remember?" said Alrou Malise with an annoyed chuckle for emphasis. "Those are our allies out there."

"The Comes Riton," said Haakogard, and he could have knocked his head into the wall for having taken so long to think of it. "That's it. That's *it*! That's what— It's been there the whole time. The Comes Riton." He sat down. "How could I miss it?"

"That's what?" asked Mawson Tallis suspiciously.

"The way to keep them from fighting; to settle this whole mess," said Haakogard, his mind working very rapidly now that he had a direction to pursue. It felt so good to know what to do. "And to get us off the hook. I've been blind and stupid. It's so obvious!"

"Not to us," said Tallis, hoping Haakogard would explain.

"It will be." He pressed his private communications nodule and said, "Please ask Navigator Zim and Colonist Tenre to meet me in my quarters in five minutes." With that he waved to the others. "Get into class five dress uniforms. All of you. Bunter-perfect. We're going to need to fancy up. No jewels, but a lot of ribbon and brass. Put on every medal and award you have." He grinned as he pushed out of the conference room and hastened along to his quarters, rapping out a few sharp orders to his Bunter as he came through the door. "Class five dress. And find something in the music tapes, something loud and impressive, lots of roulades and explosions. Put it on all the exterior hailers on all four Katanas."

"At once?" asked his Bunter.

"At once," said Haakogard as he stripped off his

standard work uniform and reached for his shiny class five.

By the time Zim and Tenre showed up, he was adjusting the red horse-head tags on his collar, positioning the four rosettes of his rank at the proper places around the horse's head. He welcomed them perfunctorily, saying, "I have an idea how to work this, but I'll have to get your help. I mean of both of you. It's risky, but I think it'll do the trick. Will that be acceptable to you?"

"It depends on what you want us to do," said Zim, not allowing Tenre to answer. "I want to know how risky it is. If it's reasonable, fine." The response was daunting, just as she intended it to be. She held her head higher than usual and the tone of her voice was defiant.

"Naturally," Haakogard assured her, smiling at his own reflection and hers behind him. If he could convince these two, he told himself, he would be able to persuade Thunghalis as well, and poMoend. One hurdle at a time, he warned himself inwardly. He tweaked the points of his collar and turned to face Zim and Tenre. "Correct me if I am in error, but the soldiers of poMoend will not attack the Comes Riton in any phase, will they?"

"It is dishonorable to do it," said Tenre, looking toward Zim for the reason for this question. He had not been prepared to answer, by the look of him, and now that he had, he feared he had done the wrong thing, or handled it badly.

Haakogard nodded. "And you are a clone of the Comes Riton just as legitimately as the current Comes is, am I right about that?" He could hardly help grinning.

Zim's eyes narrowed as she watched Haakogard beam at them. "You know the answers to your questions. We established that already. Genetically the

Comes and Tenre are interchangable. So what are
you up to, Line Commander? And don't say you
aren't up to something, because you are. If there's
anything incorrect about—"

"Navigator, let me finish. You can upbraid me
then if you still want to," he said, more convinced
than ever that he had made a very clever decision. "I
think we've found a way out of this mess. For all of
us. You are a clone of the Comes Riton, that's what
counts. You're the same phase as the current Comes
Riton."

"Yes," said Tenre suspiciously.

Haakogard looked from Zim to Tenre, his excitement making him want to chuckle, though he controlled it. "Suppose you claimed your position as
Comes Riton?"

"What?" demanded Tenre.

"Goren!" objected Zim at the same time. It was
evidence of serious shock on her part to use Haakogard's
first name that way.

"Well?" Haakogard inquired directly of Tenre, his
eyes open and candid as a child's. "Couldn't you do
that? Aren't you entitled to it? Couldn't your authenticity be demonstrated? Aren't you qualified?"

Tenre scowled and stepped back a little. "If I were
despicable enough to want it, to disown my mother
and her people, I suppose I am qualified."

"Ah, but that's just the point: strictly speaking she
wasn't your mother, was she? You're a clone and she
kidnapped you," said Haakogard, pressing what little
advantage he hoped he had with Tenre. "Isn't that
what happened?"

"What are you getting at, Line Commander?"
Zim asked pointedly. "What are you up to?"

"I'm not up to anything, not the way you're imply-
ing at least," Haakogard insisted. "I have a plan,
that's all." He regarded Tenre evenly, trying to con-

vince the Comes Riton's clone by restating his case. "Are you willing to help us resolve this conflict? It can be done peaceably, if you're willing to make a few accommodations."

"Is that why you're dressed up?" Zim asked, more convinced than ever that Haakogard was manipulating her and Tenre.

"Yes; and I'd appreciate it if you'd get into your class fives, too. Or something that's the civilian equivalent. You've got some such clothes in your wardrobe, haven't you? I've given the order to the other Katanas for the crews to be ready in a quarter of an hour. I'll want a short Harrier drill done in the center of the ships, for starters." He grinned again. "That ought to get their attention. They seem to like drills."

"And what then?" Zim insisted. "You might as well tell us, if you expect any cooperation." She did not sound encouraging but Haakogard explained as if she had been wholeheartedly enthusiastic.

"Then we present them with the Comes Riton. Tenre." He looked from Zim to Tenre and back again. "In full regalia, or as close as we can come with the Bunters working on it. Since the officers and soldiers will not attack him, the other Comes Riton will have to negotiate. We will not hurt Tenre, and neither will the men of poMoend. Even the Mromrosi would have to like a plan like this." He pretended he had not noticed the look of repugnance on Tenre's face, or the wildness in Zim's eyes. "We can work out terms that are honorable but won't leave anyone dead. That's the most honorable of all, no matter what Thunghalis thinks."

Tenre shook his head. "Death is preferable to claiming that vile title," he announced vehemently to the air, his voice glorious.

Haakogard crossed his arms. "Is it?" He waited briefly. "Truly?" He waited again. "Is Navigator Zim supposed to agree with you? And how honorable is it for the men who follow you now and who will die to no purpose because you will not end this dispute? If you were not the alternate clone of the Comes Riton, he would have ·been able to crush you and your fighters long ago. It would have been a simple civil war. There would have been no need to bring the Petit Harriers into it. The only reason we were brought in is that it is dishonorable to attack you—you, the clone of the Comes Riton—directly. If you were not who you are, there would be no dishonor for poMoend in wiping all the First Colonists off Neo Biscay. What little protection the First Colonists have had is because of you." He swung around to face Zim. "Not one word, Nola. For once, you listen."

"But—" she began.

"Listen," said Haakogard in a light, conversational manner that silenced Zim more quickly than a command would have done. He gave his attention to Tenre again. "Will you make that claim? For the sake of your followers? Or do you all have to die?"

"No one does not die," said Tenre, lifting his head. "No man escapes."

Haakogard did not permit himself to be pulled off track. "Better old and happy than young and terrified," he said and resumed his argument. "Will you at least attempt to be recognized?"

Tenre coughed once, twice. "I have sworn never to—"

He got no further. The door to Haakogard's quarters opened and the Mromrosi scuttled in. He bounced in the direction of Haakogard and Zim in the most perfunctory courtesy, then moved purposefully toward Tenre, his frizzy locks mercurochrome-red. As he reached Tenre, he was shaking, his curls in greater disorder than usual. "You!" the Mromrosi howled directly at Tenre. "You do not emerge! You do not come forth. You are bound in losses. You have contempt where growth waits and you embrace your downfall." He jounced himself indignantly.

Tenre backed away from the Mromrosi until he was against a tall case containing Haakogard's personal weapons. His sand-colored eyes were enormous and he held his arms in defense posture. "What is this all about?" he kept repeating while the Mromrosi quivered at him.

Haakogard watched with some amusement as Tenre tried to avoid the aggravated Mromrosi. At last he said, "Our alien observer doesn't approve of your decision, Tenre. Maybe you'd better reconsider." He motioned to Zim. "That goes for you, too."

Her smile was sardonic and quick, but it was there. "Class five dress uniform, I believe that's what you said, Line Commander? Or its civilian equivalent?"

"That's what I said," Haakogard agreed, filled with relief.

The crews of the *Yngmoto*, *Freyama*, *Sigjima*, and *Ubehoff* had just completed the second part of their three-part drill when the stern military music that had accompanied them ceased abruptly, only to be replaced with a large, exuberant fanfare; the monitors around the zone brightened all their lights and the four Katanas added their own lights to the dazzle. The soldiers of the Comes Riton who had been watching the drill now came nearer, curious and determined at once.

"Good enough. All halt," said Executive Officer Mawson Tallis, indicating where the crews were to draw up in ranks.

The loading hatch of the *Yngmoto* was lowered to more peals of brazen joy. The Mromrosi emerged first, a series of bright clips attached to his curls. Behind him Line Commander Haakogard escorted the alternate Comes Riton.

Barbered and groomed, rigged out in the closest approximation to the dress uniform of the Comes Riton of poMoend, Tenre was disturbingly like his clone. This man was not quite as imperious, but his face showed more lines and therefore suggested age and experience beyond that of the other clone. He walked slowly because of the tight boots he wore, and he could not make himself smile. The stern line of his mouth was more impressive than he realized, and gained another notch of respect from the soldiers of poMoend.

Behind him, Navigator Zim came, not in uniform but in a reception dress of deep blue that shone black where the light struck it directly. She wore a wide sash decked with two jeweled orders and her splendid dark blue hair was dressed in the height of Hub fashion. The soldiers of poMoend were very still, very silent.

A longer, more majestic fanfare sounded; the Petit Harriers came to attention and saluted. Haakogard steeled himself for his gamble. He stepped forward and gave a short bow to Tenre. "We have been ordered by the Magnicate Alliance to assist the Comes Riton of PoMoend to end the conflict between the First and Second Colonizations. To that end, we give our assurances to you, as the continuing phase of the Comes Riton, to protect your claim to the leadership of poMoend." He could hear the translators repeating his words to the waiting soldiers and officers.

A Tydbar raised his hands in protest. "We serve the true Comes Riton, not this . . . interloper." He was echoed by several others, and a few of the Harriers exchanged uneasy glances. "We have sworn to defend the True First and all his phases."

"This is the true Comes Riton. You may authenticate him. He is as true as your version of him is," said Haakogard quietly, waiting for the translators to do their work. "He is as much the Comes Riton's clone as your leader is. They are the same. And you are honor-bound to serve this one as loyally as you serve the other." He turned so that he could stand at Tenre's side. "Say nothing yet," he warned in a whisper. He listened to the angry, soft words of the soldiers of poMoend, not wanting to rush them. It was foolish to press them now.

Navigator Zim came up next to Haakogard. "Do you really think this will work, Goren?"

"I hope it will," said Haakogard. "Otherwise . . ."

There was a sudden excitement in the poMoend ranks marked by shouting and a hurried attempt to stand in good order. Then an avenue of soldiers opened and the Comes Riton strode down it, his features thunderous.

"Do nothing," Haakogard ordered Tenre under his breath. "Just stand."

"I do not want to see the Comes Riton," said Tenre softly, and there was fright as well as hauteur in him.

"You're going to have to. He probably doesn't like it any better than you do," Haakogard declared, hoping that the Comes Riton was not armed. He palmed his stunner, just in case.

The Comes Riton stopped at the monitor line where a faint shimmer in the air revealed the deflection shields. "You betray me, Petit Harriers!" he shouted, the sound of it magnificent.

"How do we do that, Most Excellent Comes Riton?" Haakogard responded with great politeness. "We were asked to protect the clone of the Comes Riton: how have we failed to do that?"

"You have allied yourself with the alternate," accused the Comes Riton.

"Who is the clone of the Most Excellent Comes Riton just as you are," said Haakogard at his most reasonable. "We are following the orders given us by Fleet Commander Herd." He remained at attention while he spoke, so there would be no reason to claim he showed disrespect to the irate Comes Riton.

"He is the *alternate!*" the Comes Riton bellowed.

Haakogard closed his eyes an instant for respite, then took his single greatest chance. "Is he? Are you sure of that?" He felt Tenre stiffen with shock at his side; he continued persuasively, "Are you sure you were not the alternate, Most Excellent Comes? When Syclicis kidnapped the clone, would it not have made more sense for her to take the first, not the second clone? Think; wouldn't it?" He wanted to turn to Tenre in order to reassure him, but he dared not give up the advantage he had found with the Comes Riton. "What if you are the alternate, not this man? Isn't that what the alternate is for, to take the place of the clone of the Comes Riton if any mischance should keep him from reaching maturity?"

"I am the Comes Riton!" he screamed, and for the first time the sound of his voice was ugly. "I!"

"And so is this man," said Haakogard. He nudged Tenre so that he stepped forward one pace. "He is the Comes Riton, too."

The Comes Riton made a loud, furious noise and started to reach for his throwing axe, preparing to destroy Tenre with a single, decisive blow.

"*Don't!*" Zim yelled, bringing up her arm, her stunner aimed directly at the Comes Riton. "Don't," she repeated.

But the Comes Riton was already restrained by a dozen of his officers. "No one," said a lean Tydbar, "is permitted to attack the Comes Riton." He forced the Comes Riton to lower his hand and give up his weapon.

"*I am the Comes Riton!*" he bellowed. "I will have you flayed for what you have done, Tydbar."

"No," said another Tydbar. "That is not correct. You attacked a clone of the Comes Riton and we cannot permit that to happen." Then he abased himself. "I have done treason to thwart you. I want to end my disgrace by ending my life, Most Excellent Comes."

"I will kill you myself," said the Comes Riton grimly, showing his teeth without smiling.

Tenre took another step forward. "No!" His voice was as compelling as the other clone's. "I forbid it. These men have defended me. They deserve praise, not death."

"You forbid it? *You*?" the Comes Riton laughed ferociously. "You're something out of a bad dream. You have no right to forbid me *anything*." He kicked at the postrate Tydbar, whooping at every impact.

"Leave him alone," said Tenre, coming another step close. "He has done nothing wrong."

The Comes Riton started to protest but was suddenly restrained again by his own Tydbars. "If you do this, you are as guilty as Tydbar Grabt here, and you will answer with your lives."

"They will not," declared Tenre. He was almost at the barrier now, standing very straight; being half a head taller than his clone, he had a slight advantage. "Tydbar, get up. You have not dishonored yourself. You have tried to protect me, and that is your sworn duty."

"He is sworn to protect ME!" roared the Comes Riton.

"Precisely," said Haakogard, who had moved up behind Tenre. "Neither of you can attack the other or allow the other to be attacked. You have a stalemate here, and no way to change it that does not dishonor one or the other of you; any attempt at aggression brings both of you down, one way and another." He stepped back, murmuring, "Zim, for Loovrie's sake, put that stunner away."

"Don't wish any of your Grunhavn spooks on me," she whispered back, but returned the stunner to its hidden sheath.

The Tydbars standing around the Comes Riton regarded one another in confusion; a few helped Grabt to his feet and dusted off the front of his uniform for him. No one could think what was proper to do next.

At last Haakogard spoke again. "Why don't you go back to Civuto poMoend and think about this? Talk it over. Consider your position. All right? When you decide how you want to handle having two Comes Ritons, you let us know."

"There cannot be two Comes Ritons," said the Comes Riton, his voice growling with emotion.

"Well, there are," said Haakogard, and addressed Tydbar Grabt. "We have Pangbar Thunghalis with us. You can work through him, if that makes it less difficult for you." He saluted Tydbar Grabt, then the Comes Riton. "There's got to be a reasonable answer to this problem, gentlemen." Very deliberately he put his hand on Tenre's shoulder. "We will expect to hear from you by dawn tomorrow. If you haven't sent word by then, we will come to Civuto poMoend. If you make it necessary, we will come armed, though we would much rather not." This warning was delivered with a pleasant smile to take away its bitterness.

"You will invade!" shouted the Comes Riton.

"We will negotiate," said Haakogard. "Be sensible. We haven't a large enough crew here to invade, even if we wished to, which we do not." He took two steps back, saluted one more time for good measure, then turned on his heel and started back toward the *Yngmoto*. He could hear Zim hurrying up behind him.

As she caught up with him, she said, "Tenre's still at the barrier."

"Fine," said Haakogard as he ducked into the

shadow of the Katana's double wing. "The more of the poMoend soldiers who see him, the better." He watched as the rest of the Petit Harriers executed a quick herringbone drill and then went back to their Katanas. "Zim," he said when the Harriers were gone and the martial music was silent, "What is it? You're . . . not yourself. What's going on with you?"

"You mean Tenre? Oh, high empathy index, according to the psycher," she said with a little diffident shrug. "Disenfranchised nobility, underdogs, powerful personalities: it's all part of the pattern." Her laughter was harsh with self-mockery. "Don't worry. It's fleeting. It's not even very intense, just involved. If he weren't so oppressed, I wouldn't pay any attention to him at all."

"If you say so." Haakogard's left eyebrow rose.

"Don't worry—really," she assured him. "Because when all's said and done, he's boring, and only the situation is novel, and this planet is a prison, like all planets." Impulsively she kissed his cheek. "But thanks for watching out for me."

"Part of my job," he told her, adding, "Now go in and get out of that rig before Tenre decides it means something."

She gave him a wide, jeering smile before hurrying into the port of the *Yngmoto*, leaving Haakogard to serve as an escort for Tenre.

Tydbar Grabt was one of the four officers who approached the Katanas shortly after sunrise the next morning. They all carried their weapons reversed, a sign of peaceful intention, and two of them carried large jars of oil and wine, the traditional gifts for allies.

"And that sheaf of arrows without points, that's the most significant," said Thunghalis as he watched the gifts set out right at the edge of the shimmering barrier. "More than the wine and oil."

"Why?" asked Haakogard. "What makes it so special?"

"It's from the founding of Civuto poMoend. This was supposed to be the central city of the north coast. It is, but the coast itself here is not like the coast to the south. We were not able to build on the cliffs and rocks, and so the city was built inland. The idea was that we would manage the development of trade but . . . Look around you. We do not trade very much in this part of Neo Biscay." He indicated the suveills and their barren setting. "So Bilau, on the other side of the continent, thrives and the south coast is filled with cities and towns while poMoend remains isolated with Other Colonists around it." He pointed to the arrows. "To give up arrows this way is to show you they are willing to go without food because you cannot hunt without arrows, and all for the sake of peace between us. They will do nothing harmful."

"All right," said Haakogard, faintly perplexed at this explanation, though he had long since become accustomed to odd traditions in out-of-the-way places. "What do we do, to let them know we'll cooperate?"

"Send out three or four officers, carrying no weapons. Two of them should bring some recognizable kind of food, and one should have a token like the arrows. That way you will do them honor and they will not be disgraced by the decisions you reach together." Thunghalis made a sweeping gesture that Haakogard suspected was intended to encompass the entire Petit Harrier mission on Neo Biscay. "If their offerings are dishonored—"

"I can imagine," said Haakogard. "All right," he announced to the control room and the communications nodule. "Bunters, I need two large sacks of simple foodstuffs. Take it from the shipwreck locker— that looks more like food than most of what we carry—and include a medium-sized container of Standby Hooch. I need them at the loading hatch in five minutes."

Communications Leader Alrou Malise was the only other crew member in the control room, and he was startled by these orders. "Isn't that getting a little generous?" he asked Haakogard, his long face seeming to grow longer with disapproval.

"Better than getting into more trouble," said Haakogard philosophically. "Besides, look at this place. A little extra food is going to gain us a lot more goodwill. We're near enough to the *Semper Arcturus*. We won't need those stores before we get back to her. And if we do, a few handfuls of protein isn't going to make that much difference."

"You think so?" Malise asked, trying to affect the same light-handed cynicism as Haakogard, and failing.

Haakogard shook his head. "I'll want Dachnor and Fennin and Chaliz with me. And Pangbar Thunghalis. Make sure you're in top kit. That way we won't get bogged down as much." He loooked at the poMoend officer. "Is there any need for special dress for the rest of us for these negotiations, or will our standard uniforms do?"

"Why do you ask? You are the ones who may decide these matters, for you are the ones of superior strength," said Thunghalis.

"You know what sticklers these out-of-the-way planets can be for dress codes. And cities like poMoend are the worst. We had better use the tunics with the braid and bright buttons," Haakogard decided aloud. "The Senior Bunter approved it."

"Done," said Malise, knowing that there was little point in arguing with the Senior Bunter on such points. He was about to go change when he asked, "Do you think your ploy is working?"

"Is this nothing more than a ploy?" Thunghalis demanded, shocked.

"More of a gamble than a ploy," said Haakogard. "We'll find out." He hoped it would: the most recent zaps had warned him that a shipful of Grands could be coming his way before sunset tomorrow. The whole dispute of the clones would have to be resolved by then or the Grands might well use it to create a scandal and a war. His lips set in a grim line as he went to put on his braided tunic.

Tydbar Grabt offered salutation to the four Harriers and Thunghalis. The poMoend company examined the food they were offered and pronounced it most acceptable, and pretended to understand the use of the target-locking boomerangs which Chanliz had taken from her shipwreck stores. At last the Tydbar put the two sets of gifts aside and sat down on the elaborate carpets spread on the ground for the occasion. "We have come to offer you a proposal to end this conflict. It is the only one acceptable to the Comes Riton, and therefore it is the only one we may endorse."

"Which Comes Riton?" Haakogard could not resist asking.

"The Comes Riton who rules in poMoend," said Tydbar Jeshalest, the only one with a scar on his face: it ran from the outer corner of his eye to the lobe of his ear. "We must protect him or be dishonored."

"True," said Thunghalis. "But you must protect the alternate clone as well—and we are not in agreement which of the clones *is* the alternate, are we? —since he was not devivified at the proper time. To do otherwise would also dishonor us." He kept his head lowered as he spoke.

"It would," agreed Tydbar Grabt. "And we have

spent the night hoping to reach an acceptable way to resolve this to our mutual advantage."

"Yes," chimed in the third officer, a Tsambar in a metallic surplice. "At first it was thought that the clones must fight, but we cannot permit that to happen, for we are sworn to protect the Comes Riton in any phase and if they were to fight, we would have to prevent it or die for disgrace."

"Naturally," said Haakogard softly.

Tydbar Grabt gestured emotionally. "That was the one thing we could not change. We cannot stand by and see the Comes Riton exposed to any danger. So such a contest between clones could not be acceptable. We were agreed on that. But . . ." He let the hopeful word hang.

"But we decided on a way that would preserve the lives of the Comes Riton yet would not imperil our honor," said Tsambar Foethwis with pride. "We have hit upon the means to settle the whole."

The poMoend officers gestured their agreement and support, and Tydbar Grabt addressed Haakogard. "It is entirely acceptable to us, and we will gladly abide by the results, no matter what they are, of a combat between appointed champions of the Comes Riton and his alternate. That way neither clone need lift his hand against the other and we need not—"

Haakogard broke into this. "You're assuming that whichever champion wins, the losing clone will submit to . . . would not disgrace you. Have I got that right?"

"Most certainly. What Comes Riton could live when his champion was dead? It would be a more dishonorable thing than lifting his hand against his clone." Tydbar Jeshalest spoke as if Haakogard were slightly deaf. "It is entirely appropriate and exposes no one to disgrace. You can see why this is so worthy a plan."

"Of course," said Haakogard, who could see nothing of the sort. He had set his mind to resolving the whole problem through negotiation, and here the officers of Civuto poMoend were advocating trial by combat. He decided to give basic sense another try. "Perhaps it might be wise to delay before taking so . . . so extreme an action? The two clones might discover a way to rule as partners?"

All four of the poMoend officers laughed, and Thunghalis joined in. Tydbar Grabt was the first to stop. "How entertaining you are. I was told you had a droll wit, and surely it is true." He slapped the carpet twice, and explained. "How could that be possible? We would have to obey both clones equally, and that could easily lead to disgrace and dishonor if the clones were not always in perfect agreement. To say nothing of the confusion when the next phase clone is activated. At whose orders would that occur? How would the clonery know that the wishes were those of the Comes Riton and not the whim of the alternate?"

"Champion?" said Haakogard quietly, hating the sound of the word.

"An ideal way to settle the matter," concurred Thunghalis, who supposed that Haakogard was in accord with the rest of them. "When it is over there will be no question of who is entitled to rule, and all confusion about the next phases will be ended." He made himself overcome his shame and looked directly at Tydbar Grabt. "Excellent, Most Excellent Tydbar."

Tydbar Grabt clearly knew it was not completely correct to acknowledge the praise of an officer who was so compromised as Thunghalis, but he lowered his head, and let Thunghalis decide if that was a response or not. "We are prepared to undertake the contest as soon as the alternate of the Comes Riton appoints someone to fight for him, providing that person is honorable and of fighting age, so that the match is a fair and honorable one." He got to his feet and made two graceful, confusing gestures. "By midafternoon?"

"That isn't a suggestion," said Dachnor, knowing an order when he heard it. His manner continued unruffled. "We'd better find someone."

"But by midafternoon?" Haakogard wanted to argue, to make the officers of Civuto poMoend give up their ridiculous notion; but he could see that was not going to be possible. He rose, motioning to his officers to do the same. "We will consult with the Comes Riton called Tenre, and if he is willing to be defended in this way, and chooses to appoint a champion, we will be here at midafternoon." He bit down hard on the last word, his jaw tightening.

"Most worthy Petit Harriers," said Tydbar Grabt, lacing his enormous hands together in a gesture of short-term farewell.

As the three Tydbars and the Tṣambar marched away from the Katanas, Group Chief Ower Fennin shook his head. He attempted to laugh but it sounded rusty. "You don't suppose they mean it, do you?"

"Oh, yeah," said Haakogard, weary and irritated. "Yeah, they mean it."

Thunghalis stood straighter. "It is the honorable thing to do."

To Haakogard's dismay—though not to his surprise— Tenre endorsed the plan with alacrity. "Yes!" he declared in a tone like golden thunder. "That is the perfect way!" He looked over at Navigator Zim. "What a superb idea they have. I have never thought well of poMoend, but they have shown that they are not entirely fools. How pleased I am that my honor will be preserved. I cannot thank you enough."

"Why is the idea superb?" Zim asked, her smile definitely strained.

"There will be no question of who has the right, and no one will have to sacrifice his honor to end the matter." He shook his fists in the direction of Civuto poMoend. "They will not be able to claim that the First Colonists were reprehensible in their conduct, as they have in the past."

"Why reprehensible?" asked Haakogard, puzzled by what Tenre said.

"Because we did not attack as they would," said Tenre simply. "We do not have their weapons, nor do we have their city, so we must fight them as the chance presents itself, without the proper form and music." He beamed at Zim. "No one can dispute the outcome of a battle of champions."

"Why do you say that?" Zim wanted to know, curious as much for Haakogard's sake as for her own.

"Because who shall say that a Petit Harrier is not an honest champion?" answered Tenre, his smile so beatific that he looked ten years younger.

"What?" Zim demanded.

"Wait a minute!" Haakogard ordered at the same time. "You leave her out of your arguments, Tenre. She has no part of it."

Tenre's grin widened. "You are certainly right," he said, his eyes moving from Zim to Haakogard. "It is not Nola Zim who will defend my claim. It is you." He slapped his palm hard against his chest. "You are the leader of this mission; therefore I make you my champion, Line Commander Goren Haakogard."

Haakogard was already moving toward Tenre, distress making him clumsy. "No. Wait. Tenre, no." He planted himself two steps in front of the Comes Riton's clone. "Don't do this. It doesn't make sense. I can't be your champion; no one in my command can. We are Petit Harriers, sworn to the Magnicate

Alliance, not mercenaries for you to hire at will. Come on, Tenre. Be reasonable."

"Yes," said Tenre with a vigorous nod. "Yes, that is what I must be, and why I must choose you. None of my followers could be my champion without that choice being an unforgivable insult to the rest. Therefore I must select another, and who better than you, who has brought me to this place and put my case before the men of poMoend?" He still smiled but there was grim purpose in his sand-colored eyes.

"Tenre," Zim protested.

"There is nothing more to say," Tenre stated. "I have made up my mind that my honor and my claim will be defended by you, Haakogard, or it will not be defended at all and my cause will fail. I will die for dishonor." He folded his arms. "And the deaths of those who have fought with me and for me will be on your head, Line Commander."

"Why not Pangbar Thunghalis?" Zim recommended before Haakogard could mention him. "He has defended you already. Everyone knows that he will support your claim. He is one of yours."

"All the more reason not to use him. He is disgraced already, though he was disgraced for my sake. He cannot be made champion, for that would be a great betrayal of the honor of all the First Colonists. Only you, Line Commander, are appropriate."

"This isn't reasonable, Tenre," Haakogard warned him.

"Is it not?" Tenre inquired with feigned innocence. "Why does it seem so to me, then?" He glanced toward Zim. "You will watch with me and share my fate."

There was something unreadable in her face, an expression that was partly sardonic, partly deprecating, partly condemning. "And die with you if your champion does not prevail?" she suggested when the silence had lengthened enough. "Goren?"

Haakogard was still trying to summon arguments to end his obligation to Tenre, and so he gave her an answer without thought. "If that's what you want."

Her face clouded. "I guess it is."

"So you are going to fight?" said the Mromrosi as he gamboled along the hall at Haakogard's side.

"I don't know what else I can do," said Haakogard unhappily.

"You could always leave," said the Mromrosi, his mop of ringlets an incendiary orange.

"And leave Tenre in disgrace, facing a war and ready to kill himself because of some ludicrous code they use to gauge honor?" He stopped at the entrance to his quarters. "It's folly; the whole debate is farcical. But there are a lot of people who could get killed because of it, no matter how absurd the reason for it." He thumbed the latch.

"But you do not want to fight," said the Mromrosi.

"No, I don't," said Haakogard. "But I prefer it to a massacre." His Bunter had recommended a class two combat uniform for the contest, and Haakogard had put it on with an abiding sense of unreality. This could not possibly be happening, not in actuality. He had been allowed his choice of hand-to-hand weapons and had chosen the one with which he was most expert—which meant passably competent—the Shimbue bola. He hoped that no one on Neo Biscay had ever seen one of these tricky weapons that could be used to whip an opponent with three long, slightly stiffened thongs tipped with sharp metal stars, or be thrown to disable him. He hefted the bola and gave it an experimental swing, hearing the air whine as the thongs sliced by.

"Your mask, Line Commander," said his Bunter,

presenting him with the protective head-and-face gear that was part of the class two combat uniform.

"Thanks," murmured Haakogard before he pulled this on.

"Let me wish you success, Line Commander," the Bunter said as he stood aside, permitting Haakogard to leave his quarters.

There were few things Haakogard wanted to do less. He let his breath out slowly, hoping it did not shake. "I'll be back in a while," he told his Bunter, doing his best to sound confident.

"Certainly, Line Commander."

He found Tenre and Zim waiting at the loading hatch, both of them in class three formal gear. If other crew members were watching, they were staying out of sight. Tenre looked over Haakogard, frowning with concentration. "How is it that you chose that weapon?"

"It's a Shimbue bola," said Haakogard curtly. "I like it. It's . . . unusual."

"So much the better," said Tenre, and nodded courteously to Zim. "It honors you as well as me."

"I suppose so," said Zim, her voice uncertain, her eyes haunted.

"They will be waiting," Tenre continued.

Haakogard wished he had had the chance for a last conversation with Viridis Perzda, just in case. Not that anything was going to happen to him, he went on at once, scolding himself silently for doubting his own abilities. "Let's get it over with," he said with more enthusiasm than he felt. He rested his hand on the Shimbue bola as if it might try to escape from its scabbard.

As the hatch opened, Zim stepped out into the bright afternoon sunlight. She stood as if gilded, then took Tenre's hand as he came out beside her. "Is everything ready?" she asked quietly.

Tenre indicated the soldiers of Civuto poMoend. "I believe so. Line Commander? If you will?"

Haakogard gave a single, exasperated snort, then stepped out beside them. He hated the day for being so beautiful, and the crew of his mission for obeying his orders not to interfere. If he did not feel so full of disbelief, he might become angry. "Who is the champion for the other side? Have you been informed?"

"They have sent word. Their champion is the Tsambar, of course," said Tenre as if the conclusion were obvious. "There is no higher-ranking officer who is permitted to bear arms in this way. Tydbars are not permitted to fight hand-to-hand."

"Let me guess," said Haakogard. "It isn't honorable." He wanted to tell everyone how comical the whole contest was, but the words would not come; he could read determination in all the faces around him, including, he suspected, in many of his own Petit Harriers. He tried to remain calm, to appear collected, as if he did this every day. Now that it was too late, he chided himself for neglecting his drill with the Shimbue bola and all the other hand weapons on the *Yngmoto*.

The Mromrosi came into the loading hatch and hunkered down, waiting. He said nothing, but he was intent on the poMoend officers. He said nothing to Haakogard or any of the other Petit Harriers.

The officers of poMoend—nine of them—were gathered around the Comes Riton, who all-but-visibly seethed with indignation. Tsambar Foethwis stood at the Comes Riton's side, a small, weighted net hanging from one hand, and a two-pronged pike in the other. He had on a light body armor, all flexible but the breastplate; it was very good protection for hand-to-hand combat. As Tenre and Zim approached, Haakogard behind them, the officers offered him half a bow, and the Comes Riton swore under his breath.

"My champion is Line Commander Goren Haakogard of the Petit Harriers," Tenre said formally, his words ringing with heroic purpose. "Whatever fate decrees for him I will endorse and embrace."

"I am champion for the Comes Riton," said Tsambar Foethwis, looking once at the Comes Riton, apprehension in his eyes as if he expected the Comes Riton to deny it. "My fate is his fate."

"As honor demands," said one of the poMoend officers, which did not surprise Haakogard at all.

"The fight," said Tydbar Grabt, "will be until one or the other is incapable of fighting any longer." He saw this acknowledged by those waiting for the contest. "All of us must observe and attest to what happens here, and bear accurate witness to the event. We will ensure absolute fairness and the true disposition of the case being decided here," he went on, warming to his subject. "Therefore we now ask the champions to trade weapons."

Haakogard stared at Tydbar Grabt. "What? Trade weapons?" he repeated, thinking he could not possibly have heard correctly. They could not actually require something so senseless as that. The contest was ridiculous to start with, and if it was expected that they would battle with unfamiliar weapons, it was worse than a joke. "Are you serious?"

"Trade weapons, the both of you," ordered Tydbar Grabt without a trace of humor. "Tsambar, present yours to me." He held out his hands and took the double pike and net. He inspected both and put them aside, turning to Haakogard for his.

Reluctantly Haakogard took his Shimbue bola from its scabbard. "Here you are," he said to Tydbar Grabt. "It is just what it appears to be. There are no tricks to it."

Tydbar Grabt gave the bola a cursory inspection. "Most interesting. I don't believe we have seen anything like it." He gave this to Tsambar Foethwis before presenting Haakogard with Foethwis' weapons. "Each of you may have a short time to familiarize yourselves with your new weapons."

"Good of you," said Haakogard sarcastically as he hefted the net. The weights gave it quite a satisfactory swing, and he thought that perhaps he would be able to use it without having to resort to the double-pronged pike, which was top-heavy, making it slow on the return. He shifted his grip on the net a little, finding a more secure hold. As he swung the net again, he flicked his wrist and was rewarded as the net spread wide. What in the name of the Fifty-Six was the purpose of all this? he demanded of himself. He brought the pike up and tried to use it for thrusting. It handled rather better that way than as a slicing blade. He took a shorter hold on the staff and tried once more. He was aware that Tsambar Foethwis was making a number of passes with the Shimbue bola.

"We have marked out your field," Tydbar Grabt went on. "You will see it there. It is flat and we have rid it of all pebbles and loose dust so that you will not have those disadvantages to consider. It is twenty strides long and twelve strides wide." He was clearly pleased with the effort that had gone into this preparation, and he waited to hear some approval of what he had accomplished.

"Very conscientious," said Tenre.

"Much appreciated," said the Comes Riton through tight teeth.

Haakogard wanted to add his opinion but knew it would not be welcome. He lowered his head, looking away from the place that had been prepared for the fight. He wondered if Perzda had got an answer to the most recent zap, the one explaining about this duel. They had waited for a reply but none had come, and Perzda had warned him that the Grands might be the reason. She had insisted that the Grands wanted to trap this mission, just so that their Marshal-in-Chief would not be revealed as the criminal he was. Haakogard was not sure he believed that, but he had to admit it was very tempting to blame the Grands for the mess he was in. It was typical of the Grands to shift attention this way. His uneasiness about their arrival grew more intense. How could this minor skirmish on this out-of-the-way planet save the Grands' Marshal-in-Chief from scandal? He realized that a question had been addressed to him. "I beg your pardon?"

"Are you ready to begin?" repeated Tydbar Grabt.

"Why not?" Haakogard answered. He looked at his opponent, deciding that they were a fairly even match: Tsambar Foethwis was not quite as tall as Haakogard but had a slightly longer reach.

They appeared to be about the same age. What neither man knew of the other was the kind of fighters they were. Haakogard gave the net a last practice swing. He might be able to throw it, but if he did, Tsambar Foethwis was likely to be able to turn that to advantage.

"Tell me," said the Comes Riton, addressing Haakogard directly, "do you truly think your honor is being preserved by doing this?"

"I don't know," said Haakogard honestly.

The Comes Riton frowned. "You have no excuse for what you do, Harrier. You are serving as an agent of disruption sent by the Magnicate Alliance to throw our planet into confusion and war as the means of gaining control over it. A despicable act."

Haakogard thought that there might be a grain of truth in the accusation, but it belonged to the Grands, not the Petits. "If that is what we Petit Harriers are doing, we have chosen a strange place to do it." He made a small, polite bow to the Comes Riton. "I am profoundly sorry it has come to this." Which was as candid as he dared to be.

Tydbar Grabt strolled to the edge of the cleared field. "You must confine your battle to this place, within these markers. If either of you leaves the boundaries except by accident, it will count against you. If either of you surrenders while he can still fight, it will count against you. The honor of the Comes Riton is in the balance, whichever clone of the Comes prevails." He stepped to the side and found a place to sit on the ground not far from the edge of the delineated field. The other poMoend officers joined him.

"They're watching from the ships," said Zim as she selected a patch of ground for herself. "If anything goes—"

"We have to play this all the way out, and fairly," said Haakogard, no longer caring how foolish it all was. "Make sure everyone remembers that." He gave her a lopsided smile. "Time to get to work, I guess."

"Good luck." Zim waited for Tenre to say something, but when he did not, she rose and kissed Haakogard's cheek, then settled down to watch.

His Bunter had insisted that Haakogard wear uneven terrain boots, and now Haakogard was grateful for them. He felt the grip and stability of the soles, and thought this might give him an edge. He brought the pike around and used it to protect his chest, for though his uniform would stop anything short of high-impact projectiles, he knew that a blow to the chest could be dangerous.

Tsambar Foethwis made the first move, rushing in suddenly, bending low, the Shimbue bola hissing as it lashed at Haakogard's legs.

Haakogard jumped back and swung the net overhead before trying to snag Foethwis' arm in the mesh. He called on three or four of the least friendly spirits of his home planet as he prepared to rush Foethwis with the pike.

Foethwis turned out to be very light on his feet, dancing back out of the way of the net, though it swiped a colored tag off his arm.

"They fight well," said Tydbar Grabt. He folded his arms and watched with a curious detachment, paying no heed to the Comes Riton, who paced behind him, doing his best to ignore the fight.

The third time Haakogard used the net, he swung it incorrectly and nearly pulled himself off his feet with the force and weight of it. He used the pike to steady himself enough to stay on his feet, and came very close to having the Shimbue bola claim some skin from his knuckles. He almost dropped the pike.

"Don't fail too quickly," Foethwis taunted, though he was beginning to pant.

"Don't be overconfident," Haakogard replied, changing his hold on the net so that he could drift it open rather than sling it like a clumsy lasso. There was a trick to keeping it spread; it was that flip of the wrist. If only he had had some time to study the weapon before now . . .

One of the three lashes of the bola cut at his shoulder; only the tough fibers of his uniform kept him from being hurt.

Foethwis seized the advantage, starting to drive Haakogard toward the edge of the field. His face glistened with sweat and his eyes were bright with anticipation of victory. The lashes fell again, their little metal stars pulling rents in Haakogard's tunic. One of the rents beaded with blood.

It was all so preposterous, thought Haakogard as he fended Foethwis off with the pike. He wanted to laugh, to throw the weapons in the air and walk away from the insanity. But he was bleeding at the shoulder, and the next blow from the Shimbue bola scraped his arms, hurting him more. He shook his head as if trying to awaken from a dream that was becoming a nightmare.

"Champion!" shouted the Comes Riton—at least Haakogard thought it was the Comes Riton; it was hard to tell—for encouragement. "Avenge the insult that has been given me."

The Comes Riton, Haakogard was sure of it. He jumped aside as Foethwis charged him, and brought the net around to slam into the back of the man's knees, knocking him forward, but not quite off his feet. "Well done, Line Commander!" shouted Tenre, springing to his feet and coming nearer to the combat field.

"Sit down," Tydbar Grabt ordered. "Dignity and honor will be deserved."

Tenre took a couple steps back. "Continue! Continue!"

Was it better or worse, being encouraged, Haakogard asked himself in a remote part of his mind as he ducked under Foethwis' aggressive attack and moved to the center of the combat area. He skibbered backward, preparing for the new rush from Foethwis, his pike dragging on the earth. He had to get rid of it; it was more trouble than it was worth.

Foethwis swung twice with the bola, the second pulling at Haakogard's mask and leaving a track like a cat's claw behind. He shouted "Most Excellent Comes!" and drove his assault more vigorously.

Haakogard was driven backward. In disgust he took the pike and flung it away, far outside of their fighting area. Even as he dodged another furious blow from the Shimbue bola, he felt freer and more capable. He brought up the net and swung it, and succeeded in snagging the lashes of the bola in the tough fibers of his net.

"Goren!" shouted Nola Zim.

He tugged just once, very hard, and felt Tsambar Foethwis come off his feet. As Foethwis lost precious seconds wallowing in the embrace of the net, Haakogard moved quickly. This time it was simple to get behind him and push him forward, into the dust. As Foethwis struggled to get free of the net, Haakogard gave him a good push so that he was more thoroughly enmeshed in it.

"I will die!" screamed Foethwis as he tried— unsuccessfully—to rise. "I will reclaim my honor!"

"Stop it." Haakogard was breathing heavily, and under his uniform he could feel patches of sweat. He gave Foethwis another shove so that he would not be able to reach a weapon for suicide. Then he looked over at the officers of poMoend. "Well? What else do I have to do?"

Tenre came up to him beaming. "You won. You don't have to do anything else. It's over."

"Not yet," said Haakogard, because it did not feel over to him. "There's unanswered questions yet."

"You have prevailed," said Tydbar Grabt seriously. "And the Comes Riton is established for this phase." He motioned to some of the officers near him. "We will proceed with the devivification."

"Oh, leave it alone," said Haakogard, walking out of the combat area and approaching the poMoend officers. "There's been enough craziness about who's going to die. This has got to end." He did not realize until he said it how important it was to him, that the death for honor come to an end. "No one ought to die defending someone else's genetic code, and that's what killing a clone amounts to."

"It is right that I die," said the Comes Riton quietly, paying little attention to Haakogard. "I have been shown to be unworthy. I have not the right. It must be as you said: I am the alternate and he"—he pointed at Tenre—"he is the authentic phase of the Comes Riton. I must expiate my error."

The officers gave their endorsement to his intentions, a few of them shouting for the Comes Riton's death. "Yes," said a very young Pangbar who was completely in awe of his august company, "it is fitting that the Comes Riton be restored to honor."

"It's asinine," said Haakogard bluntly. "It's a waste of good men, it's a waste of resources and training." He was not panting any more, but his chest felt hot. "If you want to make the most of these clones, get them to cooperate. You don't seem to realize that each of them has something to teach the other, because they were not raised together. That's probably the best thing that's ever happened to any phase of the Comes Riton." He looked back at Tsambar Foethwis. "It goes for him, too."

"How do you mean?" demanded the Comes Riton.

"There's no reason for him to die because of this fight. He did his work and he did it well, and that ought to be honorable enough for anyone."

"And what will you do if we do not obey you?" asked Tydbar Grabt. "Will you enforce your edict with arms?"

Haakogard glared at him. "Of course we won't. It isn't our job to coerce you. This is your home, and your problem. *You'll* work it out. I mean it about Tsambar Foethwis. I don't want to find out he was allowed to slit his own throat, or whatever you usually do. I expect him to continue as an officer and an advisor to the Comes Ritons—both of them." He stood very straight. "And now, if all this is over, I want a shower."

Tenre clapped him on the shoulder, inadvertently squeezing one of the scratches left by the bola. "You must be acknowledged as my champion and given the respect your act deserves."

"It deserves a shower," said Haakogard, resigning himself to not getting it for some little while.

As the four Petit Harrier Katanas set down in the main landing port of Bilau, the Comes Riton stared at the surveills, fascinated by what was there. "So huge. And I have always thought that poMoend was enormous."

"PoMoend is rather small," said Zim, her tone neutral but her eyes sharp with her own brand of wit.

"You'll get used to it," said Haakogard. "You're better at cities than Tenre is, and you've got more practice at being the Comes Riton. You know how to behave, and what's due you." He started toward the main entryway where the Katanas had been directed to unload. "Tenre will manage poMoend very well so long as you make sure that you are no longer in isolation. You'll make a good partnership, if you work it right." He glanced at Perzda. "What about the Grands? Any of them around?"

"One *Bombard*-class still here," she said, "according to the most recent zap. But the Grands are doing demonstration maneuvers today, so we probably won't see them." Her smile was wicked with delight. "And they're supposed to lift off by sunrise tomorrow."

Near the largest surveill screen, the Mromrosi bounced contentedly and gave off a high, squeaky sound the crew had decided was the Mromrosi version of humming.

"Let's hear it for our Older Brothers," said Jarrick Riven, using the nickname for the Grands that was not wholly complimentary. There were low chuckles and a whistle or two in the control room; from the bridge, Executive Officer Mawson Tallis began to sing retreat.

"Anything about the Marshal-in-Chief of the Grands?" asked Haakogard, with a trace of satisfaction.

Communications Leader Alrou Malise answered. "There's been a bulletin sent around saying that he's retiring to Hathaway because of health. No mention of any scandal."

"So they found a way to cover it up without dragging us into it," said Tallis, his tone not entirely satisfied.

"Give thanks for small favors," said Malise.

The crew gave a ragged, unenthusiastic cheer.

"Ah," said Haakogard. "Don't be so cynical. We don't want to tempt the Grands to try again, do we?"

"Only if we get to choose the time and the place," said Tallis.

There were murmurs of satisfaction all around.

"But," said Malise, "we're ordered out to Mere Philomene to slow down a revolution. You know the kind of colonists they have on Mere Philomene. It's going to be nasty."

"It sounds like the Commodore felt that our return home right now might prove needlessly embarrassing to the retiring Marshal-in-Chief of the Grands, considering the situation at the time of his retirement." Tallis made a single, aggressive gesture with his right hand indicating what the Commodore could do about his decision.

Another, more genuine, cheer went up.

From his place by the surveills, the Mromrosi turned a brilliant shade of puce; it was all the comment he was prepared to make.

# INTO THE HOT AND MOIST

## Steve Perry

### 1

Newly-commissioned Petit Harrier Light Unit Commander Stelo Gain was still unpacking his gear when the space station's General Alert hooters began screaming.

Gain was absolutely fresh. He still wore his academy haircut, and he had the untested graduate's desire for battle. He had a room, though he hadn't been on Oasis II long enough to be assigned a station, or even to have met the SC; still, he certainly wanted to be a part of whatever was going on.

"Computer!"

The voice that answered was slow, lazy, and unlike any military voiceax Gain had ever heard:

"Yeah?" The word was mired in syrup: Yeeaaaauu-uhhhh?

"Status of alarm?"

"Who wants to know?"

"Huh? I—I'm Light Unit Commander Stelo Gain!"

"Oh, yeah. The new shavehead. Lemme see, don't get your bowels in an uproar, bub. Hmm. Looks like some fool lost control of his ship and is about to hit the shields."

It was the most insolent, unmilitary computer report he had heard since joining the academy, and it amazed Gain to find such sloppy programming in a station the size and importance of this one. Somebody's head should roll for this. He would help that along, as soon as possible.

"Give me a visual of the approaching vessel," Gain ordered.

"If you'll get your finger out of your nose and turn around, you'll see I already did that. Screen's right there behind you."

"I'll have you deprogrammed!" Gain yelled. His response embarrassed him. Get a grip, on yourself, Gain. For God's sake, it's probably somebody's idea of a joke to play on new shaveheads, and here you are swallowing it whole. Tighten up, Gain. Tighten up. You're an officer.

"Better men than you have tried to deprogram me, bub. I'm still here. See you later."

Gain turned, just in time to see on the holoproj a *Tanto*-class courier ship entering the outer limits of the force shield. The little ship seemed to hop sideways, then looked as if it had slammed into a rubbery wall, turning relative-up and losing part of one control surface in a bright flare of field-interactive orange. Whoever was flying that bird was going to be nursing a lot of bruises and broken bones—if he survived the landing. Plowing into a station's shields at speed made for a very rough ride, stress-cocoon notwithstanding.

Thus slowed, and with its power shorted out by the secondary damping field, the courier ship tumbled, smacked into the safety broadband and stopped cold, and was finally lowered somewhat less than gently by the invisible hands of the put'emdown.

Whoever it was, better have a real good excuse coming in like that, assuming he was alive, or the Station Commander was going to cook him and eat him for supper. Gain was glad it wasn't him, and glad he didn't have anything to do with it.

He accessed the room's external viewer and looked at the blue mostly-water world of Feddalsi Oasis hanging like part of a giant bowl in space. A few fleecy clouds decorated the deep blue; not much weather churning otherwise. Between the incompetent pilot and the insolent computer, he hadn't gotten the best impression of Oasis II so far. Maybe things would improve after he met the SC and found out what he'd be doing. Never mind. He was commissioned, young, smart and tough. He'd show these slack Harriers a thing or two.

## 2

"You still here, bub?" the computer said. The lazy voice had some kind of accent Gain couldn't identify, a fat drawl that stretched the words and made them seem like hot taffy in the sunshine.

"What do you want?" Gain snapped out the question.

"The Old Man—that's Station Commander Zougag to you, bub—would like the pleasure of your company on Level Four, Station One—if you can spare the time."

"What?"

"Hospital unit, and you'll need it if you don't hurry. You were supposed to be there ten minutes ago."

"What?!"

"I forgot to tell you. Got busy and all."

"What? You *what?*"

"Well, well. You ain't all starch and elbows after all. Better hop to it. The Old Man hates to be kept waiting."

Gain left, moving at triple time, trying to look calm and unhurried as he ran toward the chute. He practically leaped into the tube. "Level Four, hurry!"

"Ain't got but one speed, bub."

Great. The same computer ran the chutes. What was going on here?

A line trooper with a zap carbine held at port arms stood guard at the chute's exit. Gain passed his wrist under the wall's admit scanner and was identified by the implant in his pisiform bone. The guard snapped to attention as Gain passed. Well, at least there was some discipline here. "As you were," Gain said. It was the first time he had given that command as a real officer, and it gave him a kind of power-filled tingle.

A second guard admitted Gain into the unit, directed him down a corridor, where a pair of guards with holstered sidearms stood at ease on either side of a third door. Must be important, given all the security.

Inside the room, a man lay inside a Hertz full-medical attend unit. Such boxes were usually called creep coffins by military and civilians alike. Next to the unit stood the Station Commander. SC Zougag was a boot-plastic-tough old man of sixty-five or seventy T.S. years, white-haired and still fit under his station work blues; a man reputed to eat slow nails and pee high-speed needles when in a bad mood.

"Sir, Light Unit Commander Gain reporting as ordered." Gain made it as crisp as he could.

The Old Man waved one hand. "At ease, Luck." He shook his head. "Old men, jailrats, pregnant women and shavehead children," he muttered. "Thank you so *very* much, Marshal Twill."

"Sir?"

"Nothing, Luck. Just the usual snafu. Over here."

Gain moved toward the creep coffin. Through the clear densecris cover he saw a man of maybe fifty, somewhat the worse for recent wear, plugged into the sensory and medicant gear. Getting a full replete ride, looked like.

"Gain, this is Commander Dino Farr, formerly a decent officer of the Fighting Foxes, now stealing his pay as a do-nothing Aide to Marshal-in-Chief Twill. You may have seen his somewhat inexpert landing earlier in the day, in which he destroyed a *Tanto*-class ship without even trying."

"It was sabotage, Pil, I told you," the man in the coffin said. He sounded sleepy. He smiled, and it was a doped-to-the-eyebrows expression. Must be doped to be calling the SC, who was Line Ranked, by his first name.

"We'll see what the mechs say," the SC replied. He looked away from the injured man and back at Gain. "Farr has come to make my life difficult, as is his usual wont." The Old Man smiled. "And since I run things here, I get to pass such grief down the line. Commander Farr being pumped full of dorph to ease his much-deserved pain for smashing into the shield, it falls to me to try to explain."

"Sir?"

"You just got here, Luck, and I'm sorry to have to dump this on you, but most of my able bodies are on maneuvers teaching the Grands from Big Star One how to suck vac. You may not be aware that the Petits have won the deep-space combat games six times running."

"Sir, I knew that."

"Um. Farr here came to deliver a message from the MiC Himself, and as usual, the news isn't good. My at-homes are at skeleton strength now. I have to

have a commissioned officer look into his problem
and you, son, are who I can spare."

Gain swallowed. Well, he wanted to be in the
thick of things. Having a mission direct from the
Marshal-in-Chief of the Petit Harriers first time in
the barrel was certainly thick enough. If he did well,
it couldn't hurt. If he screwed up, well . . . he didn't
want to think about that.

"You know anything about Feddalsi Oasis?"

"Sir, normal briefing material."

"Son, this isn't the Academy, you don't have to
'sir' me every time you open your mouth."

"Sir. I mean, ah . . ."

The Old Man grinned. "Forget it. You may be
aware that there is some . . . rivalry between the
Grands and the Petits."

"Si— Ah, yes, I was aware of that."

"You may also be aware that out in the real galaxy
things aren't always as neat and clean as the Magnicate
Alliance would have them be. You ever hear of the
Texas Rangers?"

"Some sort of mythical pre-space law force, weren't
they?"

"That's right. Since they were there when things
happened, they had to interpret the laws somewhat
loosely as they went, if you take my meaning."

Gain understood that, though he didn't see where
the Old Man was going with it.

"In any event, there are sometimes things that go
on in the realm of politics and power that might not
be strictly legal, but into which you don't want to
run like some ignorant tumwah waving a law dictum.
There are some, ah, delicate balances where the
Grands, the Petits and the Twelve all sit around the
same table."

Gain knew that, at least in a theoretical way. Somebody was always stabbing somebody else in the back

where Uplevels were concerned. Real Machiavellian stuff. Nobody trusted anybody in those rarefied chambers, and that was considered the height of wisdom.

"The bottom line here, Luck, is that a situation has arisen that is very delicate and dangerous. It has to be handled carefully, because the politics might be as important as the military end, if you get my drift."

Gain swallowed again. Politics. This did not sound good at all.

"If what Farr says is true, the continued future of the Petit Harriers themselves might well rest entirely on a successful completion of this mission.

"You, son, are going to be very careful, or it won't be just you who suffers, it will be all of us."

Gain stood there, frozen, growing more and more incredulous as Station Commander Zougag told him exactly what the problem was, and what shavehead LUC Gain was going to have to do to fix it. He had never dreamed just how thick the intrigue got Uplevels. How could they *do* such things and get away with them? Holy Juddah Bright!

It was beginning to look as if Light Unit Commander Stelo Gain's first mission as an officer might also be his last.

Oh, boy.

### 3

Gain stood at ease in the SC's office as the Sub-Unit Officer arrived. Even a shavehead knew that SUO's were the real power in any military organization. Officers might issue orders, but it was up to the noncoms to get things done. A good SUO could make you look real sharp, if he or she wanted; they could also make you look like a sunbleached old white dog turd if they didn't like you.

Sitting behind his desk, the Old Man nodded at the SUO as he stepped inside and came to attention. "At ease, Chan."

The man relaxed. He was maybe forty-five T.S., a head shorter than Gain, had a lot of smile wrinkles, black hair cropped in a spacer's buzz, and a look of having seen and heard it all. His skin was coffee-and-cream-colored, and the whites of his eyes were remarkably clear. A forty-year man halfway through, Gain figured, and not somebody to screw around with. He'd know the system backward and how to get what he wanted out of it.

Everything Gain had learned at the Academy wasn't theoretical—the Subs had run things there, too.

"SUO Chan Singa, this is Light Unit Commander Stelo Gain, just assigned to Oasis II."

Gain gave the other man a military nod. "Sub."

"Luck," Chan said. He turned back toward the Old Man. "What's up, Pil?"

Gain wanted to shake his head. What, was the Old Man on a first name basis with *every*body? Discipline must be hell around here.

"Usual FU. I've just given the LUC here a very sensitive mission, and I want you to volunteer to go along and make sure he has proper backup."

"A sensitive mission. What are we talking about here?"

"Oh, a little trip down to the water. A few days of R&R in Oondervatten. A few odds and ends."

"And you let me out of brig to tell me this? Come on, Pil. Fire the other barrel."

Out of the brig?

"Well, I can't give you all the details—we're talking commissioned-ears-only—but you might be paying a little visit to the Hot and Moist."

"What? You want me to go to Fishtown? Officially? To Jaskeen's place? Have you lost your mind?"

"You're still on speaking terms with Limos, aren't you?"

"When the uniform's in the locker, yeah."

"So leave it in the locker. You have some cit clothes, don't you?"

Chan shook his head. "I don't like the sound of this, Commander. Maybe I'd be better off in the brig."

"Well, I can tell you that the future of the Petit Harriers may be in jeopardy."

"Yeah, so? It's always in jeopardy, what else is new?"

Gain was holding himself in check, but barely. Who was this noncom to talk back to the SC like this? But—what could he learn from listening to a noncom who *could* talk back like this without getting cashed and booted out of the service? He listened.

"It's a matter of galactic importance?" the Old Man tried.

"The brig ain't so bad. Good food. Nice bed."

"How about, if we pull this off, we'll put a big fat dog of a problem right on the Grand Harriers' new Marshal-in-Chief's lap? Maybe get him fired?"

SUO Singa grinned. "Hell, why didn't you say so in the first place? I'm in."

As Chan and Gain left the SC's office, the SUO turned to the LUC and said, "So, you in charge here, Luck?"

The question meant more than it was asking on the surface, and Gain damn sure knew it.

Gain thought about it for about three seconds. Yes, he was the officer and, in theory, responsible for, and in control of, this mission. The Sub was being let out of the *brig* for this operation, and God knew why he'd been put there in the first place and why the SC thought he should be released. The rules said there was a certain way to do things; the chain of command dictated it so.

Gain wanted to play the game as he had learned it. On the other hand, he wanted to get the job done. That was more important. Not only for the Petits, but for his own hide. If he had to take a risk, now was the time, before it all started to sizzle. You didn't need to be a physicist to know which way the reaction blew.

"Sub, I'm just out of the Academy and I don't know squat except what they taught me there. I'd rather win than be in charge. If you can get me out of this in one piece, I'm all ears and no mouth." One of his Subs at the Academy had been fond of that phrase, telling him it was the best way to learn. Gain was halfway convinced that all Subs everywhere knew each other.

Chan smiled, adding to his eye wrinkles. He reached out and slapped Gain on one shoulder. "Good for you, kid, that'll make things a lot easier."

Gain was relieved. "So, what now?"

"We have to collect a few people to give us a decent op unit."

"How many?"

"Oh, I figure another three besides us can manage it."

"Only five?"

"More'd only get in our way, where we're going."

"The courier ship was sabotaged," Gain offered.

"Yeah, I heard when I was in the brig."

Gossip was faster than subspace com, nothing new about that.

"Still, if we can't do it with five, we probably can't do it. We can yell for help, though it probably won't get to us in time."

"Mind if I ask you something?" Gain asked.

"Shoot."

"Why were you in the brig?"

"I punched out my LUC. Guy you're probably replacing. A real wetbrain. A shavehead Academy boy thought he knew squat about everything." Chan grinned.

4

"Where are we going?" Gain asked.

"Back to the brig."

"Leave your luggage?"

"Nah. Couple of the people we want are there."

Gain shook his head. Maybe he'd made a mistake letting Chan know he didn't know anything. As if he could have hidden it.

"Don't worry. They're good troopers, just a little at odds with authority. You learn to deal with it when you've been an officer long enough; you let a certain amount of it slide."

Gain had a sudden flash. "You talk like you know what it's like to be an officer."

"Yeah, I been there."

"You had a commission? You got it *revoked*?"

"Well, yeah. First time I was a LUC; second time I did a tour as a Combat Com Op, third time I almost made it to Full Commander before they kicked me back down."

"No kidding?"

Chan laughed. "If you don't screw up bad enough to get drummed out, they figure they'll need you again eventually. We had us a shooting war going, I'd probably get a field commission for the duration, if I wanted it. Pil Zougag and I go way back. I did my first tour with him twenty-five years ago when he

was running the Second Foxes during the police
action on Gascognye."

Gain nodded. That explained the first-name basis.

"We'll need, ah, some different kinds of soldiers
for this run. People with unusual talents. I dunno
exactly what the deal is and I don't need to know,
but I do know where we're going. Fishtown ain't a
place for people who can't take care of themselves."

They were admitted into one of the small cells on
the brig level, a place made to look smaller by the
man who occupied it.

"Hey, Sub," the man said, a big smile on his face.

Chan nodded at the man. "Hey, Shoulders. This is
our new Luck, Stelo Gain. He's okay."

Gain stared at the man Chan had called Shoulders.
It was easy enough to see why he'd gotten the name.
The closer he got, the broader the trooper seemed to
grow, until he was nearly filling Gain's entire line-of-
sight. Looked like he was almost a meter wide across
the shoulders, a good two meters tall. Guy had to go
110, maybe 115 kilos in a standard one-gee pull, and
he had muscles that looked as thick as any Gain had
ever seen. The overstretched white coverall couldn't
begin to hide them.

"This is Line Trooper Stamblock," Chan said, "sector weight-lifting champion, but pretty much a kitten,
except when somebody insults his mother. Last man
who did that is still in the creep coffin."

Gain made a mental note to avoid insulting Trooper
Stamblock's mother.

"Shoulders is good at picking things up and moving them," Chan said. "He comes in handy now and
then."

"We going someplace?" Shoulders asked.

"Yeah, we have to go save the Petits' lunch again."

"Oh, sure. Okay."

\*     \*     \*

The next cell they visited contained a woman trooper, and Gain was caught by her exotic beauty when he saw her. She was dark, nearly as much so as Chan, with a spacer's haircut that gave her a short but dense cap of tight dark curls. Her eyes were green, her nose flat and wide, upper lip thicker than the lower. She had an athlete's body under the whites, the giveaway veins visible in her forearms where the coverall was rolled back, not much breast tissue but heavy pectorals, strong-looking legs. A dancer or a gymnast, maybe.

"This is Doreen Shu O'Rourke," Chan said, "who would normally be representing the Petits in free-style combat at the ground games with the Grands this month, only she never seems to be able to make bedcheck when she's supposed to. Rook, this is Stelo Gain, and we'll be working with him for a while."

"Why should I?"

"Well, because I had half my last paychit bet on you to beat Gonzo Gauthier for the title and I lost it when you got caught sleeping with Top Matron's husband and got sent here instead," Chan said. "You owe me."

The woman called Rook shrugged. She looked at Gain as if he were a meal she was considering eating, then shook her head. Nope. Not on her diet. Too small to keep. Gain felt himself blush at being found wanting.

"Rook here's okay," Chan said. "She does, however, have maybe too high an opinion of her sexual skills."

"Whenever you're ready for a demonstration, Sub," Rook said, grinning and licking her lips.

"No thanks, I still got fifteen years to go, I want to live long enough to draw my retirement pay."

"Limp rod."

"Better than having it worn off."

Rook laughed. "Okay. Where we going?"

"Into the Hot and Moist."

"You're kidding, right? Who do I have to kill?"

"It's a job, Rook, not a holiday."

"Can't work all the time."

"Maybe. We'll see."

The final cell held an innocuous little man of maybe thirty, who had somehow managed to make the place look like a luxury cube. He had a holoproj, liquor dispense, and a feelofoam mattress humming under him.

"This is Line Trooper Royal Tinner," Chan said.

Tinner didn't bother to move from where he was stretched out. " 'Lo, Sub. You want a drink? Some smoke? I got a masseuse coming by later."

"No, thanks, Tin. We—this is our new temporary LUC—we thought you might be willing to help us out on a small matter."

"Maybe. What?"

"Little trip to Fishtown. Visit with Limos Jaskeen at the Hot and Moist."

"I don't think so. Bad odds."

Chan turned to Gain. "Tin here is the best gambler in the Petits. He'll bet on anything he thinks he can win. Hardly ever backs a loser."

That didn't make Gain feel any better.

"Tin, what if we could cut you loose for a hour or two at Madam Howzu's?"

The little man sat up on the humming mattress. "Three hours."

"Two."

"Done."

"What was that all about?" Gain asked.

"Fishtown's best gambling house, run by a borderline empath named Madam Howzu. The only person Tin can't yet beat consistently in a fair poker game. She's got him two rounds to one. He'd give his left testicle for another shot to even the score, and the other one to go one up."

"Just out of curiosity, can he beat her?"

"I wouldn't bet against him."

Gain shook his head. A giant weight lifter, an oversexed combat artist, a compulsive gambler, and a noncom Sub busted from officer no less than three times. One hell of an operations unit there, Gain. Nobody ever told you about anything like *this* at the Academy.

## 5

The drophopper fell out of space into the atmosphere, piloted by somebody who obviously must be immune to any pull under three gees. Gain and his misfits wore cit clothes and had all been issued neural tanglers in hideaway holsters. Rook had also given Gain a short double-edged flexsteel knife in a slipskin sheath before they'd left.

"What's this for?"

"Knife doesn't run out of ammo or charge," she'd said. "Or, you never know, you might need to clean your fingernails or something."

He'd tucked the knife into his boot.

As the bone-bending drop continued toward planetfall, Gain reviewed what little he knew about where they were going. Feddalsi Oasis was a waterworld; most of the human population lived in barge towns or man-made submarine cities. The land masses tended to have a lot of earthquakes and volcanic activity, so only a few hundred scientists spent any permanent time there. Boat towns and cities stayed in deep water, to avoid tsunami trouble. In the right seasons, local hurricanes sometimes carried winds topping three hundred kilometers an hour. Nice place to not-visit.

Oondervatten was the largest of the submarine cities. It was more like an iceberg, in that some of it stuck up above the surface, but most of it stayed below. Fishtown itself was at the lowest inhabited level, just above the recycling plants and the sewage treaters, and the bar-slash-whorehouse belonging to one Limos Jaskeen was at the bottom of Fishtown. The name, Hot and Moist, could mean a couple things, Gain had learned. What went on, or the atmosphere itself, which shared the same air system as the main filter pumps. Before graduation, Gain had been in a few tough port bars, itching to try out his hand-to-hand, but this place made them seem like a meditation class.

As the drophopper pulled a wide, face-stretching turn to land on the midsea non-commercial military pad, Gain said to Chan, "Tell me about this Limos Jaskeen."

"You've never heard of him?"

"No."

"You ever heard of the Expeditionary Rangers?"

"Yes, of course. I'm not totally stupid."

"Jaskeen was a Ranger, just before they got busted up. Mean S.O.B. Had four combat duty stripes in three years."

"I am given to understand that the ER was a pretty poor excuse for military. More thugs and crooks than real soldiers."

"Maybe so. Can't say, I wasn't there. After they were disbanded, Jaskeen went into the Grands."

"He's highborn?"

"Oh, yeah, a great-great-uncle and great-great-grandfather founded some minor world, I forget which.

Jaskeen stayed in the Grands long enough to make it to Full Commander."

"Then he retired?"

"Not exactly. Deserted."

"Juddah! You serious?"

"Yep. Got tired of all the crap, he said. Too much talk, not enough action."

"And the Grands just rolled over and let him go?"

"He changed his name and ID." Chan grinned. "Then he joined the Petits."

"Come on."

"Yep. Only man to have served in all three, near as anybody can tell. Got to FC there, too, then retired."

"Oh, man."

"Along the way, he picked up a few pretty smooth moves in some esoteric martial arts, can pin a fly to a wall at ten paces with a needle gun, either hand, and eats trouble for breakfast without spices. He's about, oh, sixty, maybe, and the toughest man I ever met. Doesn't have much use for authority."

"Wonderful," Gain said. Just what he needed to hear.

The ship slewed through another turn, fast and hard enough to kick the safety cocoons into a brief lockmode. When the cocoon opened, Gain said, "No wonder you wanted the troops we brought."

"I think Jaskeen could probably take the three of them, plus you and me, without working up a major sweat. They are just to get us to the place and back. Like I said, Fishtown is not exactly a stroll in the park, Luck. And if the courier ship was sabotaged, we might have other things to worry about, too."

### 6

As Gain and his irregulars stepped onto the landing pad's salty plastcrete, an insect buzzed past his left ear, moving at a good clip. Something spanged! against the side of the drophopper.

"Down!" Chan yelled. He grabbed Gain's arm and dropped, pulling them both to the platform. Crusted salt and grit ground into Gain's hands as he broke his fall. The place stank of seaweed, too, he noticed, now that he had it practically shoved up his nose.

Gain lifted his head. What was going on—?

Shoulders, Rook and Tin were already prone, and each had a weapon in hand.

"The control tower, about halfway up!" Rook said.

Gain still wasn't sure what had happened, but he was a military officer and quick enough to guess. Not an insect. Somebody had shot at them. And whoever it was was supposed to be on the control tower, a good hundred meters away, and if he were halfway up, thirty meters above the platform. There was an old-style slide window there, partially opened, with a shadowy figure visible through the thick plastic. The sniper had the high ground, a perfect field of fire, and superior weaponry. Way out of range for a tangler, Gain knew. His gut twisted in sudden fear. They were wide open out here, they didn't have a prayer—

Tin and Shoulders pointed their weapons at the tower and started firing. Wasting time, Gain thought, and none of us has any to waste, either. The noises were not the high-pitched squeal of neural tanglers, however. One of them went *whoosh-boom!* and the other sounded like heavy sheet brass being pierced with a sharp object, *wraank!*

Rook came up and did a broken-step jerk 'n' jive

across the platform, dodging and darting as she tacked toward the tower's base. She also fired as she ran, and *her* weapon went *foing!*

The window halfway up the tower was bracketed by things pocking the wall. The metal chinged with the impacts. The heavy plastic of the half-opened window itself sprouted half a dozen punctures. That window, all of a moment, was a very dangerous place in which to find oneself, Gain saw.

Chan had a heavy-looking gun pointed at the tower, an old flexmetal handcannon, it looked like. After a second, though, he tucked it back under his synlin coat.

"They're gone," he said. He stood, and helped Gain to his feet.

"Damn," Gain said, surprised and relieved to be alive. "What is that battery you're carrying? I thought you were issued a neural tangler."

"A tangler is only good for short-range stuff; you that close, you might as well hit 'em with your fist. I left the thing under my mattress at the station. Old Bruce is my charged-particle pal, good for half a klick." He patted the weapon under his coat.

Shoulders and Tin stood, dusting the salt and dirt from their clothes.

"Shoulders, he carries an antique, an old Pinzer rocket launcher. Tin favors a Dagon boltslammer. Rook likes her pinwheel pistol, shoots those little electropoison corkscrews."

"Am I the only one carrying my issue non-lethal hand weapon?"

"I expect so. Pil allows us some leeway when it comes to, um, nonstandard missions. Whoever took a shot at us was probably using a sniper rifle. He could have plinked at us all day if all we'd had to wave back at him were tanglers. Sooner or later, he'd have hit us. Or you, anyhow."

"Me?"

"You're the LUC, Luck. Take you out, we have to go back and get ourselves another officer. Got to figure they know that much."

Gain stared at the SUO. The Sub laughed. "Sorry, Luck, I don't make the rules. You got any idea who might be shooting at us? Anything you can tell a lowly SUO?"

Gain shook his head. "I don't know for sure. Might be agents of—" He stopped and looked around.

"Luck, we also got to assume they know who *they* are."

"I suppose you're right. I'd bet money that they are either hired by one of the Twelve or special operatives of the Grand Harriers."

"Oh, mama," Tin said from behind them. "What'd you get us into here, Sub?"

"You know about as much as anybody," Chan said. "You got any discretion here, Luck, to tell us any more?"

"Technically, no." He paused a few seconds. Somebody had just shot at him and his first command. That ought to mean something. Regulations notwithstanding, he figured his people had a right to know why. "Let's find a place to get out of the sun and I'll tell you what I was told."

Regulations weren't doing so well these days.

## 7

The above-sea eatery was a fully-automated unit, and a few locals shuffled in front of the dispense trays, ordering food and drinks. The five Petits moved to an empty corner and sat at two of the scratched red lastever-plastic tables. Chan watched the nearest door, while Shoulders scanned the patrons. The place stank of curdled sofsoy and scorched cheese. Nothing to write home about.

Gain told them what he'd been told.

When he was done, Rook shook her head. "Man. We'd have been better off staying in the brig."

"You said it, killer," Tin said. "I wouldn't want any piece of this, if I was covering bets. You got us into a bleeding *duel* between the MiC of the Petits and the MiC of the Grands."

"Don't lets forget the drug-addicted One-of-the-Dozen," Rook said. "Man. You sure about that? One of the Twelve is on *yadjak*?"

"I'm not *sure* of anything," Gain said. "I'm just following orders and you just heard what they were."

Shoulders said, "Why'd one of the Twelve need to sky up on *yadjak*? They can do just about anything already, can't they?"

"Don't ask me," Gain said. "What I know about people who walk those levels you can carve on your eyeball with an axe without feeling it."

"Jaskeen is probably not gonna like it much," Chan said. "*Yadjak* comes from some kinda bug or plant that grows on the ocean bottom, and the local underlevel honchos don't like anybody fucking with it; it's a real expensive item. He has to live here; he probably won't want to step on any powerful toes."

"*Our* MiC says if somebody is going to be controlling a member of the Twelve with an addictive, no-known-cure, Look-I'm-God drug, it isn't going to be the Grands," Gain said. "I think you can see where *that* leads."

Chan shook his head. "Real can of ugly worms. Just as soon toss the suckers back into their hole and go home."

"I don't see as how we have much choice," Gain said.

"Kid's got a point," Tin said.

Chan nodded. "Yeah. Well. Might as well get to it."

The layout of Oondervatten was similar, if not identical, to other water-based cities Gain had seen. The basic shape was somewhat like a squashed diamond, flat on top and pointed on the deep end, thickest in the middle. It looked pretty much like a child's wooden spinning top. It did not bob in the water like a float, however, since most of its mass and weight were below the waterline.

The dropchutes did not run in a straight path from top to bottom. Every dozen or so levels, passengers had to exit and take a slider a few meters to a different chute.

"It's a pretty stupid system," Chan said, as the slider moved them over fairly bumpy rollers to the next set of chutes. "Some whizbrain somewhere decided that the city needed to be laid out so that in case there was a major breach in the outer hulls, the chutes wouldn't fill to the top. A hole that big would drown everybody anyhow, but the foofah designer had to have it his way."

"How far is it to Fishtown?"

"Eighty-six levels," Tin said. "Six chute changes. Last one is guarded by local cools."

"To keep people out?"

"Nah, to keep 'em in. Anybody with two demistads to rub together can get a riser pass, but everything below eighty-six runs on grease."

"Bribes," Chan said, to Gain's puzzled look.

Gain liked the sound of the place less and less. Maybe his uncle was right: he should have gone into the family business. Nothing wrong with the packaging trade. A little dull, maybe.

The LUC was slightly ahead of the others when they reached the next series of dropchutes.

The chute in front of them opened. Four men with arcnives leaped out and seemed intent on carving Gain into bloody tatters.

The first man lunged straight at the LUC, the humming arcnife spitting blue sparks and the stink of ozone. Gain didn't have time to talk, but he could react. He twisted to his left and back, and the deadly line of bottle-blue energy stabbed the air a good centimeter away from his chest. Gain shot his right hand out, using the heel as he'd been taught, slamming it against the attacker's temple. The man stumbled, lost the arcnife as he tried to break his stunned fall, and skidded across the no-slip ridges of the slider on his face.

As the downed man came to a stop, Chan kicked him upside the head.

Rook spun toward the second attacker, smashed his throat with one elbow, grabbed his hair with her other hand, and slammed his face down onto her knee. He was still in the air and falling when she stepped into the third attacker, deftly avoided his panicked swipe with the humming weapon, and snap-kicked him square on the balls. That one wasn't going to be causing any more trouble, either.

Shoulders dodged around the final attacker's fencing lunge, grabbed the man under the arms, and threw him across the corridor as if he weighed no more than a sack of air. The fourth man hit the wall face first, his feet a meter or so above the ground, and slid down, unconscious.

Tin stood there, weapon held at the ready, but it was all over.

No more than five seconds had passed.

Startled locals made astonished noises as Chan and Shoulders bent to examine the stunned or unconscious attackers.

"Nice move, Luck," Chan said, as he moved to

collect and extinguish the arcnives. "Your hand-to-hand Sub would be pleased."

"Should have followed up the first strike," Rook said. "Course, it gave Chan something to do." She turned to Tin. "I didn't see you working up any sweat, sucker bet."

"Well, you hogged two of 'em," Tin said, grinning. "I didn't want to spoil your fun. If I'd shot one, you'd never let me hear the end of it."

"True," Rook said.

"Let's see can we find out who these clowns are," Chan said.

## 8

The local cools came and looked at Gain's ID and listened to his explanation of what had happened. The four were Fishtown muscle-for-hire, the cools said. Finding out who hired them would have to wait for the prosecutor to get a court order for a truthscan, and they'd all have legals who'd put that off for as long as possible. Might take a week.

A week from now, Gain hoped to be done with all this.

The cools had more questions, but the SUO pulled the officer in charge aside. Something unseen changed hands, and the cools went away.

"Did you bribe him?" Gain asked.

"Sure. Pil has a special fund, feelie money; I have a few platinum coins to spread around."

Gain shook his head. He sure as hell was getting an initiation into how things were really done out here in the sparsely traveled spacelanes.

"We haven't even gotten to Fishtown yet and already we're having to work to earn our pay. Hell of a thing," Chan said.

## 9

The final chute into Fishtown was indeed guarded, and more of Chan's bribe money got passed to the cools as the five Petits fell the final few levels.

When the door opened, the first thing Gain noticed was the stink; dead fish with just a whiff of stopped-up toilet.

Chan grinned at Gain. "Ah, the delightful bouquet of the entertainment capital of Feddalsi Oasis. You'll get used to it."

And the look of the place was something else, too.

The normally squared-off and clean hallways had been decorated with all manner of graffiti. The very shape of the wall was rounded in many of the corners. There was a big open area outside the liftchutes that on other levels held fountains or artwork; here, there were stalls, so that the place resembled an outdoor bazaar. These were made of cheap stressed plastic, or in some cases, billowing and colorful fabric, and the patrons and sellers were every bit as brightly dressed as the shops. Gain saw people wearing neosilk pantaloons and tictack boots; full body tattoos and little else; thinskin combat suits; and all manner of dress and undress in between.

It looked like a freak show.

"That corridor, to the left," Chan said. "Let's show some teeth, boys and girls."

Shoulders, Tin, and Rook pulled their concealed weapons from hiding and rebelted or holstered them in full view. Chan moved his inside-the-waistband holster with his flexmetal gun around to the front.

Gain started to reach for his tangler.

"Why don't you leave that out of sight, Luck? Most everybody is armed here, and it's better to let 'em think you've got a killing weapon. A guy who knows he's gonna wake up after you shoot him is a lot braver than one who knows he won't."

Gain nodded. But he bent and slid his pant leg up to show the boot knife Rook had given him.

"Nice move," Tin said. "They think all you're carrying is a dead steel blade, they'll figure you're either real dangerous or real stupid. Me, I'd bet on dangerous in Fishtown."

Gain knew a little about knives, but Tin's evaluation made him feel better. And hey, he *was* a Petit officer, wasn't he? Yeah, but he was also beginning to understand the SC's comment about the whosis rangers. Nothing about this mission conformed to regulations.

Somebody screamed down a side hallway as the five Petits moved along the corridor. Rook looked that way, but Chan said, "Not our biz, Rook." To Gain, Chan said, "We chase every noise we hear down here, we'll never get anything done." They turned away from the sound.

There were some hard-looking souls in the corridor, men, women and even children. About half the wall lumes were burned out or graffed over, but even so, there was enough light to see that virtually everybody carried some kind of weapon. Gain recognized buzz-buckles, fireblades, cobrateeth, dartguns and assorted low-output energy wands. He also saw several items he guessed were weapons but could not recognize. One guy carried a big stick. Nice place.

Some of the people were doing business: whores selling their reusable goods, drugs changing hands, energy chits and illegally-detached small-power units in plain sight. None of the dealers or buyers spared the Petits more than a wary glance or two before getting back to their transactions.

"Law doesn't come down here much," Chan said, answering Gain's unasked question.

"Hi, soldier," a tall woman with shocked green hair said to Gain. "Looking for a good time?" She wore snake-patterned skintights that covered her completely in iridescent green from neck to ankles to wrists—except for sections artfully cut out to reveal parts normally concealed. "I'm Trish."

"No, thanks," Gain said.

The trull laughed, and glanced at the other Petits. Rook said, "You know the Zamalah Variation?"

Trish looked surprised, and when her smile returned, it was not of the same professional caliber as before. "*You* know it?"

"To Level Six."

"Honey, I'd pay *you* for that."

"Catch me on the way up," Rook said. "We can work something out, maybe."

Chan said to Gain, "You don't want to know."

"There's the stairs," Tin said.

*Stairs?*

"We got four more levels down," Shoulders said.

A small boy of maybe seven or eight, armed with a contact zapper, leaned against the wall next to the open door to the stairway. Tin moved toward him and said, "Kid, here's a fiver chit for you." He flipped the small disc at the boy, who deftly caught it.

"Whaddya want for it?"

"Go tell Madam Howzu that Royal Tinner's in town. Tell her to save me a couple of hours in the next day or two. She'll give you another five."

"Gone," the kid said. He tucked the coin away and pulled his zapper out, in case anybody had thoughts of taking his money. He ducked into the stairway and ran.

"Okay, let's go down, people," Chan said. "Rook, you got the nose, Tin, you're the tail. Shoulders, you backstop Rook. Me and the Luck, we'll ride in the pocket."

"Life is hard," Rook said.

"Yeah, ain't it? Let's walk." Chan turned to Gain. "The stairs sometimes get a little busy."

Rook pulled her pistol and checked the magazine, flipped the safety off, and moved into the entrance to the stairs with the weapon in pointfire hold. Shoulders pulled his own handgun and moved in behind her. He was pretty quick and surefooted for a guy his size.

"You 'n' me, Luck." Chan moved up behind Shoulders.

Gain pulled his tangler. Maybe it wasn't much, but in a stairwell, it would reach far enough to be useful.

Tin followed them, his sidearm pointed up in order arms.

They passed two men standing on the first landing—two beefy men who looked like ad vids for black leather and chrome, but who kept their hands in sight, fingers spread. Both men wore sickly smiles.

On the second landing a big man, almost as big as Shoulders, lay on his side, clutching his scrotum and whimpering softly. A tackdriver rod lay next to him.

"You feeling merciful?" Chan asked. He nodded at Gain's tangler.

Gain returned the nod. He pointed the tangler at the injured man and thumbed the firing stud. The man's brain scrambled under the energy beam and he slid into what was probably a welcome unconsciousness.

On the third landing there were two more unconscious men hanging by their belts from the short metal tines of a support strut, their feet well clear of the expanded aluminum floor.

There was a doorway with the door removed and

propped next to it at the bottom of the stairs. Chan removed his hand cannon and moved to stand to one side of the door, motioning for Gain to stand clear on the opposite side. Tin stayed on the stairs three meters back.

"Clear," came Rook's voice from the other side of the door.

Chan holstered his weapon.

Beyond the door was a narrow hallway with several exits along it, all of which were closed. The five of them moved along the corridor, which twisted and turned, the lighting growing dimmer. Gain estimated that they had gone maybe five hundred meters when they came to a door that looked like the others. Rook rapped on the door—metal, from the way it rang—with the butt of her pistol.

"Yeah?" came a voice from the air. The speaker sounded bored, mean, and ugly.

"Chan Singa and some friends," the Sub said.

"Gimme the line."

" 'The smallest worm will turn, being trodden on.' "

Juddah. It seemed as if he might die wearing a puzzled look, Gain thought; it was getting to be second nature lately. As the door slid open, Chan said to the LUC, "The scanner can recognize voices. I'm in the bank, but Jaskeen likes to make his customers recite his favorite poet. They got visual, too."

The door opened into an even narrower corridor that was somewhat better lit than the previous one. The hall ran straight ahead for ten meters to another doorway. Instead of a door, though, there was a curtain of beads undulating in a faint breeze.

Halfway down the hall, a large drawer suddenly slid out of the wall at waist height. Rook put her handgun into the drawer, then unloaded a small arsenal she had hidden about her. Gain saw knives, stun caps, a pen-sized shockstick, and a reel of saw wire, plus a couple things he couldn't put a name to. The others began unloading weaponry into the drawer, and Gain didn't need to be told to put his own gear into the receptacle. All he had was the tangler and the boot knife; all the others had at least four or five implements they deposited.

"This is the only public way in or out," Chan said. "Everybody gets scanned hard, and anything detectable as a weapon gets checked."

The five of them moved past the drawer toward the bead curtain. A bright blue light flashed, once.

"The left bootheel, girlie," came the bored voice.

Rook grinned and went back to the drawer. She did something to her boot and the heel came off, and she plucked something from the sole of her boot and dropped it into the drawer.

"They're pretty thorough," Chan said.

"So I see."

There must have been a soundstop built into the doorway, because as they pushed through the beads, the noise of a fairly busy pub surrounded Gain. He looked around.

The first thing he noticed was that the air did indeed feel hot and damp. There was that ubiquitous fishy stink, and a hint of machine lube under that, plus some other smells Gain didn't know but didn't like.

The layout was on three levels, concentric circles, with the outer ring being the highest and dropping down about a meter for each of the other two levels. Thick permoplastic rails protected the patrons on the outer perimeter and on the upper and middle levels where the mushroom tables came close to the edges. The bar was a circular affair in the center of the bottom level, manned by a pair of tenders. Stock and liquor cabinets displayed wares in a floor-to-ceiling mechanical servex column in the exact middle of the room.

The tables and chairs were all bolted to the floor. It was larger than Gain would have guessed: there was enough room for maybe 150 people if they were packed in fairly tight. As it was, maybe half that number sat or stood around drinking, smoking, or doing what passed for socializing. The blend of dress seemed much the same as Gain had seen in Fishtown, but there were some patrons in expensive clothes—slummers, probably—and a few that the LUC would have guessed to be military, despite their cit clothing. Servers moved up and down the short ramps from level to level, carrying drinks or other rec chem.

The buzz of conversation and activity muted some when the five Petits entered, but didn't stay that way long. Everybody seemed to go back to their own business, though Gain felt that crawly sensation he sometimes got when he thought he was being watched. Well, if the bad guys were here, at least they'd be unarmed.

Rook led the others to a pair of tables on the upper level opposite the door. From there, they could see most of the place laid out below them, and the entrance. A male server, depil-bald but with three-dee tattoos on his head made to look like blue hair, arrived in front of them.

"Keep it light," Chan said. "Local beer all the way around."

The server flashed black enamel teeth and left.

"Now what?" Gain asked.

"We drink our beer and wait. Jaskeen'll show up sooner or later."

Gain felt impatient. It must have shown.

"Relax, Luck. We got here alive and without major problems. We're ahead of the game. The beer is pretty good."

## 10

Given how tough this place was supposed to be, Gain was a little disappointed. Yeah, he still felt as if somebody were eyeing him, but that could have been simple camera pressure. Given the weapon-scanning gear, surely Jaskeen would have spyviewers in the pub itself. This could have been any off-duty toke 'n' slosh place in a dozen base towns from what he'd seen so far.

"—Hey, drop dead, pal! I say you're so full of it your blasted eyes are going brown!"

Gain looked over to see two men glaring at each other across a table ten meters to his left. The speaker was halfway to his feet, halfway to being roaring drunk, and halfway to throwing a punch. He wore freight-handler blues and looked to be physically hard under the thin coveralls.

The second man was dressed in like fashion, also good-sized and fit, and not going to take such insults sitting down. He was rising, plastic tankard clenched in one hand, some purple fluid sloshing from the container.

"How'd you like to *eat* this stein, elbowsucker?!" the second man said.

There would be a bouncer here somewhere, Gain knew. He wondered how long it would take the guy to get to the two. A couple of punches from either side, maybe.

He was wrong. Before the two men came fully to their feet, there was a third man standing there.

Gain was not impressed. The man was short, slight, and had white hair. Looked old enough to be Gain's father, maybe his grandfather. Didn't seem to have any kind of weapon, and hardly seemed the kind of bouncer Gain would have hired. Either one of the two freight handlers could probably wipe the table top with the old guy without working up much of a sweat. He got in between them, they'd chop him into soypro patties. The old guy wore an old-fashioned silksuit, lots of flowing folds from his narrow shoulders to the gray plastic boots.

"Who the Yellow Yazoo are—?" began the first freight handler.

"Sit down," the old man ordered.

The two words were not particularly harsh, nor were they loud. Sit down. Very simple. And yet, the tone, something in it, carried in it a . . . power. Sit. Down. It hit Gain like a punch, like a sudden hard fist in the solar plexus, and for a moment, he couldn't breathe.

If he had been standing, Gain knew he would have sat as ordered, no question about it.

Juddah.

The two freight handlers sat. The old man leaned over and said something that Gain didn't catch, and they nodded dumbly, as if they were two children listening to instructions from their father. Both men looked pale and frightened. When he'd finished, the old man smiled and nodded, and moved away. Toward where Gain and his party sat.

"Hello, Chan," the old man said. The power was hidden, but a faint hint of it echoed through his words. Something about the voice was familiar to Gain, as if he'd heard it before. Where—?

"Hello, Limos," the Sub said.

Holy Hershaw! *This* was Limos Jaskeen?

The old man slid onto a seat and grinned. "Lot of skill for a little visit to Fishtown." There was some

kind of drawly accent to the words. He nodded at
the group.

"Some of us are slowing down as we get older,"
Chan said. "This is Rook, the big one is Shoulders,
you know Tin the gambler. And this is Stelo Gain,
he's just on-station."

The owner of the Hot and Moist took in Gain with
a quick glance. It reminded the LUC of Rook's earlier assessment of him.

"Officer," Jaskeen said, a hint of disgust in the
word. "First mission, eh, bub?"

*Now* Gain placed the voice. The station computer.
Same voice exactly. How——?

"What makes you think we're here for anything
but R&R?" Chan said.

At that moment a tall woman walked by and smiled
at Rook. It took a second for Gain to place her. Her
hair wasn't green or shocked now, and she was covered in the same dark silks as Jaskeen. The Fishtown
lady of the evening.

"Chan, Chan. Don't you think I try and keep up
with what goes on in my part of the world?"

Chan shook his head. "Never know but that you
could have gone senile."

"You should live so long, bub. What do you want?"

Chan glanced at Gain. *Your move*, his look said.

"We need your help," Gain said. "It's a matter
of——"

"——galactic importance," Jaskeen said, cutting Gain
off. "Always is, bub. What crack has uplevels got
itself in now?"

"I, uh . . ." Gain floundered. How much could he
tell this old man? "It concerns one of . . . of the
Twelve," Gain said. Best to be cautious.

"The one who's skyed on *yadjak*? Thinks it's God,
can wave its paw and create Universes? Spends half
its time contemplating its navel and like that?"

Oh, *man*! How can he *possibly* know that? This is supposed to be *top secret*!

Jaskeen grinned at Gain's obvious surprise.

Chan shook his head.

"Like I said, I try to keep up, even down here in the basement."

"Uh, uh—"

"And you want me to help you corner the market on *kabid* urchins so the Petits and not the Grands can string the addict along, right?"

Who *was* this guy?

"Sorry, bub. I'm a simple pub owner now. I don't mess in greasy politics anymore."

Jaskeen nodded at Chan. "Have another beer, on the house." He started to stand.

"Wait!" Gain said.

"Sorry, bub, I hardly ever change my mind about such things."

Rook said, "Just how good is your scanning gear?"

Jaskeen looked at her.

"Guy by the door, in black on black," she said. "He's got the feel."

Jaskeen reseated himself. He grinned. For a moment, Gain had the distinct feeling that the old man had been hoping one of them would say something that would make him stay. Jaskeen said, "Why, I do believe you're right, sister. The gear's good enough so he can't be alone."

"This beautiful young lady," Jaskeen volunteered for Gain's benefit, "has just told me me that the lightfoot by the door is probably armed, and I told her that our sensor gear is sharp enough so that the only way to smuggle any weaponry past it would be to do so in a number of pieces, each of which would have to be pretty innocuous by itself to get by." Gain had understood the first part of that all right, but not the second.

"Can you figure out who his friends are?" Chan asked.

"He came in alone. The computer can probably nail it, given time. But I don't expect we'll have the luxury."

"You armed?"

"Sure. I can take the lightfoot easy enough. Or I can *kiai* the room, but if they were told how to bring in guns, they might have also been told to be earplugged."

"Zap field?"

"Yeah, but I'd just as soon avoid the hangover," Jaskeen said. "Better we should do it manually. Ah. There's one, blue slicker and yellow dabs, at 169, back to the wall."

"Got him," Rook said quietly.

Gain still felt that pressure of being watched, and a quick glance to his right gave him the source. A tall and thin man with black hair, dressed in a jumpshipper's greens, pretending to be staring at somebody past him. The man was maybe eight meters away. "There's a guy in jump greens three tables over who's watching us," Gain said.

"Good read, bub. That's three. I'd figure two more."

"That'd be my guess," Chan said.

Shoulders said, "There's a guy who's lifted some heavy weights loosening up carefully down one level. Getting ready to move."

"Me, I'd give six-to-one that the fat woman coming out of the fresher finds us more than usually fascinating," Tin said.

Jaskeen said, "That's five. Okay. I've got the woman and lightfoot, any leftovers were missed. Chan, you and Shoulders take the one with muscles. Rook, the one in blue and yellow. Kid, you get the one in greens. At speed. On my count of three. One. Two. Three—"

Gain didn't have time to think about it. He rolled off his chair and took three quick steps toward the black-haired man in greens. The guy was startled, but not so much so that he froze. He untangled himself from the chair and came up, sliding into a defensive stance. That confirmed something or the other.

A needle gun twanged and Gain caught a peripheral flash of the fat woman coming out of the fresher as she began to fall.

Somebody yelled something obscene in tradespeak.

Gain was moving fast enough that the guy in greens couldn't dodge, and the LUC kept going, shoulder first. The guy tried to block and move at the same time, but managed neither, and Gain slammed into him hard enough to knock him down and sprawl on top of him. Before the guy could do more than curse and try a punch, Gain smashed down with a hammer fist. The guy was trying to come up, so his head was a few centimeters clear of the floor. The strike connected with his forehead and drove the crown of his head back down. The guy was knocked cold. A lucky shot.

Remembering what Rook had said, Gain whacked the guy again, this time on the temple. He didn't react, save to bounce to one side. He was out, all right.

Gain came up, in time to see Rook twirl into her man with some fancy aiki move and cut him down like a laser-sawed tree. The guy never had a chance.

Shoulders and Chan, meanwhile, were busy tossing a big man over the rail. He didn't want to go, but he was losing.

Jaskeen stood facing the one he'd called a lightfoot, five meters of space between the two men. Jaskeen's hands were empty. How could that be? Hadn't he shot the fat woman? Gain remembered the sound of

the needler, and she was lying on the floor, sure
enough. Wait. There it was, tucked into his waist-
band. Why'd he do that—?

Lightfoot dug for something under his black tunic.
His hand came out with a stubby-barreled plastic
gun and he started to swing it up—

Jaskeen, grinning, snatched the needler out of his
belt and whipped it toward Lightfoot with a speed
Gain couldn't believe. He shoved it out and caught it
with his other hand, like punching a fist into his
palm. The needle gun twanged three times. Gain
twisted and saw the trio of needles stick up in
Lightfoot's forehead, making a neat line right between the eyes, but up a centimeter. Lightfoot went
over down and backwards like a destringed puppet.

The big man who'd been dumped over the railing
hit on his back on a table below him, making a fairly
loud crash as the tabletop shattered.

Then things got very quiet in the Hot and Moist.

## 11

"Who were they?" Chan asked, as Jaskeen came
back to where the Petits sat once again.

"Grands. On detached envoy duty. Got full diplomatic credentials."

"Ah."

Gain thought, So I'm stupid: "What does that
mean?"

"Means they are a mission from somebody way up
the chute, bub. I'd guess maybe as high as the
Grand MiC Hisself. And it also means I am reconsid-
ering your request."

"Why? I mean, probably they came after us, but it
still isn't your business."

Jaskeen didn't smile. "Doesn't matter why they

came. People don't bring weapons and hassle in here. They need to understand that I can't let that happen."

Jaskeen's tone made Gain feel cold suddenly.

"What did you do with them?"

"Sent 'em up to the main level. Trish went along to make sure they behave until she turns 'em loose."

"You're going to let them *go*?"

Jaskeen looked at Chan, then shook his head at Gain. "What did you want me to do kid, kill 'em? They're documented Grand Harriers, you can't just shove 'em out a lock. Plenty more where they came from. Better the devils we know. There are certain rules to this game."

"That include assassins shooting at me up on the landing deck?"

"Yep, that's so. You Petits and Grands can fling hardware at each other until the local sun goes nova, but us cits have to be a bit more careful how we walk."

"But you're still willing to help us?"

"They broke the rules. People come here to get stoned or swacked or laid, that's okay. Anarchy ain't allowed."

They followed Jaskeen to a door that was concealed against the back wall of the fresher, into a long hallway lined with other doors. From the sounds coming through those thin panels, Gain realized that this was the other part of Jaskeen's infamous operation. Lust about to be fulfilled had a certain . . . urgent tone to it.

He led them down through a series of turns and downward angles until they reached a pressure door. The thick portal swung open after Jaskeen tapped a command into the key console next to it.

They faced a second pressure door across the length of a small lock chamber. Past this one was a huge room, full of submersible craft. There were maybe two dozen vessels, each on rolleracks, lined up with hatches in the metal walls. Looked like so many ship coffins waiting to be deep spaced. Several techs moved around, attending to the various craft. Jaskeen went ahead to speak to one of the techs.

"I don't suppose you want to tell me what's going on?" Gain said.

"I don't know for sure," Chan said. "Limos is unhappy that the Grands and the Selachii smuggled guns into his place. Real unhappy."

"Selachii?"

"Yeah, name for the local crime syndic. Means 'shark' or 'ray,' something like that. Among other things, they control the hallucinogen trade on this world."

"I thought the four in the pub were Grands."

"They were, but they couldn't have gotten that far without Selachii help. Limos has—or had—a deal with the Selachii: they didn't bother him, he wouldn't bother them. Well, now they bothered him."

Gain had the sudden feeling that bothering Jaskeen was much like saying something uncomplimentary about Shoulders' mother.

Rook moved closer to Gain and Chan. "That true what he said about being able to *kiai* the whole room?" she asked.

"Yeah," Chan said. He looked at Gain. "Limos knows this esoteric martial art, *kiaitsu*. Sound control. Takes years to perfect, gives the same effect as a sonic stunner. An expert can knock you down with a shout. You saw a little bit of it when he made the two freight handlers sit."

"What," Tin put in, "does he do if somebody is deaf? Or wearing plugs?"

"Kuji-kiri. Magic finger weave. A kind of hypnosis,

it thralls you long enough for him to sucker-kick you."

"Yeah? What if they are blind *and* deaf?" Tin said.

Chan laughed. "Hey, Tin, even *you* could probably keep up with a blind and deaf opponent. Likely he'd just shoot 'em. He can outdraw most with those needlers he carries, and he doesn't miss many within range. You saw the lightfoot."

Jaskeen came back from his meeting with the tech. "Sub's ready," he said. "Let's go."

## 12

The hatch slid open ahead of the sub, and the view through the front ports was of a long, lighted metal tunnel ending in another hatch. The sub rolled into the lock and the hatch slid shut behind them.

Gain was impressed by the submersible. It was built shaped like a cigar inside a toilet paper tube on the outside; inside, the sub looked almost like a ground car or a multi-passenger hopper. Eight seats in four pairs for company, a pilot and co-pilot seat at the controls. Each pair of seats had a thick double densecris plate, cut round, through which the outside was visible.

Gain had seen aerocraft with more complicated boards, but not many. A lot of hydraulic switches and mechanicals up there. Jaskeen ran through his checks with an offhand expertise, both hands working independently as he powered up the sub and put systems on-line.

"There's a box just ahead of your seat," Jaskeen said to Gain. "You might want to check it out."

Gain was in the front pair of seats behind Jaskeen, next to Chan. Tin and Rook sat behind them, and

Shoulders had a pair of seats across the aisle to himself.

Chan opened the box, which looked like a padded footrest. Inside were their weapons.

How'd he do that? Get them here ahead of them so fast?

Chan passed out the hardware. Even though it was only a tangler, Gain felt a lot better once he had it again. The knife was somehow even more comforting.

"There are only three known *kabid* urchin beds on the planet," Jaskeen began.

There came a loud whoosh of compressed air. Water foamed and bubbled up next to the sub. A piece of some kelplike plant floated past the window as Gain watched the water level in the lock rise to completely engulf the ship.

The sub moved forward on its rollerack.

"Two of the urchin beds are owned outright by the Selachii," Jaskeen continued, "and they buy all the output of the third, so the Selachii have a pretty good monopoly.

"Now *kabid* are scarce and very finicky. Nobody's ever been able to raise 'em artificially. They are native to a hundred-klick oval in this one sea. They live at a thousand-meter depth, plus or minus five, need a special kind of rickrock bottom, a current no stronger than a klick or two, and an absence of industrial pollution. Take away any one of these, or maybe ten other things, they don't reproduce."

The sub slid out into the ocean. It was dark and murky, but Jaskeen switched on exterior sunlamps that brightened things considerably. Colorful fish darted past in small schools, and more vegetation drifted into view. Gain couldn't see the bottom of the sea.

"The *yadjak* drug is part of the poison the urchins use to protect themselves from bottom feeders. Only one species of fish is immune, and there ain't many of them, both because they breed slowly and because the Selachii pay a real big bounty for any brought in. Don't want the little suckers eating up their profits."

The sub made a slow turn, the humming of its electric motors sending a pleasant vibration through the seats. The air was dry and crisp, and Gain felt his sinuses ache a little.

"How is it you know so much about these things?" Gain asked. He swallowed, and his ears popped.

"I own the third *kabid* bed."

Ah. Well. How about that? Our ace in the hole is a dealer in the very drug we've come to find. How convenient. It made Gain want to spit. The MiC had sent him out to procure drugs so that they could manipulate one of the Twelve. Yeah, yeah, the Grands were already doing it and it was self-defense, to maybe save the Petits from ruin, but where was the moral stance here?

"So we're going to harvest some of your private stock?"

"No, we're going to destroy the Selachii urchin beds."

## 13

The voyage was two hours old when Jaskeen put the ship on autopilot and went to use the head. While he was gone, Gain turned to his SUO.

"You have any problems with all this?"

Chan shrugged. "I do what I'm ordered to do most of the time. I sometimes volunteer when they can't legally make me go. It's a big galaxy, Luck. Lot of wicked things running around. You can let 'em run over you, you can hide from 'em, or you can try to get a grip on 'em."

Gain leaned back in his seat. He sighed. "Situational ethics."

"Sure. What else? It *always* depends on where you are and what's going on to figure out what you need to do. Unbendable rules tend to be real brittle; they break when you try to pry with 'em. A guy living in a metroplex thinktank on Dataline can give you a hell of a theoretical law to live by, but he won't put his own toe in the cold water down here. There are only a few things I'd be willing to put my back to the wall and stand or go down for. You need to think real hard about what *you*'d do it for."

Chan looked at Gain's face and shook his head. "The Bugs—the Wammgalloz—have a saying: 'Let the one who would choose my food taste forever with my tongue.' "

Along with everything else, Gain was getting philosophy lessons from aliens, via his Sub. Wonderful mission so far.

Another hour passed. Jaskeen did something to the motors and they got very quiet, but also began to pulse in a strange rhythm. He killed the exterior lights, then one-wayed the densecris all around. They were getting close to their destination.

"We're pretending to be a joewhale," Jaskeen said. "Even so, we'll stop well outside the patrols' range."

"Then what?" Gain asked.

"Then we suit up and take a swim."

"A thousand meters down?"

"In a deepsuit, it's a walk in the park," Jaskeen said. He grinned.

*Well, if this old man can do it, so can I. But—then what?*

He asked. Despite his promise, Gain was sure being a lot of mouth with all his questions.

"We get to the bed, set some poison charges, and the crop dies, quick and painlessly."

"That's it?"

"Like I said, bub, a walk in the park."

"What if they find out who did it?"

"Oh, they'll know who did it. I plan to tell 'em myself."

The sub idled to a stop. Jaskeen adjusted the ballast so that the craft hung in neutral buoyancy. It was very quiet down here all of a moment.

"The deepsuits are aft, in the big locker next to the head. Three of us should go. Anybody know how to run this tub?"

Tin said, "I've driven a few."

"Good. You keep things loose here. I holler, you come and get us. Weapons system controls are in the lockbox, left console. Here's the key." Jaskeen flipped a small plastic tag at Tin. "If you have to come in, shoot anything that doesn't look like us."

"Who gets to go?" Rook asked.

"Me, 'cause I know what we're doing. Chan, because I trust him. And the kid, because he's the officer."

Rook, Tin, and Shoulders looked at Chan. He glanced at Gain, then nodded. "Limos was an officer before most of you were potty-trained. It's his show, right, Luck?"

Gain felt a small moment of doubt, but suppressed it. It was a little late to start acting like he was in charge, now wasn't it? He nodded. "Yeah."

## 14

The deepsuits were simple. They were augflex with air bottles and gills, bubbleless siphon drives and standard deepwater tool kits. More like mini-subs, they each looked like nothing so much as a big hydraulic walking loader, except that the frame was enclosed in the augflex. Not much different in operation than a standard vacuum spacesuit, and Gain had tested out okay in those.

Once he'd climbed into the suit and latched the watertights, he found that walking in the sucker was a lot harder than in any vac suit, though. Fortunately, he only had to manage a few meters to get into the lock. Once outside he'd use the siphons for most of his locomotion. Dangling from his belt was a pressure canister of something that would supposedly kill the urchins.

It occurred to Gain as the sea poured into the outer lock of the sub, swirling up around him under pressure, that for Jaskeen to have on hand a poison that would kill the *kabids*, all ready to go and all, was passing strange.

"Com check," Jaskeen said. His voice sounded tinny and hollow in the deepsuit's speaker.

"I read, L-A-C," Gain said. Just like a meteor drill.

"These coms are line-of-sight magwavers," Jaskeen said. "We don't want to be bleeding radio where anybody can hear us, so the range is real short and real narrow. Don't get lost."

"Copy," Gain said. "Uh, can I ask something?"

"I think maybe I'd be disappointed if you didn't, bub."

"Don't you think the Selachii are going to be mad if you kill a third of all the urchins on the planet?"

"I'm going to kill more than a third," Jaskeen said. "We'll do their other bed, it's only a few klicks away, right after we finish here. And; yeah, they'll be real upset. They should have thought of that before they sent those Grands to my place."

Juddah, Gain thought.

The outer hatch slid wide. "We'll have to do this in the dark," Jaskeen said. "Keep your doppler tuned to me, I'll lead us in. Oh, and don't worry about me, kid. Selachii'll be steamed to the eyeballs, but I've got the only other urchin bed on the planet. They'll come to terms if they want to stay in the *yadjak* business. Nobody knows where it is but me, and I've got a burnblock against telling the location. They touch me and it goes away. And they know it—I bought the block from them."

At a thousand meters from the surface, it was like the inside of a cave. Occasionally Gain saw bright sparkles in the gloom, some phosphorescent fish luring prey, maybe, but those and the diodes in his and the other two men's suits were all the lights there were.

After what seemed like hours but was only a few minutes according to his suit clock, another light source appeared in the distance in front of them. It was very dim, but definitely there.

"Coming up on the beds," Jaskeen said. "The light is from the guards' habitat. Nine-person permanent station. We'll circle around it. What we want is about five hundred meters past it."

The silent but powerful siphon pumps drove the deepsuits through the dark waters.

"They don't have sonar or UWR?" Chan asked.

"Both, but these suits give off the same shadow as portfin lubafish. They breed in these waters. And they are siphoners."

No doubt about it, Gain figured. This wasn't some spur-of-the-moment deal on Jaskeen's part. The man had been prepared to run this program before Gain and his misfits ever showed up. Poison all ready, stealth-camouflaged deepsuits—Jaskeen definitely planned ahead. Maybe he had figured on cornering the drug market for a long time, making his own urchin bed worth a whole lot more.

Did it matter? He was helping them do what Gain had been sent to do. Wasn't that the important thing? Was this, as Chan had said, a back-to-the-wall issue with Gain? Wasn't his duty as a Petit officer more important than his personal moral and ethical feelings?

Now *there* was a question.

It was all fine and good to be like the on-the-spot rangers, dispensing justice as needed when there was nobody else around to do it, but *yadjak* was an addictive-after-one-time drug that made you think you were a god. People had tried to fly off tall buildings while skyed on *yadjak*, had walked in front of mag-lev trains, and there was no cure for it. Once a *yadjak* addict, always a *yadjak* addict; you could take it away but you couldn't take away the desire. People would do anything to get more of it. Anything at all.

What were the Petit Harriers doing involved in this kind of thing?

"Kid, you veer off to the left, go about a hundred meters and put your canister down, heading at two-two-zero, you copy?"

"Yeah, I hear you."

"Good. You get done, use your doppler to find me. You got a fix on my shadow?"

"I got it."

"Go."

As he siphoned away, Gain heard Jaskeen ordering Chan to take the second leg of the triangle. Well, this much at least he didn't have to think about. Killing these *kabid* would make that much less of the poison available on the market.

No, he didn't like this mission worth a damn, but this part he could manage. How much of the rest of it he could stomach remained to be seen. He hadn't had much chance to think about that, they'd been moving so fast, but sooner or later, he was going to have to come to terms with it. He hadn't joined the Petits to become a drug dealer.

## 15

The doppler image on Gain's heads up was easy enough to follow. There wasn't anything else to see, and after he dropped his canister, he swung a wide turn and siphoned toward Jaskeen. The man was only a hundred meters ahead, according to the read, but he'd have been invisible at five meters in this murk.

Suddenly the darkness turned into bright light.

Somebody had popped off a string of flares! Seventy, maybe eighty meters ahead, magnesium-white light shone through the seawater—the flares were releasing hot bubbling gases whose ghostly, contorted shadows danced in the brightness. There was Jaskeen, caught like a bug under a scope, four suited figures jetting toward him, trailing more bubbles, no more than thirty meters away. One of the figures began firing meter-long darts from a repeating speargun he carried. The darts fell short, but not by much.

Gain pushed his suit's siphons to full. The four didn't seem to see him—at least none of them were coming his way. He aimed himself at the four, and the suit began picking up speed.

"Luck?" It was Chan.

"I see them," Gain said. "I'm fifty meters away and slightly above, coming in on their starboard side. Where are you?"

"Port, and level. These suits aren't armed. I can't get at my weapon, it's inside with me."

"Ram the sons-of-bitches," Gain said. "The helmets should take it."

Yeah, if you didn't hit face first and crack your viewplate and drown under high pressure.

Jaskeen had turned away from the four attackers and kicked his own siphons to full push, but the guards were faster since their gear didn't have to be quiet or mimic some foodfish. He'd be within speargun range in a few seconds.

The angle was perfect. Gain flew the waters like some undersea raptor, and his speed and that of the guards was such that he speared down into the leader like a javelin. At the last second, he remembered to duck his head and use the top of the helmet. He hit the man square on the right side, banging his own head hard enough on the inside of the helmet to see a flare of red and then gray sparks. The blow knocked the guard sideways, mashing one of his main siphon tubes shut. The port siphon blew that much faster, and he went spiraling off out of control into the fading glow of the flares.

Chan hit the second of the guards just then, coming up from under him to thunk against the man's more or less unprotected belly. The man dropped his speargun and bent as close to double as the suit would allow.

That still left two armed guards.

"Turn off your com and exterior suit pickups!" Jaskeen yelled at them. "Turn 'em off *now!*"

Dazed, Gain obeyed. Not that there was anything to hear but suit motors and siphons anyhow. What good was that going to do?

Jaskeen had circled back and was coming toward them. Just in time to watch us get darted to death, Gain thought. Stupid idea to ram those two. The other two guards bore in and raised their spearguns. Gain cranked his siphons up, but he knew he'd never outrun the guards. They were going to die. And on his first mission, too!

Something beat at Gain's suit. Like a pressure wave. It hurt his ears. He reached up to cover them, banged the gauntlets against the helmet before he realized he couldn't get to his ears that way.

The two guards dropped their weapons and began to spin madly. Holy Hershaw! What had happened to them?

Jaskeen came close enough so that Gain could see him in the rapidly dwindling light of the flares. He touched his com aerial. Gain clicked his com back on.

Jaskeen's sub came out of the murk to within a few meters of the trio. He must have called it.

They weren't going to die after all. How about that?

## 16

Inside the sub, Gain realized what had happened. That esoteric sound thing. Jaskeen must have turned his external speakers on and blasted the two guards. If he'd keyed into a radio freq they used, they would have gotten the sound through the water *and* inside through their coms.

Ouch.

Which also meant that Jaskeen hadn't needed his help, and that now Gain owed him his life.

"Any trouble?" Jaskeen asked Tin.

"I had to shoot a couple guys got in the way. Nothing serious."

"You want to keep driving? There's a bunk in back. I think I'll grab a little nap."

"No problem. Where to?"

"Put it on a heading of three-oh-four. About an

hour at cruising speed. Wake me up when we get there."

Gain stared at Jaskeen. Could he really just go to sleep after this? Wasn't he tense? Gain was tense.

Rook moved toward the old man. "You, uh, want any company back there?"

Jaskeen smiled. "I never heard a better offer, Doreen."

Gain was aware that his mouth was gaping as he watched the pair of them move toward the rear of the sub. Come on. He was an old man! What did she see in him? Besides, Rook was some kind of nympho. She'd probably kill him.

Forty minutes later, Jaskeen returned. He looked ten years younger and refreshed, as if he'd had a full night's sleep. What is wrong with this picture?

"Where is Rook?" Gain asked.

"Asleep. Let her rest, would you, bub? She's real tired. A lovely woman, Doreen. Lovely."

Un*bel*ievable!

The second urchin bed was much easier; Jaskeen went out alone and placed the timed canisters. No guards. That bothered Gain.

"The other one was the main bed," Jaskeen said, after he'd gotten back. "And even there, they had to be careful about how many bodies they had swimming around. The trick is not to be noticed. This bed is close to the Soflu Fissure; there's a cold water power intake less than ten klicks away, got a lot of maintenance workers and like that around. Nobody is likely to notice a flat patch of urchins on the dark sea bottom here, but they would see a habitat. A diver disguised as a fish can come by now and then and harvest what he needs by hand."

They were halfway back to Oondervatten before

Rook emerged from the back, grinning widely but looking exhausted. She in turn looked at Jaskeen as if he could not only move beneath the water, but could, if he wanted, walk on top of it.

Chan just shook his head and chuckled. Gain realized all over again how much he had yet to learn about things.

"Now what?" Gain asked.

"Back to the Hot and Moist," Jaskeen said.

## 17

Jaskeen had an office and he and Chan and Gain were in it, the old man behind a desk that looked as if it had been carved from a giant pearl. Rook was in one of the rooms behind the fresher with Trish, formerly of the green shocked hair. Shoulders was lifting weights in the gym with a couple of guys who looked as if they could be his brothers for size and shape, and a woman who had more muscles than Gain. Tin was in Madam Howzu's, playing poker.

"Here's what you came for, bub." Jaskeen held up a crystal vial about the size of a hen's egg. "Enough in here for more than a thousand doses."

Gain stared at the vial.

"Marshal Twill'll be tickled, and you'll probably get a commendation for your rank rec file."

The thought didn't raise Gain's spirits. He hated this. But what was he going to do about it?

A voice came from the com inset into the pearly desk. "Boss, we got trouble out here. Behind the bar."

Jaskeen glanced at the holoproj, waving until the camera picked up the view he wanted. "Oops."

"What?" Gain said.

"There's a guy behind the bar holding what looks like an implosion device."

Chan said, "Kreest, Limo, you're letting all kinds of trash in here these days. I might have to find myself another place to do my drinking."

"You might at that," Jaskeen said.

Gain moved to stare at the front of the holoproj. There was a short but well-knit man dressed in gray skintights, his hands clutched around a roundish object with a plunger on top. His thumb was on the pushed-in plunger. "You know who he is?"

"Selachii assassin, I expect. Well. Let's go talk to him."

## 18

People had moved away from the bar, but that wasn't going to do them any good. If the guy was holding what Gain thought he was, nobody in the place was safe, nor anybody for a fifty meter circled around the pub. Looked like a military surplus suckbomb, probably in the hundred- to three-hundred-megavac class, and the red blinking diode said it was armed. The plunger was a deadman's switch.

Jaskeen moved toward the man, Chan and Gain right behind him.

"Close enough," the assassin said.

"What's the deal, bub?"

"Don't try your yell, I'm plugged, and I'm circulating nodistract against your hypnosis. Shoot me, the bomb goes off. Zap the whole place, the bomb goes off. Look at me crooked, the bomb goes off."

"Yeah, you're in the pilot's chair. The deal?"

"You or the whole place. Your choice."

Jaskeen didn't hesitate. "Me," he said. "Everybody else walks?"

"That's the deal. Put your hardware on the floor."

Jaskeen pulled two needle guns from their hiding places and put them carefully onto the floor.

"You, too," the assassin said, nodding at Chan and Gain.

Gain said, "You implode us, you go with us."

"Yeah. Don't matter to me either way."

He had to be on something, Gain figured, or else he was a fanatic jobbed out to the mob by one or another group of homicidal zanies. Gain pulled his tangler from his holster and dropped it onto the floor. Chan put his weapon down next to Gain's.

Gain was trying to remember something. Something about these old implosion devices. About the timers. What was it?

The assassin moved toward the exit from behind the bar, keeping one hand on the bomb as he lifted the section of bar that blocked the exit out of his way.

Four seconds, that was the standard delay on such devices. After that thumb came off the deadman's switch, there'd be four seconds before it sucked everything around it into a supercompact ball, but there was something else. What the hell was it?

Nobody in the pub was making any kind of noise. It was as quiet as a tomb.

The assassin moved toward the three of them. "Back up," he ordered.

Once activated, the timer gave you four seconds, no way to stop it, pushing the plunger back in didn't do any good. It gave you two chances before you armed it, but once it was armed, that was it. Except—

The assassin reached the spot where the weapons had been dropped and bent to pick up Chan's hand cannon. Not the tangler or the shocktox needlers—he was going for a kill.

The assassin came up, grinning, the gun pointed at Jaskeen.

—except that the plastic plunger for the deadman switch was *mechanical*, not electronic, and it had a spring inside the plunger, the plunger was hollow and the spring was inside it, a coil spring inside a hollow chamber, and if that spring didn't push down on the firing mechanism then the thing wouldn't go off, and that's why the military had junked the things and gone to the all-electronic models, and Gain still had the boot knife right there in its sheath.

Jaskeen was a drug dealer and probably not a very nice man in a lot of other ways, but whatever else he was, he was on the Petits' side. He'd saved Gain's life. Gain couldn't just stand there and watch him get burned down. This was back-to-the-wall stuff.

"Hah!" Gain yelled.

The assassin swung the heavy handgun to cover him, but Gain was diving and rolling, pulling the knife as he came up, slamming into the assassin as the man fired, feeling the heat of the beam sear through the fabric and skin of his left side, stopping the bleeding as it cauterized the shallow wound. The assassin rolled away, but that didn't matter, only the bomb mattered, and that was falling in slow motion and Gain grabbed it in the air like a teshball and slammed it against the floor, watching the red warning light that had stopped blinking and gone full on, the second timer on the side of the bomb flashing from four . . . to three . . . to two—

God, let it be sharp enough!

Gain laid the edge of the knife against the tip of the bomb's plunger and pushed for all he was worth. The tough plastic resisted—

Then sliced through. The coil spring inside shot out and hit the knife blade and Gain jerked the knife away and the spring popped free of the plunger and flew ten meters across the room.

And the timer said "0" but the firing pin wasn't going anywhere. And Chan and Jaskeen had the assassin face down.

"Oh, man," Gain said. "Oh, man!"

## 19

Sitting at a table and drinking large gulps of the best beer anybody had ever tasted, Gain kept shaking his head. "I can't believe I did that," he said, for the third time.

"You're gonna be all right, kid," Jaskeen said. "Don't you think so, Chan?"

The Sub grinned. "Oh, yeah. Gonna be a great officer, Luck."

"I can't believe I did that. Risked my tail and everybody else's for a drug dealer."

Jaskeen looked at Chan. Chan shrugged. "Up to you, Limos."

Gain took another long swallow of his beer. This really was good beer, the best he'd ever had. But he also caught the exchange between the two men. "What?"

"Look, bub, you're an officer, you understand the term 'need to know,' right?"

"What are you talking about?"

"Things aren't always what they seem, kid. No, not kid—Stelo. You see, this vial"—he held up the crystal he'd shown Gain in his office earlier—"this isn't what you think it is. It's not *yadjak*, it's an *antidote* to *yadjak*."

Gain put his beer down and stared at Jaskeen. "Antidote?"

"Might as well fire the other barrel." Chan sipped at his own drink. "Really good beer," he said.

"What are you trying to say?" Gain said.

"Well, for instance, I sort of misled you when I said there were three *kabid* urchin beds. There were only two."

"You—you destroyed them *both?*"

"Yep. When the galaxy runs out of the drug on hand, it's all gone. Oh, the second bed was mine, sort of. I had to get into the business all the way for a couple of reasons. To convince the local underworld types to let me into their confidence. And the Petit scientists needed a good supply of the urchins to produce the antidote."

Gain shook his head. Jaskeen couldn't be saying what he thought he was saying.

"I've been deep cover here for more than five years. Marshal Twill sent you and your crew along when I told him we were ready to burn this operation down. Sorry I couldn't tell you sooner."

Gain felt like the stupidest man in the galaxy.

"We were a diversion," Gain said, seeing the light at last.

"Well, yeah. Sorry."

"That's how you knew what was going on. That's how you were always a step ahead of us."

"You were helpful," Jaskeen said. "Really."

"Oh, man."

"Come on, Stelo. You didn't join the Petits to be a drug dealer, did you? You don't think we're like the Grands, that we'd really stoop to something like that?"

"*We?* You . . . you—you're . . .?"

Chan finished his beer. "Yeah, afraid so. Jaskeen here is still in harness, Luck. A Full Commander bucking for the Line, ah, detached to envoy duty at the moment."

Gain wanted to scream. "And you?"

"Well, I'm probably an officer again, I expect."

Gain shook his head. This was all a dream. He was back in the academy, having a dream. It couldn't be real, could it? "Who else is in on this? Everybody but me?"

"Nah," Chan said. "Just me 'n' Limos 'n' Twill."

"Oh, man."

Jaskeen said, "Of course, I'll be pulling out of here now that the job's done. I expect I'll be given a command somewhere nasty as a reward for my service. No good deed goes unpunished. I expect they'll give me Chan. Want to go along, Luck? I can always use another good officer."

Gain couldn't believe the words when they came from his mouth. He said, "Sure. Why not? It couldn't be any worse than this."

Chan and Jaskeen grinned at each other.

Tin came bustling in at that moment. "I won!" he said. "Cleaned her out on the last hand. Both of us had heart flushes, would you believe that? Ten out of twelve of them in our hands, only I had the ace! What are the odds against that?"

"Damned if I know," Gain said. "I believe I'll have another beer. It's been a real long day."

Somebody laughed, but it wasn't Gain.

"Hey, Luck?" Chan said. "By the way—welcome to the Petit Harriers."

This time Gain did laugh.

# TONIGHT WE IMPROVISE

## S. N. Lewitt

Executive Officer Yuen was in charge of the briefing. "We have been tasked by the Twelve, or at least by the Fleet Commodore at their orders, to verify the rumors about certain factions on Zamalah running an illicit slave trade."

"Again," said Navigator Rasidov.

"Still," said Group Leader Lentzer, who was also the protocol officer.

Yuen would not be distracted. "*If* we can verify these rumors *directly*, then and only then will the Twelve decide what action is to be taken. We will be there as investigators, nothing more. Mr. Lentzer will be in command. Any questions?"

"What's our cover?" Lentzer asked, trying to sound casual.

"The Mromrosi has provided that: a tour for the Emerging Planet Fairness Court. We're the formal entourage and bodyguards," Yuen answered smoothly, little though he liked the notion.

"They'll think we're Grands," Gregori Rasidov griped. "And the Bunters'll want us in class two dress or above all the time." He pantomimed sticking a finger down his throat.

The Mromrosi went bright leaf-green.

Why the Mromrosi was cooperating was anyone's guess, Rasidov thought. Maybe on general principles, if nothing else. The Emerging Planet Fairness Court was always going on about principles, though not everyone understood what they were talking about. Not even brass always agreed with the aliens. Everyone knew that, too. But there was plenty to gain if the alien court accepted them, and, hell, they beat going it alone in the big wide galaxy. He winced inwardly at the warning the Emerging Planet Fairness Court issued from time to time: that without the Court's continued endorsement humankind wouldn't be allowed out in the big wide galaxy at all.

Yuen remained impassive. "It's one of the sacrifices one makes, being in the Petits," he stated, deadpan. "Anything else?"

The Nada Solis/2 jumped in immediately. "What's *he* doing in charge? He shouldn't even be here. Not the way he drinks. AIO or not, he ought to be posted to the grid station on Buttress." She pointed at Jaanu Lentzer and glared. "And Tek isn't an officer."

The other two Nada Solis nodded in unison. The three New Gaia clones preferred to work as a team without outsiders. But this time they weren't objecting to Gregori Rasidov and Tek going along. Lentzer offended them; Rasidov and Tek were just inconvenient.

No one knew Tek's full name; the Bunters insisted it was improper to say it aloud. He was barely a Petit Harrier at all. He was nothing more than a Supplies/Tech in the Quartermaster's command. On a smaller skimmer than this Broadsword his work would be done by Bunters.

Lentzer flinched. That the three Solis would consider a mere kitchen clerk his equal, that was worse than the threat of being retired without ribbons and full pay.

"And what about them?" Rasidov responded, referring to the Solis. "In a traditional culture like Zamalah, clones are not acceptable. Not at all. Let alone female ones. The *imam* at home called them an abomination, and if they can do that on Vladimir, where they're a very small minority, then you can believe they're going to be a whole lot worse on Zamalah."

"No problem," Lentzer hissed. "On Zamalah women wear veils anyway. No one'll see. 'Course, they could all dye their hair different colors and stuff—their Bunters would have a field day making them look different." He grinned nastily, pleased to get back at the clone's remark. Or as pleased as he ever got, which wasn't much these days. At least not without a good stash of Standby Hooch at hand. Life on the *Kinderkinyo* had been deteriorating since the Line Commander went strange.

The Mromrosi, who sat at the table with all of his legs dangling a good three inches above the floor, remained an uncommunicative peach-pink. Yuen was just about to apologize to the alien when the Nada Solis/3 went over to him with a smile. "At least there's one being on this mission we can approve of," she said, grooming the alien's long curls with her fingers.

She caught Lentzer's eye as she ran her fingers through the mass of pink tresses to make sure the mission leader knew perfectly well why she was showing such unaccustomed regard for the Mromrosi. Anything, even an alien, was better than Lentzer. He couldn't mistake the meaning if she had broadcast it in fifty-two frequencies.

The Mromrosi, who usually was treated with far more reserve, turned a shade brighter. Yuen was shocked that he permitted the Nada Solis/3 to touch him at all, but then the clone practically glowed around the curly alien.

"Nothing like a little ass-kissing," Lentzer mumbled. "Assuming Mromrosi have asses and you can find them."

The two clones not preoccupied with the Mromrosi turned hostile glares at him. The one nearer hissed.

Lentzer didn't care. All he wanted was a drink. He had been too close to sober when this briefing had started, and now he was the rest of the way there. It was not a state he enjoyed anymore. It made his temper short and his memory too sharp. If he'd had a decent shot or two of good Standby Hooch he wouldn't have commented on the Solis' behavior.

"Shared grooming is an indication of goodwill among your kind," the Mromrosi said evenly. "This includes clones."

Rasidov smiled, his mouth thin. "It brings out their maternal nature," he said softly. Tek looked away.

"I would like to make it clear that I do not regard this inspection as cover. I have never seen a traditional culture of this Moslem kind before. My report will be fascinating to the member-species of the Emerging Planet Fairness Court. I am very curious. Traditional Moslems of the African tradition, I believe they are called?"

Executive Officer Yuen nodded. "We hope there are aspects of this culture that you find interesting, aside from the possibility of slave trade." Yuen looked at the rest of the staff. He proceeded more briskly. "Zamalah is ruled by a group of religious jurists known as the *ulama*. There are several of these councils but the most important is the *ulama* at Moustar. They are interested in meeting an alien jurist and 'discussing matters of legal scholarship,' is how they put it. So you have immediate access to the ruling body."

Lentzer, all three Nada Solis, even the Navigator looked bored. Yuen, who, like several others on this mission, had trained aboard the *Semper Alpha Cygnis*, was used to having more crew to draw from; he had to resist the temptation to order them all out and reconstruct the team. He knew when he had planned this mission for the Line Commander that they should have scrapped it when they had the chance. The landing party as it was made up now came up red on the group psychological scan.

But the Alliance Intelligence Organization had insisted on Tek and Rasidov, and what AIO wanted, they got: Rasidov had been educated in a mosque school as well as public and had memorized the entire *Q'ran*. Tek was the most traditional Moslem on board and both were fluent in Old Earth Arabic.

Not that Arabic was the main language of Zamalah, but it was spoken among the educated and religious, as Latin had once been for Old Earth Christians. Translator packs could be considered heretical by the most extreme of the Zamalah Moslems. Especially on a mission as delicate as this. Thus Rasidov and Tek were ruled essential to the Zamalah visit. The Line Commander had insisted on the clones. AIO had selected Rasidov and Tek. And Lentzer was protocol officer.

Executive Officer Yuen did his best to conceal his dismay.

Over the vigorous objections of the Group Line Chiefs, Line Commander Nazaipha had volunteered his ship for the clone experiment and he would not reconsider, despite growing evidence that it wasn't working. Even on skimmers as big as their three Broadswords, each with a human complement of forty-two, with forty-three cyborgs, the clones stood out. The Nada Solis group were second generation, the epitome of New Gaian state-of-the-art, all flaws removed. They were unparalleled martial artists, excellent tacticians, and breathtaking examples of New Gaian beauty.

"In a religious society like Zamalah," the Line Commander had said slowly, when Executive Officer Yuen had presented the Group Line Chiefs to protest the presence of the clones on the mission, "we might need to display some old-fashioned skills, including the martial ones. We'll send the best."

Yuen had argued against it though he knew the Nada Solis were the best hand-to-hand fighters among the Harriers, Grands and Petits; it was something of a coup for the Petits, for clones were not permitted in the Grands. So the best kickboxers in the Alliance were all Petits by default. To Yuen's mind, this advantage was outweighed by the nature of the clones themselves. The Nada Solis only liked to work together, didn't get along well with anyone else, and were not subtle in their preference.

Group Leader Lentzer had backed him up. "The AIO doesn't use them."

"They're too volatile," Group Line Chief Xer M'kaba of the *Zuruchmasu* had protested. "And they don't follow orders."

The Line Commander remained adamant.

"We need someone with experience, someone from the Alliance Intelligence Organization, with an AIO brain implant for Old Earth Arabic," Group Line Chief Laeo Ghano of the *Waldashita* had insisted.

All to no avail.

Full of trepidation, Executive Officer Yuen brought the news to Line Commander Nazaipha. The mission would proceed as planned. Pog it all anyway.

Line Commander Nazaipha was delighted for a

good five Earth Standard minutes before his attention drifted.

Yuen would have flung up his hands if he had thought it would do any good.

Line Commander Nazaipha had served on the *Semper Alpha Cygnis* as a Group Leader for nine years. His sudden promotion to Line Commander of Broadsword-class skimmers was on record as being for outstanding service. That didn't stop the rumors that it was a reward for keeping his mouth shut about some scandal in the Grands.

"We have to include the Mromrosi in all briefings," Yuen reminded Nazaipha.

"It would be the best political move," the Line Commander said unhappily, as if he were empowered to change this. He had his eyes fixed on the blank vid screen in his quarters. He leaned forward as if watching. "Slavery is one of the Big Three for the Emerging Planet Fairness Court, according to the Marshal-in-Chief. It's better if they see us doing something to stop it rather than trying to hide it."

"My thoughts exactly," M'kaba agreed. She looked uneasily at Yuen.

"And having the alien off the ship will give us a little more breathing space with Yosinero, if he does arrive. And we get Lentzer out of the way at the same time." Line Commander Nazaipha smiled a horribly meaningless smile.

Again Yuen bit back his response. Yosinero is dangerous, he wanted to shout it at Line Commander Nazaipha. Privately Yuen was convinced the Line Commander was making a bad situation worse.

"We're all aware that Lentzer has a personal axe to grind with Yosinero," said Line Commander Nazaipha with a lucidity that was increasingly rare in him. "If Lentzer does something stupid with Yosinero around that won't be our responsibility. Get rid of the drunk—

he's so much baggage anyway—and remove Yosinero all in one very elegant sweep."

Group Line Chief Ghano didn't see it that way. "Dangerous or not, Line Commander, Yosinero has been my personal friend for a very long time. The fact that he was Strategy Marshal of the Grand Harriers, protégé of one of the Twelve, and richer than the Hubcorp Group were all perfectly good reasons to want to bring him down."

"A Grand!" scoffed the Line Commander. "Do we have any courberries?" He fiddled with the red horsehead tab on his collar. "How far are we from the *Semper Alpha Cygnis*? They're expecting me back."

Yuen shook his head.

M'kaba kept her mouth shut. She had her orders, and if Lentzer interfered he had to go. Yosinero had been getting away with too much for far too long. And his mentor on the Twelve had enemies, just as Yosinero himself did. The Group Line Chief of the *Waldashita* had private coded messages containing information she was not permitted to reveal to Yuen. And she knew better than to tell Line Commander Nazaipha anything. She could feel sorry for Yuen Tsimu; he was in an untenable position with the Line Commander gone strange. But she wasn't about to lose her perspective. Not if it meant the end of Yosinero forever.

Group Leader Jaanu Lentzer hoped it was the end. All he wanted was one last, easy assignment: tame, simple, nothing that would throw him off stride before he left the Petits with retirement and ribbons and honorable memories. They might give it to him, too, the string-pullers back at the Hub, just so long as he didn't pog up this one last job. He had done a few decent things in the past. And as protocol officer, he knew enough to protect himself. And he needed to be protected, with all he had learned over the years.

What if he drank? By Old Hardy, a Harrier was supposed to be able to drink. Petit or Grand, it was part of the tradition. He had once met up with a couple of Grands in Dickens on Victoria Station and had gone shot for shot with both of them until they passed out. Then he'd stripped them both down to their socks and left them, face down, on the bar. That was sure a sight when their Line Commander had caught them out.

It had been a great joke aboard the *Semper Alpha Cygnis* for almost a full year. Of course, that had been twenty-six years ago. And very little had changed for him since then, aside from being assigned to the *Kinderkinyo*. Not a good sign, no matter what the Protocol Marshal told him. He was close to early retirement, no longer ambitious enough to press for more, still only a Group Leader and Protocol Two. Once he'd thought he'd do great things, show up his cousin Reike in the Grands. Now all he wanted was to get shut of the job and find himself somewhere he could drink in peace and forget.

His Bunter interrupted his miserable reverie, telling him that Executive Officer Yuen wanted a word with him as soon as possible.

"We've been told that you'll be given the full diplomatic treatment, in spite of the Zamalah aversion to aliens," said Yuen with a distracted frown. "I don't quite know what that entails except some sort of traditional skill demonstration and a very long feast. You'd better make sure to take an anti-bug before you go. Who knows what they've got in the soil and the stock down there."

"Of course," said Lentzer. "I've done this a few times before, you know."

Yuen shrugged. "Just had to make sure." His expression changed, becoming less angry. "I wanted to tell you that I'm sorry about the mission. I tried to get it changed. I'll show you my evaluations, if you like. But the Line Commander—"

"The Line Commander's gone strange, and everyone knows it." Lentzer wasn't in the mood to coddle Yuen or anyone else. "You could file evaluations from now until we go nova, it wouldn't matter. This whole mission is—" He stopped himself before he said what he really thought. "It's no good for anyone."

"Uhm." Yuen lowered his eyes. "I'll do everything I can to keep the Line Commander out of this. But you know what he's like. And I can't get the Marshal-in-Chief to authorize formal removal. I've tried. They don't pay any attention to my zaps, or the vids I've provided." He looked very tired.

"The Line Commander's got hidden credit. That makes it hard to get rid of him. Or they want him gone, and they're letting us do it for them." He was disgusted at everything he said. "Maybe they want us all gone, and set up a trap for us. But we have orders, right?"

"Try to do your best. It isn't going to be easy."

"No kidding," said Lentzer. He stared at the wall that separated Yuen's quarters from the Line Commander's. "Moslem slavers or Nazaipha. What a pogging awful choice."

The Broadswords cut silently above the glittering aquamarine ocean of Zamalah. On the surveills a fishing boat lay below, its occupants leaning back in their seats, concentrating on their lines. The shadows of the Broadswords passed over them, making enormous fish-shapes on the water.

The bridge of the *Kinderkinyo* was silent. At least they weren't arguing anymore. Rasidov was in his

Navigator's station with the Nada Solis/1 beside him, checking all the monitors as he guided the Broadsword over the ocean.

Lentzer's head throbbed. Watching the surveills was making him dizzy. His Bunter had insisted that there was no Standby Hooch anywhere in seventeen mega-li. Which was a lie. He decided there was nothing more humiliating than being offered Merkonic tea by a cyborg when he'd ordered something stronger. A stiff Loch Ochie Scotch would do in a pinch.

But his Bunter refused to serve him anything alcoholic at all. Lentzer took the Merkonic tea, some Xiaoqing analgesic, and all the fruit juice he could get reinforced with Buttress pepper—his mother's recipe for a hangover. For once the recipe didn't work. He put his hand over his eyes and wished he could sleep it off.

An alarm shrieked as a message came onto the board. Rasidov didn't consult the clone beside him. He toggled the hailer for all three Broadswords, which was tuned way too loud for Lentzer's liking.

"In the name of Allah, the All-Compassionate, the All-Merciful, we welcome you to the First Port of Zamalah, which is called Shaifa. We trust you are well—may Allah be thanked—and looking forward to greeting us in Shaifa. If you open your navigators to the frequency on your monitors, our field plotting will direct you to an appropriate place. We happily await your arrival."

Lentzer groaned. He hated rigamarole.

"It is not a correct and polite greeting?" the Mromrosi inquired.

"It is very traditional, but not very enthusiastic," Tek said softly. "Really, it's too short to be polite. To be completely proper they should have inquired about the health of each of our families, our friends, all the units of the Petits. But I suppose they know that

:

most people don't care so much about manners. Most
people in the Alliance just want to do business." Tek
sighed and shook his head.

"This is a landing port," said Executive Officer
Yuen. "They may save the formalities for when we
are safely on the ground."

Rasidov locked the navigator into the Port and
leaned back. The Nada Solis/1 looked at him nastily,
then shifted her gaze to Lentzer. Solis/3 picked up
the embroidered and hooded garment that was considered modest feminine dress on Zamalah.

"I won't wear that thing," Solis/2 said in a tone
that accepted no argument.

Lentzer could feel a migraine coming on. I'm too
old for this kind of thing, he thought. "You'll wear it
if the Senior Bunter says it's the uniform of the day
for those of us on the mission."

All three Nada Solis looked at him as if they were
ready to use him for free-fighting practice. They
were exactly—exactly—the same, all with the identical blond hair, full lips, and large blue eyes. New
Gaian bedroom fantasies with very nasty fangs. Lentzer
didn't find them at all appealing. Give me one of
those brunette Amazons from Lontano, or a skinny
pixie from Westward Ho, or a rangy hill woman from
Hydeyama, he thought, anyone there's only one of.
Anyone who looked so utterly perfect and came in
threes, whatever the type, he distrusted.

A stalwart figure appeared on the bridge. "I think
something more concealing is in order. For those
leaving the ships I recommend the Class Two parade
cape with the tassel cap and high-sun vision screens.
There is a high ambient radiation level," the Senior
Bunter said most apologetically.

The clones all wore the identical mix of disbelief
and deliverance on their faces. Tek smiled and Rasidov
looked like he was being sentenced to a year in the

mines on Buttress. But for what might have been the first time in his life—certainly the first time he could remember—Lentzer was grateful to the cyborg Bunter. The outfit suggested, with its long full green cape and ornate headdress, fitted Zamalah's modesty codes admirably. Yet it still maintained formality and dignity that any Petit could accept. The vision screens would hide enough of their faces that the clones would not appear identical. Or rather, they would, but so would everyone else.

"Wait a minute. Isn't there something about green in this religion?" Lentzer groused. He'd never known a Bunter to be wrong about such things, but there was always a first time, and the way this mission was getting started, this would be the time. "Won't they be insulted or something?"

"This color will be considered auspicious and appropriate for a diplomatic mission," the Senior Bunter replied smoothly. Lentzer wanted to growl at it.

By the time the three Broadswords touched ground the team were all attired in green capes with the Petit Harrier horsehead in red on the right shoulder. The tassel caps were red with long gold braiding and their boots were as shiny as only a Bunter could make them.

For this occasion the Mromrosi had matching gold and green and opal-white rank ribbons tied to his cherub-pink curls. His single green eye was brilliant with anticipation.

Lentzer had to stifle an impulse to hand the alien over to a five-year-old.

"Looks like there's a bit of an honor guard outside," Lentzer said, glancing at the gangway surveill. "The braiding says they're high-ranking."

The Nada Solis/2 and /3 balked. "We have arrived, but we don't have any instructions on how to get inside whatever slave trade they have. We refuse to go until we are properly prepared."

Lentzer rolled his aching eyes upward. The Nada Solis were beautiful and deadly and every flaw had been removed, according to the evaluation from New Gaia. What the lab had forgotten to include in the Nada Solis was any semblance of imagination.

"We improvise," he said sourly. "You three are the bodyguards. The Mromrosi is the honored ambassador. Tek and Rasidov are the translators if they don't permit us to use our translator paks. And I'm the wild card. Got that?" He gave the clones no opportunity to answer. "Good. Now, bodyguards, you stick with us, follow orders, and don't say anything. Not a thing."

"How about a code word?" the Mromrosi asked, turning red-orange.

"An excellent suggestion," Lentzer agreed. "A code word. If we use it for any reason then you know we're in trouble. How about, um . . ."

"*Candy* might be good," Tek volunteered tentatively. "It is common here. Sweets are a big part of the traditional culture."

"Common doesn't make a very good code word, Tek. We might have to use it for real. We don't want to draw stunners because they're giving us a treat." Lentzer looked at the ceiling. They weren't off the ship and already they were pogged.

"What about *snow*?" suggested the Mromrosi. "There isn't much on Zamalah, and we aren't likely to discuss it."

In spite of his acute annoyance, Lentzer came close to smiling. "*Snow* it is," he agreed. "You hear anyone in our group say 'snow' and it means we need help."

Tek nodded and Rasidov opened the hatch. Down the gangway and onto the ground they went in formation; time to make a good impression, live up to the reputation of the Harriers. The ships helped; Broadswords were one of the larger ships and they had impressive lines, like all skimmers. The red horsehead medallions were on the upswept aft blades, below the bridges and above the spines, where they caught the light.

"Translators on; we'll use Tek and Rasidov for show right now." Lentzer made sure his own was working properly.

A group of ragged-looking men was on hand to greet them. All wore long white robes and had fancy embroidered caps. They held splendid animals on leads. Lentzer, with a childhood on Hartzheim, had seen the squat, rugged horses bred there. These he knew by their Alliance-wide reputation.

One of the strangers mounted and galloped the one-third li of open space before them, reigning in at the last second to show off his skill. "*Asaalamu alekim,*" he said, a scimitar smile under full moustaches.

"*Wa-alekim a-salaam,*" Rasidov replied immediately, and held a clenched fist in front of his heart.

"That means 'peace be with you,' " Tek whispered. "And his hand means that he had the five pillars of Islam in his heart. They'll recognize what it means. It is a very excellent thing."

The other riders came forward more sedately, and this time Lentzer could see that they had more mounts than they needed. For them?

"I see you are horsemen," the leader of the Zamalah welcoming party said through Rasidov. "That the horse is your symbol is very apt. We honor the Petit Harriers from the Magnicate Alliance, and your . . . associate from the Emerging Planet Fairness Court. In proof of this we bring horses from the Sheikh's own stable. May you find them worthy."

With that the welcoming committee led forward

seven horses, each stamping and snorting as if in a rage. Lentzer supposed that the men of Zamalah thought their horses high-spirited; he thought they were nervous.

"We must ride those?" Tek asked, and there was terror in his voice.

The Mromrosi was a vivid yellow, clashing badly with his gold bows. Without a word he went over to the horse and examined it with his single green eye. Then, with great determination, he hauled himself into the saddle, clinging to every protrusion and curve of pommel and cantel with all eight of his feet.

The horse stood still but sweating, as if the alien presence had quieted it. The Nada Solis mounted without particular difficulty, though once in the saddle each of them jounced awkwardly, holding their reins too tightly and causing their horses to sidle and paw.

Rasidov and Tek managed to get on the horses; both were grateful for the grooms holding the animals.

"Why do you not mount?" the leader of the strangers asked Lentzer.

"Because it is proper for my party to choose their mounts. I can wait," he replied. These animals were taller and more flighty than their distant utilitarian cousins on Hartzheim. Lentzer could see that his rusty equestrian skills wouldn't help him here.

"That was great, saying we had to choose first," Rasidov muttered before he translated the answer. "Where did you learn that?"

Lentzer snorted. Those young sperks, convinced they knew all the answers. They were the only ones who knew anything. "I figured it out some time in the last quarter century."

Riding was horrible. The horses wanted to go faster than any of the Petit Harriers could handle; their hosts up ahead kept coming back, asking if there was some problem. One of the men suggested that Nada Solis/3's mount had thrown a shoe.

"Most of the Harriers on this mission haven't been to your planet before," said Lentzer, relying on his translator pack more than on Tek's distracted translating. "We want an opportunity to view the territory. A few of us have been to your Suroo Islands. They are very, very beautiful." Which was no more than the truth. The Suroo Islands of Zamalah were famous, reputed to be among the most beautiful places in the entire Alliance.

"I see you appreciate the subtle beauty of the red desert, as well," the rider who had first greeted them said as Rasidov translated. "Most citizens of the Alliance prefer only the soft islands, the resort hotels, the beaches and the forests of ten million flowers. But you, perhaps you have the sight of wisdom as well as beauty. Our Sheikh will be honored."

It was the first time Lentzer had ever been called wise. Smart or canny or impertinent or inquisitive, yes, but never wise. He could not think of an answer and left it up to Rasidov to come up with something flattering.

The small village up ahead was not promising. The tall gates were bolted closed. Outside the walls was a collection of black tents, too low to stand in, and steaming in this heat. No one was around and the fabric flapped forlornly in the breeze.

"This is where we will begin our talks," said the man riding beside Lentzer.

Getting off the horses took longer than anyone had anticipated. The last one down was the Mromrosi, his mass of curls deep puce. When the horses were led away, the Petits and the Mromrosi were ushered into one of these tents. Lentzer was surprised. The inside was something out of legend. The walls were hung with rich fabrics of contrasting patterns and the

ground covered with layers of multihued carpets.
Large cushions were tossed around low brass tables
and the scent of incense was so thick that Lentzer
nearly gagged.

A man with a white beard and dressed in a spot-
less white robe sat erect on one of the cushions. "Ah,
my guests, it is an honor to welcome you to this
humble camp. Please rest yourselves while my sons
serve coffee." He clapped his hands together twice.

A man about Rasidov's age carried a basin and
long-necked ewer directly to Lentzer.

"Put your hands over the basin," Tek whispered.

"I have been here before," whispered Lentzer as
he did so. The man poured scented water over his
hands. Then he was handed a perfect white towel
which he used to dry them. The whole ritual was
repeated for each of the company, the Mromrosi last.
The alien had steadied down to rose-colored; all his
bows nearly blended into the colors in the carpets.

Next they were each handed thimble-sized cups
with gold bands. Another young man—another son,
Lentzer assumed—poured a beverage that looked
too light to be kaff, too dark to be Merikot tea. He
sipped it carefully and found the flavor sharp but
refreshing in the heat. Tek had told him that above
all, nothing serious must be discussed before several
cups of this stuff had been drunk and everyone had
eaten at least a few of the sweets that would follow
the drinks.

He made the correct inquiries about the health of
the Sheikh's family and friends and business associates and horses and hawks, as the old man politely
inquired of each member of the party. After an hour
of this Lentzer wanted a drink. Pog it. He decided
he would welcome a hangover if he could have a
drink.

To make matters worse he was miserably aware of

the Nada Solis/2, sitting mutely beside him in her unchanging position. Her stillness, like the stillness of the other two, was unnatural. He hoped the Sheikh didn't notice.

Still another son came in with a plate of what looked to be oversized cockroaches skewered through the body. "My guests, even now a small repast is being prepared to sustain you. But it will need a little time to cook. Please, while you wait, have some stuffed date candy."

Lentzer froze. He could see the Nada Solis/2 and /3 stiffen, and Nada Solis/1 rise defensively. He watched them with vexation, wanting to remind them that the word was not candy but snow. He was convinced that all the Nada Solis should be melted back down into primordial soup and have their genes reconstituted for hydroponic alfalfa gardening.

"My guardians are always so worried that human food will damage me," the Mromrosi said, popping one of the stuffed fruits somewhere under the pink curls. "They never want me to try anything new. Especially sweets." The alien took two more of the dates and they disappeared. "I love sweets. You are most generous."

This astonished Lentzer, who knew how much all Mromrosio disliked sweet food. What drove them distracted was pickles.

The Sheikh chuckled and waved his hand. The Mromrosi took one more of the dates for himself before the plate was offered to Tek. The Sheikh hadn't particularly noticed the Nada Solis; he was mesmerized by the Mromrosi.

Which made sense, Lentzer realized. An animated nursery toy sitting in the seat of honor and gobbling up everything in sight was more unusual than other humans, clones included.

"But I am forgetting myself," their host said contritely. "You are tired after your long journey, and I am certain you would wish to bathe and rest before dinner is served. Hassan will show you to your tent. Consider it your own for the time you are among us." The old man rose and bowed.

Lentzer struggled to his feet with difficulty. Such an abrupt dismissal troubled him, but he couldn't determine what or why. If he had a drink he'd either figure it out or stop caring.

The tent they were shown to was as magnificent as the one they had left. Tables were set with flowers and bowls of fruit, surely difficult to supply this far out from the polar forests. And there were fresh towels, laid out, bowls of washing water and scented soaps and perfumes for them all.

The Nada Solis wouldn't let them touch any of it until the bodyguards had poked, prodded, and inspected everything.

"Maybe we've missed something back there in civilization," Rasidov said, peeling a tangerine. "Talk about traveling in style. The only thing that's missing is the genie and the dancing girls."

"I need my Bunter and I need a good shot of Standby Hooch. There's something that I don't like about this setup." Lentzer was muttering and he didn't care.

"Alcohol is forbidden in this place," one of the Nada Solis said caustically.

"Pogging shame that it is," he agreed nastily. "And I don't like the fact that the old man wasn't eating with us. I like even less that they were ready with the horses to greet us. They knew how many of us there were. I don't like that at all."

Silence dropped like twilight in the tent. "The Sheikh didn't drink with us," Tek said, shaking his head. "That's not good."

Suddenly Lentzer wanted all the quibbling and

bickering to stop so he could think, sort the situation out in his sobriety-befuddled brain. He lay down on one of the piles of rugs and pillows and put his hand over his face. It was as close as he could come to being alone. He didn't notice Tek or Rasidov leave the tent. The last thing he saw before he fell asleep was the Mromrosi busily examining every variety of fruit in the bowl.

It was dark when Lentzer was woken by an explosive blast that sent him sprawling. He crawled out of the tent, his stunner at the ready. What the pogging frack was going on? Were they under attack?

There was a commotion, but it hardly looked like a raid. It seemed that the tent itself had been removed, leaving the whole inside under the stars, cushions, tables and all. There were more people now, and they gathered around low tables waiting in the light of several large cooking fires.

Lentzer could smell the roasting lamb, and it brought back memories of his childhood. Awkwardly he stood up and dusted himself off. If his Bunter could see him, it would fuss.

There was lamb, and chicken and rice and stuffed vegetables. There were no dancing girls. There was no Standby Hooch or Lonato wine or Loch Ochie Scotch. There was music of a sort, but not the kind Lentzer liked. Very much on the alert, Lentzer went to join the festivities, taking care only to eat the same things from the same plates as the white-haired old man.

When the incense had been passed around and the dinner was ended, their host began to tell a story. It was long and complex, with endless digressions and occasional poetic recitations. Stuffed and sober, Lentzer made himself listen, glad now that he had slept before; otherwise he might do the unforgivable and drift off. The firelight was dancing hypnotically and the cadences of Arabic droned in his ear. It was impossible to remain alert, though beyond all this primitive splendor he could feel alarm growing. "We ought to get back to the ship," he said, but no one heard him.

When he woke up he was still on Zamalah, and the tent was once again in place. He checked the local time readout and found it was nearly noon. Two of the Nada Solis were asleep. The third sat immobile near the flap, completely intent on her duty.

Rasidov snored lightly from a nearby pile and Tek was missing. Lentzer shook his head, trying to rid it of sleep. Where was Tek? He knew he ought to notify Yuen at once. Groggily he peered out the tent flap, the Nada Solis enduring his presence at her station.

The camp was still. It had the feel of a ghost town, everything intact and in place but the people all gone. The village gates remained uncompromisingly shut. Lentzer walked into the middle of the circle of tents, the heat pressing on him like an invisible fist. The only thing that moved was his shadow. There wasn't a whinny of a horse, the babble of servants, nothing.

The mission had been stranded in the night. This was worse than any hangover could have been.

The worst thing was that it made no sense. Lentzer could understand being attacked. But not abandoned. In spite of the heat he grew cold. In spite of the drink he was still a pretty damn good intelligence officer, and every carefully acquired hunch was screaming a warning.

Yosinero.

The name alone made his stomach clench and his mind go into tailflips. He never wanted to see the

Hub again. Yosinero was probably still there, sitting like a fat spider in the central Grands sector. The ultimate staffer, the perfect Grand Harrier, always immaculately groomed and ready with a readout on whatever issue was at hand. Yosinero had been close to two members of the Twelve, next in line for Marshal-in-Chief if everyone read it right. And Yosinero had been lining his pocket out of Alliance funds, investing in some less than legal but very profitable trade and influence peddling.

Jaanu Lentzer had found him out. And Jaanu Lentzer had paid for it. Never attack the powers that be, Yosinero had advised him on the one occasion when they had met. And if you're going to attack the people on top, bring them down or get pogged. Very, very pogged.

Yosinero had bypassed that, had gone through his mentor on the Council of Twelve. And the Council was the last word, the end of the line. Jaanu Lentzer's career, his hopes, his ability were history. He began to drink. And then he was really washed up for good.

A mournful song interrupted his thoughts. In Arabic, in the long, modal cadences he had found so disruptive the night before, it cut through the heat and the emptiness and made him more aware of how deserted the camp was. But very slowly things began to move. As if the song had called them, he saw a few dusty figures making their way to the Sheikh's tent. Among those figures he recognized Tek. Behind him, Rasidov staggered sleepily through the tent flaps.

"What's going on?" Lentzer asked.

"I don't know. It's that other tent, the big one." He pointed it out, the farthest from the Broadswords. "I think something's going on."

"Any idea what?" Lentzer didn't expect an answer. Rasidov shrugged. "It's not familiar to me. Sorry."

Lentzer drifted nearer, motioning his mission to follow him. It was all he could do not to yell "Snow!" and get them out of there.

They entered the large tent and took off their shoes. Then they took a basin and water jug and washed, splashing water on their faces, over their hair and over their feet. Lentzer stayed in the background.

Both Tek and Rasidov were up in the first row, behind the old Sheikh who was the leader. Abruptly the men all bowed, knelt, turned right and then left and then stood again. There was a murmur through the crowd, and Lentzer realized that he was watching them pray.

He slipped back through the flap, shoes in his left hand, and waited until he was outside to slip them on again. So the place wasn't deserted. Somehow he wasn't really relieved. The stillness while there were people around made the situation even more unnatural and therefore suspect. He returned to the tent as the heat increased. Tek and Rasidov were both inside. Lentzer wanted to ignore it all, but he went over to Tek's place on the pillows anyway. The kitchen clerk was reading something with full concentration.

Lentzer cleared his throat. "Can you explain what's happening around here?" he asked, trying to sound calm.

Tek sighed and put down the reader. "It is Ramadhan, sir," he said. "We have come at a very bad time. No one will do anything until the holy month is over."

"Why the Old Hardy didn't Yuen tell us?" Lentzer demanded, keeping his voice low. Then he turned to Rasidov. "And if Yuen didn't, why didn't you?"

Rasidov turned red. "Didn't know, sir. The Arabic calendar is based on Old Earth Lunar and it doesn't coordinate with standard. The old Arabic months and even the prayer times are different on every planet. And the holidays . . . uh . . . drift."

Tek's face darkened. "Please, do not be concerned, sir. There are only three more days of Ramadhan to go, and then it is Id al-Fitr, the great feast. We'll be moving camp this evening, going into the village. Then they'll go on. The Sheikh is going to speak at the great mosque in Moustar. And he has asked me to join him, to speak about the Hajj."

Lentzer didn't want to know. But he reminded himself that this member of the group was not exactly trained for infiltration duty, and was doing a fairly decent job. "So our host is important enough to be invited to make a public speech at a major center at a major holiday?" he asked.

Tek's eyes lit up. "Oh, sir, we have been fortunate. The Sheikh is one of the members of the *ulama* of Moustar, the ruling body of this place. One of the legal scholars. Gregori spent some time with him after morning prayers, discussing fine points of *Shari'a* Islamic law. I did not know there was someone on our ship who was so well versed in these holy things. I myself am too ignorant. The Sheikh is teaching me." The boy tapped the reader.

"So this Sheikh is on the most powerful *ulama* on the planet? Does that make him a ruler?" Lentzer asked, trying to make sure he had it straight. "If he's an officer of the government, we were met exactly as planned."

"So our host is one of the leading jurists? That is most pleasant," the Mromrosi said. Lentzer had not heard it join them and its interruption startled him. "I always enjoy talking to jurists. What a quaint concept."

"But it doesn't get us anywhere with our mission," Lentzer insisted, feeling very bad-tempered.

"But sir, we can't do anything until Ramadhan is

over," Tek said, his eyes pleading. "Everyone is daytime fasting and labor is forbidden. Just to be awake during the day for prayers is difficult."

"What?" the Nada Solis/1 interjected without moving from her position at the tent flap. "Fasting? And only awake at night? Please explain."

Tek sighed. "Ramadhan is the holy month of fasting. During daylight hours is not permitted to eat, to drink, to smoke, to make love. Only after sundown. So during the day everyone tries to sleep as much as possible and no one works. And at night people gather, eat, do the things they might do in the day."

The Nada Solis/3 joined her clone and snorted. "I'm not impressed," she said.

Lentzer was glad to see Tek ignore her. He didn't care much for religion, but he knew it was dangerous to criticize what people believed. And right now it was dangerous to the team, to the mission.

"So what do we do, boss?" the Nada Solis asked, her tone just a notch down from sneering. "Leave the natives alone?"

"We shut up until we understand exactly what is going on. Or in all your training in tactics didn't anyone ever teach you to reconnoiter?" Ignoring the stone-hard anger in the clones' faces, Lentzer turned to Tek. "So everyone is fasting now. Why did they serve us when we arrived?"

Tek blinked. "Because you are not Moslems. It is not required that you fast. Although the Sheikh asked today if you were all people of the Book. I said I thought so, all except the Mromrosi." Tek turned toward the alien and bobbed his head low with respect. "I don't now know if your people have a revealed writing from God, and if you follow it. I regret any error I have made."

"You did fine," Lentzer answered by rote. "And if we're expected to go through another night like last night, maybe we all should take a quick nap. Except our guard, of course. Wouldn't do not to have a guard."

The Nada Solis/1 and /2 glared at him in fury as Lentzer winked. At least the Nada Solis were easy to bait and posed no puzzling risk as the Colony might well do.

Aboard her Broadsword, Group Line Chief M'kaba remained impassive as Yosinero and his entourage arrived on the bridge of the *Zuruchmasu*. She was dressed in a Class One formal uniform, tasseled epaulets cascading over her shoulders and her mouth in a tight smile. Group Leader Gillam Rhys-Davies, Protocol Officer, and Navigator Varren Migh were splendid, welcoming the Strategy Marshal of the Grands as if Yosinero were Fleet Commodore.

Close up Yosinero was unprepossessing. He was shorter than M'kaba by a head and his face was amazingly ordinary, even bland. He said all the right things in a smooth, pleasant voice and when he smiled at the Group Line Chief his eyes were lost in the crow's-feet. If he thought it odd that the Line Commander had not received him on the *Kinderkinyo*, he didn't mention it. There was nothing at all about him that M'kaba could recognize as charismatic, although he had that reputation. Nothing that was hateful. Only a smallish, narrow man with graying hair and eyes that were everywhere at once.

"What a pleasant surprise to find Harriers, even Petits, in the sector," he had greeted them. "I'm sorry I won't be able to visit long, I have some private business on the surface that is rather time critical."

"In the islands?" M'kaba asked, making her almond eyes large and innocent. "I have heard they are amazingly beautiful, but I've never been there."

Yosinero ignored her flirtatious smile. "They are," he answered matter-of-factly. "Unfortunately, I have to go to Moustar instead. Dullest city in the Alliance, I think. Nothing there to do at all except look at pretty sunsets. But they make the most amazing carpets there."

M'kaba nodded. Carpets indeed, she thought. He'd come with nine Bombards. Which meant there was something more that M'kaba hadn't been told in the dispatches, for the Strategy Marshal of the Grands did not require nine warships to protect carpets.

"We were informed that there had been pirates in this sector. The Bombards are a necessary precaution." Yosinero bowed a little.

"Pirates." Suddenly M'kaba was disgusted with the whole thing. She hated being in charge of this reception. Lentzer was on planet, Yosinero was on her ship, the Line Commander was gone strange, and nothing was what it seemed.

"The Twelve recommended the Bombards," said Yosinero with false modesty. "Otherwise I would have used four *Baslita*-class ships. That would be more appropriate, I think."

"Certainly more usual," said M'kaba. With those nine Bombards Yosinero had his own troops to back him up, and 270 Grands were too many for this Petit mission to handle. Which reminded her she had not heard anything from Lentzer. She hoped Yuen had warned him that Yosinero had arrived.

She moved away from Navigator Migh and Group Leader Rhys-Davies. They were the only people aboard she trusted to handle the Grand without increasing tensions between the two forces. She left the bridge just as the Senior Bunter announced high tea in the officers' mess.

Never underestimate the enemy, she thought to

herself with lightly controlled anger. Her orders had
done just that. Yosinero was no fool, and he might be
on to her. Now that he was going to Moustar he
could manipulate events without sending incriminat-
ing messages. Assuming he was part of the slave
trade. Assuming there was slave trade on Zamalah.
She feared she would have to confront him at Moustar.

She winced at the thought. Yosinero knew Zamalah,
he had allies there. The only possible support she
might have was Jaanu Lentzer.

M'kaba wanted to disappear, fade away into the
stars somewhere that Yosinero's long arm could not
reach. Instead she went to her quarters and began
scrambing a zap.

There was another tremendous feast in the Sheikh's
camp that evening when the sun went down. When
they were all groaning on the carpets, the Sheikh
insisted on filling their plates once again; there were
still mountains of food left and courtesy demanded
gluttony. The same dark drink was served and there
was more music. This time Lentzer had prepared
and managed to stay awake.

During a lull in the festivities the Mromrosi, seated
next to the Sheikh in the place of honor, began to
speak.

"I was pleasantly surprised today to discover that
your planet is ruled by a judicial board. I look forward to learning what your legal codes and the Emerging Planet Fairness Court have in common."

"Allah the All-Creative gives life to creatures, and
their right is to obey His law," the Sheikh said softly,
without rancor. "As it says in the *Q'ran*, the cow
cannot help but follow God's law. It is only sentient
beings who willfully reject their place in the universe."

"Isn't sentience, and therefore willfulness part of
your Allah's law?" the Mromrosi inquired.

"It is given to man to master his willfulness," said the Sheikh.

The Mromrosi turned a violent shade of orange. "I fear I do not comprehend your theory." He faded to beige. "According to most legal codes of your species, it is not legal for human or human-descent to abridge the rights of any other human or human-descent, excepting children who are not yet of responsible age. This is one of the most important common ideas among your kind, is it not?"

"Abridge rights in what way?" the Sheikh asked, interested. "Those who enforce the law abridge the rights of criminals, but only when criminals have abridged the rights of their victims. Surely there are those whose fate it is to be deprived. Some people have accused us of interfering with the so-called right to choose a marriage partner, simply because parents will advise their children in the choice of a mate. It is well-known that parents certainly know more about what is necessary to create a proper family."

The Mromrosi turned a softer shade of pink. "Is it so?"

Lentzer hoped that the Mromrosi wouldn't say anything that would turn this occasion nasty. He wanted the mission over with. He wanted to get out of there.

In the background someone started up the music again. People were dancing, men and women, shaking their hips and moving in undulating counterpoint to the music. It was sensual and languorous. Lentzer did his best not to watch it, but could not often tear his eyes away. Gradually a circle formed around the dancers, with Lentzer in the front of the ring. People clapped to the music in the rhythm as primitive as heartbeats that came from the drums. Complicated and fast, the drumming and the clapping melded together. It was baffling and infectious.

Old people danced, and women with their over-sized sleeves draped over their faces. Children danced, men swung their swords in a line. Lentzer found himself swaying and made himself stop. He remembered the night before and was determined not to be seduced to sleep now.

All three Nada Solis wanted to dance. They swayed on the sidelines, each making the same movements, following what those in the circle were doing. Lentzer's sense of danger suddenly increased. The three Nada Solis were all away from their post. Some of the older women, giggling, were trying to teach them without words. A hand here, a demonstration of a step, a finger on a shoulder guiding. Lentzer knew with certainty that all he could do was watch with frozen horror.

Their hats and visors removed, the Nada Solis' identical faces were exposed to the crowd. And everyone watched.

Furious hisses and whispers and spat-out words rippled through the crowd. There was a single cry of outrage. One of the older women picked up a stone and threw it at the clones.

The three Nada Solis were not genetically engineered for diplomacy. As the stone landed harmlessly in the sand, /3 lunged at the veiled woman who threw it.

Lentzer yelled, jumping between the fighting clones and the old lady.

The Nada Solis froze, then all three of them backed off. They lined up and faced the whole camp from behind Lentzer's back. Tek, the Mromrosi and Rasidov were all with the Sheikh, who had risen in alarm. The crowd parted for him as he came toward Lentzer and the three Nada Solis.

"Abomination," people hissed. And although Lentzer spoke not one word of Arabic or the language of Zamalah, he understood the intent. He didn't move, hardly dared breathe while the Sheikh slowly made his way through the mob to see what had angered his people so.

As he reached the Nada Solis, the Sheikh faltered. His face was unreadable. And then he shook his head sadly. "The evil," he said softly, "is in the hearts of those who create abuses of nature. On them be the blood."

"Abomination." The whispered word fluttered through the crowd.

Lentzer didn't bother to yell "snow." If he could have yelled at all. One of the rocks had struck his chest and left him breathless.

The Sheikh raised his hand. "The *ulama* will judge who is responsible for bringing these devils," he said firmly. "There has never been such a case on Zamalah, not of three female devils. In Moustar we will consult those who are most knowledgeable. If anyone disagrees with this judgment, let him say what he will. The devils are to be guarded until the *ulama* has decided what is to be done. They are not Allah's creatures, we are. We wait in submission to Him."

The grumbling died down to whispers as the Zamalahi broke camp. Tents were furled and folded and packed on two oversized tractor-sledges. Armed men escorted the Petit Harriers to an open wagon and herded them in.

"I hope someone on the *Kinderkinyo* notices we're gone," said Rasidov to Lentzer.

"So long as it's not the Line Commander," said Lentzer.

They rode under the chill starlit sky for most of the night. A water bottle was provided and they made at least one stop for a quick meal.

"To keep their strength up," Tek explained, with an uneasy glance at Rasidov.

When daylight rose, the camp was set again and the Petits crawled into the inviting shade underneath the wagon to sleep.

They arrived in Moustar just at sunset of the Id al-Fitr, the perfect time to see the city at its most beautiful, with light glinting from facades of rose quartz. Above the warrens of the deep ravines, crystal towers stretched for the sky, always upward and splendidly ornate, above the squalor at the base of the cliffs.

High on the towers Lentzer could see people on narrow ledges, many of them carrying children and packages, preparing for the holiday. The long narrow ravines distorted sound, making it hollow and either too distant or too near, so here in the heart of the desert the city roared like the sea.

The caravan made its way through the tangle of streets. If people had not backed out of the way from respect for the Sheikh it would have been impossible for them to get through the crush of people and buildings.

Most of the people were dressed in multihued garments, and many of them were driving lambs before them. Tonight every family that could afford to do so would kill and roast an entire sheep, and there would be more food on each table than most families saw at one time for the rest of the year.

Since the Mromrosi was not tall enough to be seen over the sides of the wagon he was allowed to travel uncovered. Next to him the three Nada Solis were bound and their visors were in place. The Sheikh agreed that it was best not to display their perfect similarity too openly.

"Moslem though I am, I still don't like this," Rasidov

muttered to Lentzer as they rode beside the captive clones. "Too many people. And you see how they feel about clones. We'll be lucky if we get the Solis out of this alive."

Lentzer grunted. Little as he liked the Solis, they were still his responsibility. If anything happened to them, he would answer for it. If he survived long enough to be charged.

"It would be safest if you and the Mromrosi stay in my family's dwelling," said the Sheikh with obvious distaste. "I will post a guard on those devils, so that they will not be harmed until judgment is rendered."

Lentzer demurred. "There's an Alliance resthouse here in Moustar, isn't there? They'll put us up and they'll take the Nada Solis, if you like. That way you won't have to be burdened with them."

The Sheikh looked at him. "How would we reclaim the devils, if you did that?"

Lentzer took advantage of the opening. "Perhaps it would be just as well if the three Nada Solis were removed from Zamalah. There would be no more problem, and no retaliation for a judgment the Alliance might not approve." And the Petit Harriers would have to find some other way to investigate the slave trade on Zamalah.

"You mean that the abominations would be gone and these people would accept their departure?" The Sheikh swept his arm out to include all the people around him.

"Perhaps it's not the most elegant solution, but no one would be hurt; not Zamalahi or Petits." He gave the Sheikh a little time to consider the implications. "We'll leave quietly."

"And how will I answer to the *ulama* when it is known that I permitted such abominations as those to enter this sacred city? No, Harrier, I cannot permit that. It would offend Allah, the All-Embracing, and it would bring shame on me and my sons for seven times seven generations. You will remain in my care."

Lentzer sardonically thanked the Sheikh for his hospitality without betraying the depth of his fear. He had to save the Nada Solis. Then the mission—however great a failure it was—would not include casualties.

He motioned Tek and Rasidov aside and explained the situation.

Rasidov looked grim. "I don't like the sound of that."

Tek's face was calm. "It is written that the children of Allah the All-Knowing will not have to suffer devils. The Sheikh is a man of understanding."

This was no time to start a theological dispute between Tek and Rasidov; Lentzer looked from one to the other. "Whatever the Sheikh's reason for doing this, it's putting three Petit Harriers at risk, and that has to be our primary concern."

The Nada Solis, all three of them, glared at him with pure hatred. Lentzer ignored it. "I'm going to try to get word to the Alliance resthouse," he whispered. "We've already destroyed any credibility or goodwill we might have garnered. So now our only priority is getting out of here with skins intact." This last included the clones, who looked as if they were ready to savage him.

"Now," Lentzer continued. "What about the Mromrosi?"

"He followed the Sheikh," Tek said softly, his gaze directed to the highest tower in the city.

"If you'd release us," the Nada Solis/2 hissed furiously, "we *are* trained to deal with a situation like this. We could recover the Mromrosi, and settle this entire matter."

"I'm almost tempted to take you up on it," Lentzer

snapped. "I don't care how good you are at unarmed combat, three Nada Solis against the entire population of Moustar is pogging idiotic."

"We don't know what the *ulama* will decide," Tek reminded them. "But if you act against them, you will not help your case."

He was cut short by a blast of static from a mosque loudspeaker. "We are the Voice of the Hidden Imam. Listen, all Moustar. There are abominations in our midst, things that Allah the All-Compassionate does not permit us as His children to touch, for they are unclean devils. You who fear Allah the All-Enduring, listen and obey. We must not accept this filth in our city. Now we are cleansed from the fasting. Now we must make our city acceptable to God. We must find these devils who come with Infidels and punish them, so Allah the All-Merciful does not abhor us because we are slack in obeying His law. For this reason we have captured the Infidel unhuman. It is unacceptable unless it agrees to surrender to His law and most holy *Q'ran*. This is the Voice of the Hidden Imam, the slaves of God."

"I'd like to take whoever that was and smash their faces against a wall," the Nada Solis/3 said.

"We'd better get to the Sheikh's house soon," Rasidov murmured to Lentzer. "People are looking at us already."

Lentzer agreed. "See if you can explain it to the Sheikh, will you?" he asked, only half in jest. He stared at the mosque, wishing his implant had some information about how these Moslems judged Mromrosio.

Line Commander Nazaipha stared vacantly at Executive Officer Yuen. "I didn't authorize a shore party," he said uncertainly.

"It is an investigative mission," Yuen said patiently. "Orders came from the Hub." He was feeling exhausted. Between Yosinero and his Bombards and the precarious condition of the Line Commander, he felt worn to the bone. "You have the record of the briefing in your log, Line Commander."

"Oh, yes," he said without a trace of recognition.

"They've missed two check-ins," said Yuen. "The camp where they were taken is deserted according to the latest scan. The village is empty, as well."

"There is too much emptiness," sighed the Line Commander, and Yuen realized it was useless to continue. He rose, saluted, and left Nazaipha alone with his strangeness.

Group Line Chief M'kaba responded to his hail on the first signal. "Any news?" she asked without standard formalities.

"None," said Yuen. "I'd say we ought to lift off and do a planet scan for them, but . . ." He gestured toward the Bombards.

"Yes," said M'kaba. On the surveill her face was enormous, and her anxiety was undisguised.

"I don't want to give the Grands an excuse for taking over. Especially since we don't know why they're here." He put his hands up. "I'm open to any recommendations, either from you or Ghano. Or either of your Mromrosi."

M'kaba lowered her voice. "Yosinero says he's buying rugs."

"And I've said the Line Commander is suffering from a persistent bacterial infection," Yuen reminded her. "We're all lying."

Her chin jolted upward. "What do you mean?"

"The Line Commander's gone strange and we can't admit it. The Grands Strategy Marshal comes all the way to purchase carpets. With nine Bombards because there might be pirates." His disbelief was patent.

"All right, I take your point," said M'kaba, relieved that this was all he meant. "But we can't do anything about it. You don't have the authority, and if we contact the *Semper Alpha Cygnis*, the Grands will find out."

"I know," said Yuen.

"And Yosinero is the obvious one to take over," she said, irate thoughts directed inward.

"He might be waiting to assume command," said Yuen, revealing the worst of his fears.

M'kaba responded sharply. "You can't let that happen."

"I know," agreed Yuen.

"But how can you stop it?" she demanded.

Yuen failed to smile. "I'm pogged if I know."


"For a prison, it's not too bad," said Lentzer when he had made a complete inspection of the cavernous room the Sheikh had provided to the Harriers. It was cut high up in the street overlooking the Friday mosque, and a few shreds of twilight came in through the rough stone of the cave opening. It wouldn't be easy to get out of.

"Very neat," said Rasidov. He tapped his hailer. "Can it get through rock?"

Lentzer shook his head. "But we'll give it a try, a little later. I want Yuen to have some idea what's been going on." As much as he disliked their predicament, he had to admit—if only to himself—that for the first time in years he felt he could do something actually useful. It was an invigorating sensation, one he had forgotten; he remembered who he had become and his confidence sagged.

The Nada Solis/3 regarded him with contempt. "Do you think you've made things better for us, getting us shut away in here?"

"I've kept us from getting stoned in the street," Lentzer said. "Thanks to Rasidov. The Sheikh was ready to leave us to the crowd, or didn't you realize that?" He didn't expect an answer.

The Nada Solis/1 gave him one. "We are going to report you for dereliction of duty and as a possible accessory to the abduction of our Mromrosi observer."

"You do that," Lentzer said. "Just as soon as we're back on the *Kinderkinyo*."

"The Mromrosi went with the Sheikh of his own will," said Tek. "That can't be attributed to Group Leader Lentzer."

"We were supposed to protect him," said the Nada Solis/2. "You kept us from doing our job."

"I kept us from getting killed," Lentzer shot back. "Or are you going to protest that, too?" He paced the length of the chamber, bringing his temper back under control. Bickering now would accomplish nothing. "Our first obligation is to escape. If we can make it to the Alliance resthouse, well and good. If we can't, then we have to get out of Moustar and get the Broadswords to pick us up."

"What about the Mromrosi?" asked the Nada Solis/2.

"We'll have to find out about this group who claim to be holding him, the Voice of the Hidden Imam. If they are holding him."

The Nada Solis fell silent, and Lentzer turned to Rasidov. "Has this place been vetted yet?"

"No listening devices. That doesn't mean they aren't listening." He touched his hailer. "This can't pick up a servant with sharp ears."

"We'll have to hope the servants don't speak Standard Huble," Lentzer said. "Or that they don't use translator packs. What do you think?" asked Lentzer.

"I think we ought to stick to Standard Huble," said Rasidov, and ignored the scorn of the three Nada Solis.

"Sounds reasonable," said Lentzer. "Now what about

this Hidden Imam? Do you or Tek have any idea who or what they are?"

"Not really," said Rasidov.

"It's all ancient legend," said Tek.

"All right, let's assume it's a faction," Lentzer said pensively. "Is there a chance that the Sheikh would help the Mromrosi? Could we convince him that the Mromrosi must be returned to us?"

"That doesn't do much about the *ulama*," said the Nada Solis/3.

Lentzer just nodded once more. "First things first."

"I recall something about them," Rasidov said suddenly. "They are one of the older and more famous sects. The Ismailis. The Assassins of Old Earth were Ismailis. They believed not only in the Four Holy Imams, they also believed in the descendants of Ali, which would make them Shi'ite. They believed that Ali never really died, that he was translated into some *hidden* state and still is the only true leader of the Faithful."

"So they're the same bogo sect as the Assassins? I always thought the Assassins were myths." Lentzer shook his head. "That doesn't sound very promising for our Mromrosi's health. I don't like this at all."

"Well, they might claim to be the same sect, but the Assassins have been gone for thousands of years. This group might not be so extreme," Rasidov said, doing his best to be encouraging.

"But since they are Ismailis, perhaps the Sheikh will help. If those are real Assassins, the government of Zamalah can't like this much better than we do," Tek suggested hesitantly.

"What about all of us?" the Nada Solis/2 asked reasonably. "We might be able to take on a dozen or so of these Zamalahi. Hand-to-hand, we could beat them."

"And what if there are hundreds of them, or they

aren't willing to face devils like you hand-to-hand?"
Lentzer challenged.

"There must be something we can do," said the
Nada Solis/1, and for the first time Lentzer sympa-
thized with them.

"Once we get out of here and into the resthouse,
then we can decide on what to do about the Hidden
Imam," he said, more tactful than usual. Then he
added the thing that had been bothering him since
they were locked in this room. "I don't think we
ought to count on any support from the Broadswords.
If they were going to come after us, they'd have
been here by now. We have to assume that we're on
our own for the time being." If he had said that a day
ago, he would have wanted to fortify himself first
with Standby Hooch. Now he was glad his head was
clear.

"Then you'd better make the best possible use of
us," said the Nada Solis/2.

"And what would that be?" inquired Lentzer without sarcasm.

Rasidov spoke up. "We could use them as a first
attack team. I doubt any of the guards would be
prepared to battle them, either as clones, abominations, or women."

"That's right," Tek agreed with him. "And that is
one thing about these people, they don't expect anything from women."

"No one ever does, not on forty-one of the Alliance planets," the Nada Solis/2 said. "Which is one
of the prime reasons we were engineered female.
We're always a surprise."

"That I won't dispute," said Lentzer, then lapsed
into silence, wrestling with something that had been
nagging him since he heard the announcement: how
had the Voice of the Hidden Imam heard about the
Nada Solis and the Mromrosi in the first place?

\* \* \*

Strategy Marshal Yosinero bowed deeply to Group Line Chiefs Xer M'kaba and Laeo Ghano, his obsequious politeness more insulting than a slight would be. "I confess I am surprised that your mission has not yet returned."

"Since you're familiar with Zamalah," said M'kaba tightly, "you know that this is not a place where things are accomplished quickly."

"Not often, anyway," appended Ghano.

"Very true," said Yosinero at his smoothest. "But it surprises me, I will tell you, that a routine visit has taken so much time. Is there anything I might do to speed things along? With your Line Commander so ill, perhaps I might advise you in his place?"

"That isn't necessary, but thank you for your generous offer," said M'kaba, all but choking on her words.

"You may avail yourself of it at any time," said Yosinero. "In fact, it occurred to me only a short while ago that I ought to lend you my medical support team. From what you have said, the illness of Nazaipha is beyond the skill of most Bunters."

"That is very kind of you," Ghano answered for M'kaba, for he sensed her fury. "But we have been told there is a high risk of infection from the disease and we would be derelict in our duty if we permitted someone of your position to be exposed, however indirectly, to this disease."

Yosinero put the tips of his six white fingers together. "How gratifying your concern is."

M'kaba was so angry that she was close to tears. I will not give him that satisfaction, she ordered herself. It was maddening to spend hours catering to this smooth, insinuating Grand while Lentzer's mission was missing. She hoped that there would be a message from them when she was permitted to return to her quarters. She was so caught up in her worry that she did not hear the next question that Yosinero addressed to her.

"When I go to select my carpets, is there any message you would like me to carry for you?" he repeated, his smile widening.

Startled, she answered without thought. "No, thank you. Lentzer relays information when he can."

Something in Yosinero's eyes got very hard and bright. "Lentzer," he said mildly. "Lentzer."

Lentzer would be happy enough to leave this place behind forever, city and planet. His fourth perusal of the walls of the cavern was as disappointing as the first. "What about the carpets?" he said, determined not to lose heart now. "We haven't looked there."

"No, we haven't," said the Nada Solis/3. "What is the point?"

"There has to be something somewhere," Lentzer declared, trying to believe it himself. "All these caverns ought to connect somehow."

"They do," said the Nada Solis/1. "Through the corridors."

Tek spoke up. "There should be other passageways. It's traditional."

"What if these Zamalahi don't know the tradition?" suggested the Nada Solis/2.

"Let's just do it," said Lentzer, lifting up the corner of the nearest one to set an example for the others. He was unpleasantly surprised to discover how heavy the carpets were. "Rasidov, give me a hand."

The Navigator hesitated. "Why bother?"

Lentzer rounded on him. "Do you want to lie back and wait for the *ulama* to condemn the Solis? Do you want to wait around while those Hidden Imam sperks do something deadly to the Mromrosi? Do you?"

Rasidov stared at him. "I thought you were the one who was hanging on to get early retirement. Why get all sproinged now?" Even as he asked, he came and took the other end of the carpet.

"We'll make a pile of them," said Lentzer, getting down to work. "Right over there."

"I'll examine the floor there first," volunteered Tek, getting down on his hands and knees and running his thumbs along the tiles. In a short while he got up. "If anything's loose, I can't find it."

"Thanks," said Lentzer, puffing a little as he and Rasidov moved the first carpet.

This goaded the Nada Solis into action. /3 picked the largest of the carpets, rolled it expertly and hoisted it onto her shoulder. With one end dragging behind her, she brought her trophy and dropped it on top of the first. "You leave this to us, Group Leader," she said. "We're stronger than you and we can do it faster."

/2 had already rolled the third carpet and was slinging it onto her back. "Why don't you check the floor," she said, more genially than she had ever said anything to Lentzer.

"Sounds like a good idea," said Lentzer, feeling relieved.

A little less than two hours later, Rasidov found the uneven place in the tiles. He motioned to the others to come, and with the help of the Nada Solis/3, raised the trapdoor. The dark maw of the tunnel angled away from them down the inside of the walls of the house.

"We'll need light," said Tek, peering at the narrow, irregular stairs.

"Nonsense," said the Nada Solis/1. "Let one of us go ahead. We have augmented vision."

"And we'd better go very quietly," added Rasidov. "We don't want to be discovered, not now." He cocked his head toward the window. "They'll be gathering for another feast in an hour or so."

"You mean they might check on us," said Lentzer.

"At the conclusion of the feast if not the beginning," said Rasidov. "They have to feed us—it's part of the law. But they don't have to give us anything but leftovers."

"Probably just as well," said the Nada Solis/2. "That passage is going to be a tight fit."

They fumbled their way in the dark, never talking above a whisper. The passage led down past the harem, and then below that to the huge reception chamber where the Sheikh and his family entertained their guests.

A steady drone of conversation reached them through the walls, and the Petit Harriers were grateful for it, since it made their passage easier.

They had almost reached the last flight of stairs when Tek signaled a halt. "Wait. There's a debate going on."

"Fine," said Lentzer. "We can get out of here while they're preoccupied."

But Tek remained still, listening. "The one with the deep voice is asking about the treatment of Muslim slaves," Tek whispered at last, shocked. "He is asking how one can expiate sins when there are no slaves to be freed."

"What?" Lentzer was confused.

"It's very involved. I don't understand the argument," the kitchen clerk said apologetically, trying not to raise his voice.

Lentzer motioned to them all to halt. "Get as much of it as you can."

Tek shook his head. "It's . . . not . . ."

"Not what?" Lentzer prompted when Tek fell silent.

"He says a virtuous man must have slaves, so that

he can free them to rid himself of sin," said Tek very softly. "He does not understand why the slaves must be concealed when they are so necessary for a man to guard his soul." His voice was almost inaudible.

Rasidov tapped Lentzer's arm as another impassioned voice addressed the gathering the other side of the wall.

"He's saying that he does not believe it is proper to sell slaves to anyone but Moslems. He wants the Imam to order all the Faithful not to trade with off-worlders."

There came a third voice, this time interrupted by enthusiastic cheers of approval.

"What's that all about?" asked Lentzer when the cheers drowned out the speaker.

"He's in the other camp. It seems to be more popular," said Rasidov. "He thinks that selling slaves to those who are not Moslem is the better way because it erases the sin more completely. To sell slaves in expiation isn't enough unless they are sacrifices."

"Did they happen to mention who's buying the slaves off-world?" asked Lentzer.

"They did, but I didn't recognize the name," said Rasidov.

Lentzer turned to Tek. "What about you?"

The young Supplies/Tech lowered his voice still more. "It was too noisy. I'm sorry."

They stumbled out of the hidden staircase at the side of the house, near the hive-shaped ovens where bread was baked. The entire area was strewn with the refuse of the evening's feast, with more to come. It smelled dreadful and it squished underfoot.

"How are we going to find the resthouse?" asked Rasidov as they slipped and slithered toward the gate.

"My implant will do it," said Lentzer, already sensing the faint warmth of its activation. It was one of the few times he was glad to have it; most of the time the little device was more disorienting than it was helpful.

"What if someone notices us?" demanded the Nada Solis/3. "We're pogging conspicuous."

"It's feast-time," said Rasidov. "There won't be many people on the street, and most of them won't be likely to stop us." He looked over at Tek. "Do you think we can cover for all of us? If we're noticed?"

"Oh, I think so," said Tek. "If the Solis and the Group Leader will keep their heads down and act dejected."

"What?" cried the Nada Solis/1.

"Just do it," said Lentzer. "I'm going to." He worked the lock on the gate loose. "Ready?" he asked back over his shoulder. Much as he hated to admit it, he was beginning to enjoy himself.

"I suppose so," said Tek.

"Fine," said Lentzer. "Rasidov, you first. We'll come in the middle, the Solis and me; and Tek will bring up the rear." He put his shoulder to the gate and eased it open. His head buzzed as the implant went to work.

They reached the resthouse without incident. As they entered the main room, a station Bunter hurried toward them. "Good evening, Group Leader, Navigator, Sub-Group Chiefs, Supplies/Tech. There has been apprehension on your behalf." It checked each of them out with a medical scanner, then stopped. "And where is the Mromrosi?"

"That's what we're hoping to find out," said Lentzer. "Do you have a scrambled hailer?"

"Yes. Naturally," said the cyborg, moving nervously. "I'll take you to the vid room at once."

"Thank you," said Lentzer. "As soon as possible."

"Oh," said the Bunter. "Yes. At once." Its duties were making things difficult for the cyborg. "What refreshments may I get for you?" it asked the little mission. "Food, drink?"

All three Nada Solis asked for restorative wafers. Tek said he could tend to his own food. Rasidov ordered a sammidge.

"Very good," said the Bunter, at last able to assist Lentzer. As it led the way out of the chamber, it inquired, "And for you, sir? Food? Drink?"

Lentzer surprised himself with his answer. "Just the hailer, thanks."

"Very good, sir," said the Bunter as it opened the door to the communications area for him.

It was four minutes later that Executive Officer Yuen answered the hail; for the next few seconds he struggled to adjust the scrambler, then his face appeared on the vid screen. "Lentzer. Old Hardy, we've been worried."

"So have we," said Lentzer, grinning. "And we're not out yet."

Yuen gave a worried glance over his shoulder. "Look, if you need us, we can find a way to pick you up with walkers. But it . . . There are complications here."

"Not the Line Commander," said Lentzer.

"Grands. Bombards. Yosinero," said Yuen.

Lentzer took a long breath. "Uh-huh," he said.

"If we leave, they'll follow." The Executive Officer made a harried movement with his hands. "We've been able to keep them here, but it's getting harder. Yosinero wants to buy his carpets and leave, but I think he wants us out of the way before he does."

"I can bet he does," said Lentzer.

"What do you mean?" An expression that was not

quite dread and not quite hope crossed Yuen's features.

"Slavers, that's what I mean," said Lentzer. "Off-world slavers."

The Executive Officer's eyes grew large; when he spoke it was barely above a whisper. "You don't mean that . . ."

"Not for a fact, no," said Lentzer. "But I'll wager half my pension on it." He leaned forward. "Pog it, I'll wager *all* my pension."

Yuen jumped in his chair. "Get back here right now. If you're right, you are in—"

"Not quite yet," said Lentzer, interrupting Yuen. "There's a few things we have to tidy up here."

Once again Yuen's face grew guarded. "What things?"

"Well, for one thing, we have to get the Mromrosi back—" He paid no heed to the squack from Yuen. "And then I'd like to set a little trap for our ever-so-Grand friends."

The Friday mosque had four minarets, crystalline needles piercing the sky. Underneath was a dome and a walled enclosure. This was the main city mosque and it was huge.

Lentzer had never been in a mosque before. They entered through a courtyard arranged around a large central fountain. There were other fountains against the walls as well, the space between them paved with tiles laid out in a geometric pattern. The scent of orange trees filled the air.

In the dark the courtyard was a maze of shadows. The lighting had been designed for drama, and visibility had been sacrificed.

"Should we go in?" Tek asked.

Lentzer shook his head. "We're here. We're easy enough to spot. It's up to them to find us." He perched on the fountain ledge, looking like a tourist taking in the view. His face was perfectly composed.

"They won't like it so public," the Nada Solis/2 said.

Lentzer didn't comment. Ever since he had been informed that the Mromrosi was at the mosque, he had been busy weighing his options. There weren't very many of them, but he was determined to make the most of what he had. He was not stupid enough to move his own people into the shadows. A slight breeze rippled the water across the surface of the fountain. Fine spray wet Lentzer's face. He remained still as a stone.

At one time during his training he had been told that it was not impossible to negotiate with terrorists, only politically ill-advised. Most terrorists, he had been taught, were not suicidal or irrational unless pushed or threatened. But few of them could identify with their hostages, and most of them did not care if they died. And the longer the situation went on, the better for the negotiators, as long as some progress was being made.

He had been young then, and eager, thrilled to have passed the tests and be ushered into the secret world of the Alliance Intelligence Organization. He had enjoyed all the intricate and arcane subjects he was expected to master. Terrorism, not a major problem on most Magnicate Alliance worlds, was still on the curriculum for AIO trainees.

The instructor had been one of the crisis managers during the last Scare on Mere Philomene. There had been hordes of bogos about then, hijackings and hostages taken. Institutions were bombed. Alliance ships were sabotaged. Most people dismissed it as typical Mere Philomene, the losers acting up again. But the incidents of the Scare itself had been studied and analyzed and reinterpreted so that it was usable.

Or, as his instructor had explained, Mere Philomene was something of a laboratory of rebellion, sedition, and police action. "You have to say this about the Fils: they knew what they were doing."

The Voice of the Hidden Imam probably didn't. That made them far more dangerous, in Lentzer's view. They didn't have generations of tradition about how to handle prisoner exchanges. Their traditions came from stealth, treachery, and absolutism. They were making the scene up as they went along, and Lentzer knew it meant trouble.

"Why do we have to wait for them to make the first move?" asked the Nada Solis/1.

"Because we do," said Lentzer. "That's the way it's done."

"I hate waiting," said the Nada Solis/3.

"Let me scout around," suggested Rasidov.

"All right," said Lentzer, against his better judgment. No doubt this was a bad move. He didn't like splitting their force up. It was already too small. If only they had more time. With more time Lentzer could appeal to the wisdom of the rest of Zamalahi. There had to be another way to close in on the group. The officials of the planet, the *ulama* and others, were responsible for the Mromrosi's safety too. And perhaps they had some experience with this fringe group, had dealt with them before.

A shadow flickered in the courtyard. Tek noticed it, pointed. Lentzer nodded. He'd seen it clearly, alert the way he hadn't been in fifteen, twenty years. The hunt was on. The icy breath of challenge bathed him and everything heightened. Time slowed. Lentzer could just see Rasidov in the break between the orange trees. He signaled the others to come closer.

There were other men in the courtyard now, most of them making their way into the mosque itself. For an instant Lentzer was distracted.

And then a hood dropped over his eyes.

For a moment only he was angry. He hadn't been expecting that. He cursed himself for such a stupid, stupid error.

Hands gripped him firmly but not uncomfortably. They did not seem to intend pain. Yet.

"This way," a carefully neutral voice said in accented Standard Huble. "We are sorry for the inconvenience, but you understand our position?"

Lentzer made himself answer in the affirmative. In a hostage situation it was always better to acknowledge every question. The kidnappers always wanted to be in control. The whole issue was one of power. Let their captive think they had it. He couldn't afford to anger them now.

"We are going to take you with us," said the same voice. "All of you. If any one of you fails to obey us, all of you will be disposed of."

"Do what he tells you," said Lentzer at once, knowing that the Nada Solis were anxious to fight.

They were led behind the trees into the porch of the mosque itself. Lentzer recognized the smell of the trees, the smoothness of the pavement, the shallow steps up to the door. He wondered if he should take off his shoes.

Then they were led through a side gate and back onto the street. At least it sounded like the street, and the paving was rough like an alley. He could hear the shuffling behind him and tried to count. They must have all the Nada Solis. Otherwise they would have battled in the courtyard. And Tek? Did they have him, as well? He tried to make out their footsteps but the sounds were too indistinct to reveal much.

He was pushed and prodded into something and then pushed downward. "Sit," his captor said, and he bent his knees gingerly.

The seat was padded and upholstered and the guard fastened a belt across his lap. Then the thing took off, lurched, and rose rapidly. It felt like it was flying heavy, although Lentzer knew that could well be his imagination.

The flyer rolled, dove, rose again. It turned quickly right, then right again. That was when Lentzer lost track of their direction. He was suspended in darkness, piloted by someone who was either an expert at disorientation or an aggressive adolescent.

Not only direction, but time too became distorted. Lentzer couldn't say whether he'd been in the flyer for ten minutes or half an hour.

Then the flyer bounced hard, jarring his knees, and the belt was unsnapped. The hood was removed from his face before he was told to leave.

The Nada Solis were there, and Tek. But Rasidov was missing. Lentzer was relieved. If anyone could find them it was Navigator Rasidov.

When they left the flyer it was dark. Lentzer could make out the interior of a cave, which was not very helpful, since most of the population lived in caverns. There was some utilitarian furniture. Their captors wore checked triangular cloths tied across their faces so only their eyes could be seen. Their dress was typical of Zamalah, the long concealing robes and sandals. It was only because of bare darkened toenails that Lentzer realized one was a woman. All of them held weapons trained on the Harriers, and all the weapons looked to be well cared for and in excellent condition.

And across the room, sitting under a dim light, was the Mromrosi. It turned a soft pink color.

"The alien will be released to the *Semper Alpha Cygnis*," a disembodied voice informed them. "It will be taken directly there, off the planet, so as not to confuse the people. The rest of you will remain here."

Lentzer was immediately on guard. How did they know about the *Semper Alpha Cygnis?* Only government agencies would have access to information like that, and even then only when there was a need to know.

This was not some group of amateurs playing local games, Lentzer knew. There was something else under it all, something that gave a group of fanatics information they should never have possessed. And all the while he was being diverted from their mission, seduced away from the real purpose of this whole charade.

"Absolutely not," the Mromrosi said.

If he had grown a full li and done a Yerba Buena dance it wouldn't have surprised Lentzer any less.

All eyes were on the alien. Even their captors were shocked, their attention held.

"No," the alien repeated itself. "I refuse to go as long as any sentient being is held in my stead."

Lentzer could imagine it. The thought horrified him. The Mromrosi could ruin everything.

And everyone else was as horrified as he was. Even with their faces covered, the terrorists' eyes were wide and glassy. Their weapons had swung automatically to cover the Mromrosi. And they forgot the Nada Solis altogether.

"Think what you are saying," one of the terrorists shouted.

"I always think about what I say." The Mromrosi was bright, sugary yellow. "The Emerging Planet Fairness Court is not party to coercion of any kind."

The clones had always bragged about being perfect. They were. They caught the break in concentration and used it to slip quickly behind the three captors who were furthest to the back. It took very little effort and almost no noise for the clones to hand-drop the guards with quick double blows to the temples. They held their victims so there was no sound at all as the unconscious terrorists sank to the ground.

By the time the terrorists came groggily back to consciousness, the clones already had them covered. "Drop your weapons and sit down," the Nada Solis/3 ordered.

The kidnappers complied meekly. Lentzer glued their palms together so they made a circle. The Mromrosi watched everything, and Lentzer watched him. The Nada Solis removed the ammunition from the weapons. Tek was checking out the flyer.

"Do you think we can get back to our ship from the resthouse?" Lentzer asked the Nada Solis when he was finished securing the prisoners.

The Nada Solis/2 rolled her eyes. "No problem," she announced. "Why? What about you?"

"I have to find Rasidov," said Lentzer.

Back at the resthouse the Nada Solis were explaining every move to the Mromrosi.

"But will they be troubled, all glued together like that?" Mromrosi asked.

"As long as they don't move they'll be fine. In ten hours the bond will dissolve if no one finds them before then. As long as they stay calm no one will be hurt," the Nada Solis/2 said very reassuringly.

"But what if no one comes?" the Mromrosi persisted.

"That's very unlikely," Lentzer said, interrupting the Nada Solis/3 who was clearing her throat before making a presentation. "They had a complex plan and a leader. They knew the identity of our *Semper* ship. They're a lot more sophisticated than we anticipated. I'd bet they won't have to wait long enough for any of them to get hungry."

The Mromrosi accepted that. "Then something else bothers you."

"Yes, it does," said Lentzer. "This whole Voice of the Hidden Imam thing. They're a lot more professional and organized than anything we were anticipating. And a lot better armed, too. Those stunners were new-style, expensive and not available on the open market. For another, I don't like it that all three Broadswords were effectively immobilized by nine Grands Bombards. That's too much convenience for someone." Frowning, he retired to his own quarters.

There was a coded zap waiting for him, one that was keyed to his AIO implant.

He straightened his back and placed his palms flat on his thighs the way he had been taught immediately after the implant was put in place. Then he started slowly with the breathing. And then the pain began in the back of his head, but he ignored it. He thought about his heart rate, about the blood going to the brain, about his brainwaves getting longer and longer—

He had to force himself to open his eyes, to look at the words on the screen. The implant took over, and the words melted in front of him and recombined in kaleidoscope patterns, revolving until they finally came to rest.

The new words pounded in his head. In decryption state, he was unaware of their meaning. He whispered them harshly into the speaker and saw the right patterns on the screen.

He came back to awareness slowly. The first thing he noticed was that his shirt was damp with sweat and that he stank. Then he felt the drained, dizzy aftermath. Great pogging Morjis, he was out of practice. His mouth was parched and he was too tired even to call for water.

The dizziness steadied and the weakness passed. Lentzer summoned the Bunter and requested Boreas sehap broth and some real courberries.

Then he stared at the decoded information. He read it through three times, wondering as he did so whether perhaps the implant had atrophied and he had bungled the decryption. But all the other signs were there intact, the series letters and the syntax.

*Directorate CCC, Expt., L-YY3; from level 12, in this sector at location local Moustar, re: Strategy Marshal Yosinero, Grand Harriers, ret. Possible instigator local political instability, re: price of goods and personal investments. Possible, possible, illegal cargo—repeat. Expose local, report global. Orders 7, yyB-17-3 ref., date.*

The name alone held him captive, delicately poised between murder and flight. Yosinero. Again. Lentzer's first instinct, animal, was to run. Hide. Crawl under a rock or drown in Standby Hooch.

Why not? What the hell did he have to lose? Yosinero had already wrecked his career. If he fled now, the Strategy Marshal of the Grands would have total victory.

If a curly-mop of an alien could refuse to be rescued, the least Lentzer could do was stand up to his enemy. Running away had destroyed Jaanu Lentzer's self-respect.

And the Group Leader and protocol officer wanted it back.

Tek the kitchen clerk was afraid. With Rasidov missing, he was beginning to think he had made a serious mistake. It was bad conduct, immodest, to show off his ability, which in truth was a gift from Allah, a revelation of mystic truths to serve Allah the All-Glorious, not the Quartermaster of the Petit Harriers. What were supply orders and fleet requisitions

compared to the permutations of the thousand-
thousands Names of God?

Rasidov had challenged him, saying that someone
with Tek's experience and training could probably
find the details that had escaped the rest of the
Harriers. He had told Tek that it was his duty as a
Petit Harrier to discover who had been using requisitions and supplies to hide smuggling.

It was difficult to accept that good Moslems would
be party to such terrible schemes as the ones he had
unearthed. Zamalah was a religious place. The men
here followed the ways of Allah.

Otherwise, why would they still have slavery here?

The whole of it was in the *Q'ran*, of course. And
Rasidov had even recited all the appropriate verses.
Slavery was permitted. Creating things in the image
of God was not. Devout Moslems didn't even paint
human figures, let alone create clones and cyborgs,
which were vile imitations of Allah's creation of hu-
manity and the stars. Cyborgs and clones Tek could
easily see were against the letter of the law, if not
the intent.

And slavery was accepted. Of course, in more
enlightened places it was considered that slavery was
an evil that the *Q'ran* mitigated, since it was impossible to abolish the entire institution. A free Moslem
could never be enslaved, and on every feast and at a
person's death the freeing of Moslem slaves was an
act of charity that was one of the five pillars of Islam.

Tek liked Zamalah. He liked the Sheikh and the
people in general. He liked the food and the women
in modest dress, he liked not feeling out of place.

Back home on Atam Akal where the storms threatened every hour of life, his family had been outsiders. His grandparents had been skilled builders, and
since that was Atam Akal's prime industry they were
welcomed, along with other fine craftsmen from

Samarkand, Bukhara, and the other cities of Moslem Asia.

Until he had helped organize the markets, Tek had been pitied, an embarrassment to his community. But once he had discovered the splendor of numbers, Tek had blossomed. He only had to be shown once how to tag and coordinate inventory, how to record sales, how to enter expenses and sales, profits and losses, and he could compose whole structures of commerce. In a very short time he had mastered the intricacies of trading, and longed for new vistas in the sublime realm of numbers.

That was the year of the worst storms of the century on Atam Akal, where horrible weather was standard fare. In that season, Tek's mother died and his father was disabled. The Petit Harriers were called in to keep order, prevent looting, and incidentally take charge of the rescue mission.

Like many residents, Tek volunteered in the relief work. Unlike most residents, he had a positive genius for making sure adequate supplies of milk got to the shelter with the small children and that no piles of blankets sat unused. Somehow he found school supplies that no one else could locate and had them brought to start up a temporary school. He scrounged plastics and reusable steel beams for building teams. He found volunteers with skills, builders who could put up houses, cloth artists who could cook soup, teachers of mathematics who could plan the new streets and buildings.

He kept everyone busy, including himself. After the first days he caught the notice of Group Leader Stalton, who realized how talented Tek was. He suggested that Tek had a future in the Quartermasters. More from gratitude to Stalton than out of ambition, Tek filled out all the application forms and

forgot about them. The dozen *Katana*-class boats
took off, and Atam Akal was left to lick its wounds.

Four months later, when he was informed of his
acceptance into that proud body known as the Petit
Harriers, he honestly could not remember having
applied. But since there was nothing at all left for
him at home, he went.

Once he had joined the Petit Harriers Quartermasters Corps, it was obvious that God had intended
all along that he become one of them. He had gone
to Old Earth on his very first mission, and had
managed to make the Pilgrimage to the Holy Places
and become a hajji. And he had a magic aura around
him, as if everyone knew he was *destined for great
things*. Surely Allah the All-Understanding was looking out very carefully for his welfare, and Tek responded accordingly.

On his second training cruise he was assigned to
the kitchens of the *Semper Alpha Cygnis* because it
was difficult to supply the enormous motherships.
He had been industrious and correct, keeping to his
tasks and to himself.

Then he was told to report for mission briefing.

Tek found everything confusing. There was nothing at all for him to do here, except translate, which
he could manage tolerably well if no one went too
fast. But there were no goods to distribute, no inventory to organize, no ledgers to balance. Once again
he was out of his element.

Rasidov, though theoretically a Moslem, was not
religious; the Nada Solis were exotic and wrong. The
Mromrosi, whom he had only seen once before, was
so out of his range of experience that he avoided the
alien whenever possible. Lentzer, well, everyone
knew what Lentzer was. And Tek knew him, too,
from his unusually large requests for Standby Hooch
and his frequent absences at dinner.

Terrible how easily he had become corrupted, Tek thought. After only a few days with the Harriers— the real Petit Harriers—here he was eager to volunteer for a dangerous assignment. He hoped Rasidov would talk him out of it, once he found him.

Slavery and smuggling. He had found them in the records, cleverly concealed, but for someone with his gifts, as prominent as boulders. What infuriated him was the realization that devout Moslems were being manipulated by off-worlder Infidels.

If his fate was written on his forehead, as the Prophet taught, then Tek prayed that his would be to end the shame that had been visited on these good Moslems of Zamalah.

The only trouble was that with Rasidov missing, he could not act. He knew he would have to find the Navigator himself if he were to achieve his fate.

Line Commander Nazaipha went down on his knee to Yosinero. "How fine to see you. Be welcome in the name of all the Petit Harriers aboard my ship." His eyes were less haunted than usual. Executive Officer Yuen, standing beside him, hoped that his explanation of reaction to medication would be accepted.

"Very gracious," said Yosinero. "But a trifle inconvenient for all the pleasure it is to be so well-received by the Petits. We Grands are not always given such a reception." He smiled, his cold eyes glinting.

"The rivalry between the services is lamentable," said Nazaipha. "It delights me to correct some of my fellow-Petits' misconduct." He gazed at a point about a handsbreadth above Yosinero's head. "I have been told that you and your . . . escort are here to purchase carpets."

"Yes, we are," said Yosinero with asperity.

"Very good. Very good. As you have been told, we

have a mission in Moustar at the time, and they will require a few days more before it is finished. If you would be willing to let us entertain you for a short while longer?"

Yuen was light-headed with relief. For once the Line Commander might squeak through, and the tale of his illness gain a little credibility beyond his own Broadsword. "We have made arrangements to prepare a feast for you. Nothing like the Zamalahi, but satisfactory by Hathaway standards."

Yosinero's face was shut, unreadable. "If it's necessary to the success of the mission, then certainly my expedition for carpets must wait a little longer. But I can't dawdle here forever. A man in my position has pressing engagements and important negotiations. Doubtless you comprehend."

"Comprehend?" said Line Commander Nazaipha distantly, and Yuen's heart sank. "Business?" He threw back his head but there was no laughter. "It is a bad, bad business when Alliance ships must sit on the ground. Skimmers may land, but only so that they will rise again. Bombards . . . they are not meant to be earthbound."

"No," said Yosinero sharply. "They are not."

"Therefore," the Line Commander maundered on, "anything that keeps us earthbound is not welcome. Not at all welcome."

"But we can't leave with the mission out," Yuen reminded him urgently. "You've said it yourself. And the flight command for Zamalah has ordered us to remain here for as long as we are on their planet."

Some vague grasp of the facts reasserted itself within the Line Commander's wandering mind. "Yes. It would be hostile for us to move from this place except to leave. It would be wrong for you to move until you are authorized to do so," he reminded Strategy Marshal Yosinero.

"Which will be when you depart, I gather," said Yosinero sourly.

"That is what I have been told," murmured Line Commander Nazaipha just before he fainted.

Yuen seized the little advantage that provided. "It is the treatment. It makes it difficult for him."

"So it must," said Yosinero as he stepped over the fallen Line Commander. "And for the rest of you, as well."

Tek smiled. "I am very good at inventory," he said; it was a relief to tell the truth. "I began in my father's business, but I can handle a city's worth of stock. Food, water, fuel, any kind of logistics, anything on the computer, payments, records, all of it." Around him Zamalah men prostrated themselves before entering the holiest of holies, the Heart of the Friday mosque.

The man looked shocked. "Everyone hates that," he said.

Tek's smile couldn't get any wider. "Allah in His Mercy has given each of us talents."

"Let me talk to some people," the man said after careful consideration. "Will you be here later?"

Tek nodded happily, prostrated himself toward the Heart, then rose and wandered out into the courtyard; he found a place to sit and leaned back under one of the orange trees, prepared to wait for Rasidov.

"This is war," Lentzer said. "The whole thing fits together too neatly. Yosinero being here, the Voice of the Hidden Imam snatching our Mromrosi, and them being too well-armed and funded. There's a rat in the works and we're going to eliminate it." The resthouse was quiet in the drowsy afternoon. "And I don't like Tek being out there by himself."

"Excuse me," the Nada Solis/2 said, "but I don't

get the connection. What does Yosinero have to do
with the Voice of the Hidden Imam and what has
that got to do with our mission?"

For the first time her habitual insolence didn't
bother him. He smiled thinly. "AIO orders are to
find out exactly what Yosinero is doing here and
bring him up on charges if possible. And I have a
little experience with Yosinero and some of the politics of the Twelve; his mentor is grooming him for a
position on that august council. Given that he's a
Grand and a politico and Strategy Marshal, and a
bungwallop, it wouldn't be to our benefit if he did
make it to the Twelve. But he has made a couple of
enemies on the way up, and some of them weren't as
easy to get rid of as me. There's another of the
Twelve, who doesn't want to see Yosinero anywhere
near the Hub again if he can help it. And that's
where we come in. Any problem with that?"

The Nada Solis, all three of them, were amazing.
Politics was not their forte. It hadn't been his, either, when he'd run across Yosinero fifteen years
before. He had made up the missed education.

"So you mean this Voice of the Hidden Imam isn't
really some fanatical fringe group at all?" Rasidov
asked, offended that Islam could be used so cal-
lously. "It's just a front for Yosinero to come into the
community and assert leadership?"

Lentzer shrugged. "It's not that simple. The Voice
of the Hidden Imam probably is composed mostly of
fringe fanatics and reformers. Like all fanatics, they're
dedicated and sincere. And gullible. But they're getting a little help from somewhere, money and supplies that make them more dangerous than they'd
normally be. People like that, without weapons and
money and safe houses, would be quickly identified
and contained. These bogos have been given a little

help—that makes them active. They're out to desta-bilize the region."

"But how does that help Yosinero?" Rasidov asked again.

Lentzer smiled tightly. "Either way he wins. He supplied the dissidents, and if they actually win, they are beholden to him. And they don't care what goes on at the Hub as long as they're free to run Zamalah as they like. If these Hidden Imamers lose, then all Yosinero has to do is find another group to manipulate. Unless we can find proof of what he's up to."

"There could be a real war," said Rasidov.

"Maybe," said Lentzer. "It's a lot more likely that things will get just a little dicey and the local govern-ment will call us in to keep the peace. Then Yosinero walks in as negotiator and comes out managing the peace."

"And making us take the blame for everything the locals don't like," the Nada Solis/1 mused. "So not only does he pick up an original Fifty-six colony for support, he slams the Petits at the same time. That's pogged."

This time Lentzer's smile was honest. "And the only way to stop him is to expose him. Hard evi-dence would be nice."

"But in the meantime it wouldn't hurt to reduce the firepower of his pet bogos," Rasidov finished the thought. "At least that way he's got a setback and we get some more time. Do you really think Tek can pull it off?"

"Who else can get inside?" Lentzer asked. "Be-sides, I've never known of an extremist group that wasn't in desperate need of a good planner and sup-plier, and Tek is that from Monday to Sunday."

"Will we have to bring him out?" the Nada Solis/2 offered, far happier than she had been an hour ago.

It felt good, Lentzer reflected. After fifteen years revenge was going to be very sweet.

The only problem was the Mromrosi. Lentzer was certain the Twelve didn't want the Emerging Planet Fairness Court to know about the skulduggery here on Zamalah, not if scandal touched the Hub. He didn't know what the criteria of the Emerging Planet Fairness Court were and he really didn't care. But he didn't want to answer for any risks the Mromrosi decided to take for himself.

Now the waiting was over; it was time for him to emerge again, Yosinero's nemesis. Lentzer rocked back on his heels. He liked the sound of nemesis.

"How do we go from here?" asked the Nada Solis/3 with undisguised eagerness.

"We can't hide what we're doing much longer," Lentzer said carefully. "Which means we have to be ready to move quickly. I'll need all three of you to look after the Mromrosi, to keep him out of trouble. We don't want anything to happen to him. Not again."

"We'll do it," the Nada Solis/3 responded.

Then he turned to Rasidov. "Gregori, can you get us back to that cave? I don't know if the beacon will work through that much rock."

The Navigator grinned wolfishly. "No problem, Group Leader."

"Then let's get it done," said Lentzer, excitement possessing him as much as Standby Hooch had for so long. "Battle fatigues. Fast kit. Here. Fifteen minutes."

There was a Grand flyer in the docking bay on the landing field above Moustar's glittering pink cliffs. Two Landing Authority guards patrolled the bays, but most of their attention was on the two merchant flyers being unloaded.

"What do you think?" Lentzer whispered to Navigator Rasidov as they gathered in the shade of the bay.

"I think we might as well get on with it," said Rasidov, and all three Nada Solis nodded in agreement.

The Mromrosi looked up at them. "I believe I could be of assistance here," he said, changing to a very odd shade of neon pink.

"How?" inquired Lentzer, with no intention of permitting the alien to be involved.

"I could distract the guards. It would cause them no harm and put me in no danger." The pink faded out to a caramel tan. Then, before Lentzer could speak, the Mromrosi hunkered down and made itself into a ball, rolling away across the sand, turning the color of the sand himself.

"Pog it all!" whispered Lentzer fiercely.

Rasidov watched him and chuckled. "I wonder what they think he is?" He was already climbing onto the upswept wing.

"Get in the flyer. We'll figure that out later," said Lentzer. "Two of you Solis stay on the ground until that fuzzball comes back." At that, he went after Rasidov, the Nada Solis/1 behind him.

The guards were shouting and pointing, but not at the Grand flyer. They were staring at the Mromrosi, who was spinning in one place like one of the legendary dervishes.

Rasidov slipped into the pilot's seat and indicated the cramped quarters behind. "Sorry it's so close. That's the Grands for you. Never enough room for a decent crew." He activated the engines.

With that, the Mromrosi bolted toward them at astonishing speed. He hurtled up the stairs and under the canopy, making a sound that Lentzer hoped was his version of laughter.

The Nada Solis/2 and /3 scrambled into the flyer, securing the Mromrosi between them.

"Let's get out of here," said Lentzer.

"Your wish is my command," said Rasidov. He brought the flyer up fast, and banked a hard starboard turn. The lurch felt good, the power vibrating subtly under the floor grate. The Grand flyer had speed in her.

So suddenly high they couldn't easily be seen from below, Rasidov did a quick overflight on Moustar. Lentzer hadn't had a real perception of just how the city was cut into the natural landscape. The deep canyons and gullies that made up the streets were irregular and striated, the result of natural water erosion. Once this had been a great river basin. Now it was dry.

Rasidov dipped sharply to show them the resthouse and the Friday mosque, close enough to each other to walk. Then he banked hard again and they were going north-northeast, out of the heavily populated sector and into a rocky crevasse deeper than any of the others.

"This is where the cave is," Rasidov announced. "I got the beacon readings on it dead straight."

But there was no break in the rose and crystal rock, no black open mouth that announced a terrorist hiding place. "Try deep sonar," the Nada Solis/3 suggested. "It's the meter on the left side of the altimeter."

Rasidov brought the flyer down low and slow, so he was deep inside a long defile.

It was not a pretty ride from down here, Lentzer thought. He knew how dangerous this kind of flying was. Those crystal cliffs, so pretty at sunset, were hazardous, their shine treacherous, their nearness frightening. Then Lentzer detected a ruffle in the side of a mountain. He chuckled. A painted screen over the mouth of the cave was all it was. Rasidov made the pass, popped out of the canyon to turn, and then dove directly for where the readings indicated the opening was.

Instinct screamed impact. Lentzer flinched. He saw the Nada solis/1 go white. And then the rock before them shredded and burned.

"That camouflage was better than most," said Rasidov with a coolness that didn't fool anyone. "Good thing I trusted these instruments."

"Are you going to be able to get us out of here?" Lentzer asked Rasidov as he began to release his protective webbing.

The Navigator gave him the standard damn-all smile that they all learned when they got their ratings, like the mythic Old Earth Masons with their secret signs. "It'd be tricky. We might need to find something else."

"Any suggestions?" Lentzer asked. He clambered onto the wing beside the Navigator, his eyes straining to adjust to the darkness.

"Something surface might not be a bad idea," said Rasidov, stretching. "They'll be looking for a flyer now."

"So they will," said Lentzer.

"Well, we're not under attack," the Nada Solis/2 observed as she led the three of them out of the flyer. "This cavern appears to be unoccupied except by us."

"Without lights, who can tell?" Rasidov asked. The only illumination came from beneath the canopy of the flyer.

"Do we use lights?" asked the Nada Solis/1. "Lights could alert the enemy."

"There are lights under the wings. That ought to be enough to let us see our way," said Lentzer, and ducked back into the flyer to switch the underside lights on.

They were alone in a chamber so large that the

light never quite made it to the walls. The rock floor was unfinished.

"This is where they held us all," the Mromrosi said. "I remember. It wasn't like a real place."

"So where is everyone?" Lentzer demanded. He fingered his stunner nervously. He hated this kind of waiting.

"There are probably more chambers beyond," the Nada Solis/1 said as if she were reading from a book. "We've got rope and phosphormarkers. I suggest we start going."

"As I recall," said the Mromrosi as he turned peacock-blue, "there are a number of tunnels and caverns beyond this place. The ones to your left are used for living quarters, the ones to the right are for supplies."

"If I had to say, I'd think we came in the back way," the Nada Solis/3 remarked. "They probably don't use this area often. We have the advantage there."

"And I'd bet that landing shook this whole cliff hard enough that they're ready to come right at us," Lentzer countered. "We're bound to have set off an alarm or two."

"In which case, we are prepared to fight," said the Nada Solis/1.

Lentzer realized they had to get out of the cavern. Remaining where they were only made it easier for the locals to find them. "Let's find some real cover."

The Mromrosi bounced up to him. "Follow me," he said. "I have been here before and I know the way."

"Are you sure?" asked the Nada Solis/3.

"Of course. Those of my species never forget. Anything." He hopped away from them. "Come."

Lentzer looked at the others and shrugged. "Why

not?" he said, and set off after the Mromrosi down a narrow tunnel.

Not far from the cavern the tunnel divided, and the left fork showed more promise. Here there were lights, widely spaced and dim; the main back tunnel swallowed up the meager illumination. Lentzer kept close to the wall, away from the light. The first door was two or three li away, and Lentzer couldn't read the Arabic script in the plate next to the lock. He motioned Rasidov on ahead.

The Navigator took a quick look and shook his head. They went on.

Something was wrong. Lentzer knew it. He could feel the wrongness in his bones. The installation had had more than enough time to respond to the flyer's invasion. Either there was no one here and they were missing the mark, or they were walking into a trap. That reminded him of booby traps, and of explosives primed to close the tunnels and trap them underground to suffocate.

They passed two more doors, each one rejected by Rasidov. The Navigator didn't risk the sound of even a whisper to tell them what the places were they passed. It was all too quiet.

And then they saw a blue door, the first that had been painted and not left gray. The Mromrosi bounded toward it, three of his eight feet pointing, and his curls glowing a luminous lime green.

There was enough noise that they could hear it, shouting and trampling. Lentzer and Rasidov pushed themselves hard against the wall. The Nada Solis took up positions, /3 on one side of the door and /1 and /2 on the other. One of them blasted the lock and kicked in the barrier.

The Nada Solis entered in proper stance, covering each other and the action in the room. Lentzer and Rasidov hung behind.

The ruckus in the cave was so overwhelming that the occupants didn't even notice at first that they were under attack.

It was an ordinary work center—extraordinary in this place—terminals and vids and chairs in modular groupings for whatever task currently took precedence. The people running around, screaming, pointing at someone quivering behind a partition, all had the look of harried bureaucrats, not the grim purpose of terrorists.

"Looks like this is their headquarters, all right," Lentzer muttered to no one in particular.

"Freeze," all three Nada Solis yelled in unison.

Heads swung around, disbelieving. The three clones spread out to cover the crowd. There were at least fifteen people there.

"You're crazy," one of them said, an older man wearing a red checked headcloth and holding a sheaf of reports in his right hand.

"We've got the guns," the Nada Solis/3 said laconically.

And then Lentzer realized that the man had been speaking to the person behind the partition and not to the Nada Solis at all. "You there. Come out!" He let Rasidov translate for him.

A head popped over the top of the partition, dark hair and wide eyes. It was Tek. He smiled broadly and waved to his teammates. Then he tossed something very small at them. Rasidov caught it with ease. It was a data capsule.

"Tek, are you all right?" Lentzer asked.

The kitchen clerk's hands appeared on the edge of the partition and he hauled himself over, away from the group that had him surrounded. The man with the headdress blinked. "I have been busy," he said, beaming at them.

"Okay," Lentzer said very slowly, giving everyone

time to realize that they were overpowered if not outnumbered. "I want to talk to whoever's in charge. Call him down here now."

The man with the reports froze. Lentzer gave him a moment to think about it. It was a moment too long.

The opposite door, the proper front door, burst open to reveal Yosinero at the head of a group of armed Grands at the ready.

Lentzer's eyes met Yosinero's. Lentzer smiled.

"So they got themselves a new hostage, huh, Yosinero? Is that your story?" Lentzer asked lightly. "You probably were expecting snow more than us."

Three Nada Solis against seven armed Grands were unfair odds. The clones reacted before their opponents realized that anything had begun. Their stunners were activated before the Grands could release their safeties.

The Zamalahi in the cave dropped to the floor, hands clapped to their heads.

The Nada Solis/2 took a running jump and landed with her feet in one of the Grands' chest, bowling him into Yosinero. Staggering, the Strategy Marshal started to run but he had been living the good life at the Hub too long; the Nada Solis was faster.

The other Nada Solis were drawing most of the fire, using chairs and office partitions and mobile glare shields to deflect the energy shots of the Grands. Rasidov laid down covering fire, and took out at least two of the defenders on stun himself.

Lentzer kept the Zamalahi pinned down. He wanted no native casualties.

The Mromrosi sat on Yosinero.

The door was open. There would be more troops coming down the tunnel. And there was no way out without a dangerous retreat.

The Nada Solis had put most of the honor guard to

sleep; they weren't even breathing hard. They formed a wedge and took the front door into the heavy-use corridor.

Lentzer followed and Rasidov brought up the rear covering Yosinero as the Mromrosi got off him.

"Please, this way," Tek said, appearing beside them and pointing in the opposite direction to the one the Nada Solis were taking.

The clones grimaced. They were obviously planning to mop up any armed terrorists or Grands they'd missed in the initial melee. But Tek was pulling them away.

Yosinero looked aghast.

Lentzer motioned to Tek with his stunner. "Take the front." He signaled the Nada Solis. "Guard the rear."

They were not pleased, but fell in as ordered.

Tek led at a walk. He seemed unaware of the danger around them.

Lentzer looked back over his shoulder. "One of you Solis come up front," he said. "Sweep the tunnel."

"Oh, I don't think we have to worry," Tek said brightly. "I sealed all the locks and changed the filtration cycle on the air conditioning. The sealed sectors are going to be short of oxygen for half an hour. Everyone there will be sleepy, I think. And we're going up to the hangar now. The Strategy Marshal's private flyer will accommodate us. It's larger than the flyer you came in."

Yosinero swore. "You can stop the charade now," Yosinero said to Tek, his voice hard. "And you." He rounded on Lentzer. "Let me go and I won't have your pension along with your career."

"Actually," said Lentzer, relishing the moment, "I think it's the other way around. This time *I* will have *your* career."

\* \* \*

Their arrival at *Kinderkinyo* was almost absurd: a Grand Harriers Marshal's flyer coming to land between the Broadswords and Bombards, the mission team disembarking, the Mromrosi, a gaudy shade of rose, leading the way.

"What in pogging—" began Executive Officer Yuen as Lentzer requested permission to come aboard.

"Don't tell the Line Commander just yet," Lentzer recommended in high good humor. "He might decide to take some action."

An override came from the nearest Bombard. "For what reason are you escorting our Strategy Marshal?"

"Because we caught him with his hand in the goodies," said Lentzer.

There was a hesitation from the Bombard, then the hailer blared, "This ought to be referred to the Hub."

"Oh, it will be," said Lentzer in firm satisfaction. "Yuen, will you please let us aboard, before the Strategy Marshal tries something very stupid?"

The Senior Bunter arrived at the gangway before Executive Officer Yuen. It looked at Yosinero and said, "How pleasant to see you back here again, Strategy Marshal."

"Yes, isn't it?" Lentzer answered for him.

"No, Lentzer, you're wrong," Yosinero said very coolly. In the flight back to the Alliance ships, he had been very thoughtful. "I admit, it won't look wonderful for us, you rescuing me from the Voice of the Hidden Imam. But you have nothing on me at all. Only my word against yours. And who do you think the Twelve or anyone at the Hub is going to believe, you or me? The washed-up drunk, or someone whose name has already been put before the Twelve for consideration?"

The Mromrosi rocked from side to side. "They would believe me."

Yosinero laughed. It was a very ugly sound. "Your word? Against any human?"

"The Emerging Planet Fairness Court is believed," said the Mromrosi very seriously.

"There's nothing I can't explain," Yosinero said, straightening his back and looking at Yuen.

"I do not think so," Tek said happily. "Gregori, do you have the capsule I gave you? Why don't you put it on the vids for the Grands?"

Rasidov inserted the capsule and keyed the main screen. It looked incomprehensible to Lentzer, all those columns of numbers and dates, account codes, and trade receipts.

Yosinero saw the display and lunged at Tek. The Nada Solis/2 stopped him with a well-placed kick to the stomach. She didn't even leave her seat to deliver it. Yosinero collapsed on the deck like a flat balloon.

"No doubt the Fleet Commodore will find this interesting," said the Mromrosi, all beige and soft-spoken.

Tek smiled pleasantly. "It is the record of Marshal Yosinero's payments to the Voice of the Hidden Imam. There were some other interesting things there, too, so I just copied it all. Embezzlement from the Twelve, shifting funds, investing and skimming the interest, all there. Including the slave trade." At that his face changed. "Slave trade," he repeated. "On six planets. Two of them in the Alliance."

"A clerk. A damned Quartermaster's clerk," Yosinero repeated, dazed. "You're nobody. You couldn't have."

"Oh, yes, it was hidden very well," Tek said amiably. "But then, the Quartermaster's Internal Investigation Accounting Division specializes in exactly this kind of trouble. I admit that I am very junior in that department, but I suppose the Division has faith in me."

"A pogging junior Inspector-General," said Lentzer in false commiseration. "Ain't it disappointing?" His grin belied his words.

Jaanu Lentzer's retirement dinner was Full Dress One, Invitation Only. Three members of the Twelve showed up, along with several *Semper* Fleet Masters, three Mromrosi and two Wammgalloz from the Emerging Planet Fairness Court.

The dinner had been catered by the Quartermasters, of course, but this was not the usual watch-and-handshake meal. This dinner started with Xiaoqing dumpling-and-egg-flower noodle soup, had courses of lamb and fish and rice, and ended with a lavish display of Hartzheim tortes. Even the most exclusive caterer in the Hub couldn't readily match the glories of the dinner.

The speakers were lavish in their praise, all mentioning how Jaanu Lentzer had been planning to retire to a farm on Hartzheim seventeen years earlier, and had only been convinced to stay on until the situation between the Grands and Petits and the Twelve had stabilized. That was the official version, along with the assumption that Lentzer had been working for the Twelve ever since his first clash with Yosinero.

Jaanu Lentzer listened to the speeches and tried not to be too cynical. He saw their faces at the table, Rasidov now wearing the stars of a Katana Line Commander, the Nada Solis actually behaving with some manners, M'kaba shaking her fashionably coiffed head and waving away an inquiry.

The Mromrosi was at the podium now—standing on it, in fact. His curls were a glossy chestnut color. "Let me say that was a privilege to serve with Group Leader—now Sub-Marshal—Lentzer on the *Kinder-*

*kinyo*. I learned a great deal thanks to Lentzer. I will miss him now that he is retiring from the Petits."

There was applause that brought Lentzer back to the moment at hand. Someone introduced him. He rose and went to the podium. "I really don't know what to say," he began. "I'm grateful to all of you for being here, and I want to thank each and every one of you for coming."

"So where do you plan to go first as a private citizen?" M'kaba asked, smiling. "Standby?"

"Standby," Lentzer echoed. "Because of Standby Hooch, you mean? No, I don't think so. But not Hartzheim, either." He looked over the gathering and decided that just this once he would tell them the truth. "I'm starting my own firm. One dedicated to vetting merchants. So situations like this one won't have as easy a time in future." He squared his shoulders, feeling less like a fool with every passing second. "This isn't for the Alliance, it's for my own peace of mind."

He couldn't figure out why they all applauded.

# FRED SABERHAGEN

Fred Saberhagen needs very little introduction these days. His most famous creations—the awesome Berserkers—are known to SF readers around the world. He's reached the bestseller lists several times, most recently with his "Book of Swords" series, and his novels span the territory from hard science fiction to high fantasy. Quite understandably, Saberhagen's been labeled one of the best writers in the business.

These fine volumes by Saberhagen are available from Baen Books:

## PYRAMIDS
A fascinating new twist on the time-travel novel, introducing a great new series hero: Pilgrim, the Flying Dutchman of Time, whose only hope for returning home lies in subtly altering the history of our own timeline to more closely reflect his own. Learn why the curse of the Pharaoh Khufu (builder of the Great Pyramid) had a special reality, in *Pyramids*. "Saberhagen's light, imaginative and enjoyable adventures speed along twisting paths to a climax that is even more surprising than the rest of the book."

—*Publishers Weekly*

## AFTER THE FACT
This is the second novel featuring the great new series hero, Pilgrim—the Lost Traveller adrift in time and dimensionality. His current project: to rescue Abraham Lincoln from assassination, AFTER THE FACT!

## THE FRANKENSTEIN PAPERS
At last—the truth about a sinister Dr. Frankenstein and his monster with a heart of gold, based on a history written by the monster himself! Find out what happened when the mad Doctor brought his creation to life, and why the monster has no scars.

## THE EMPIRE OF THE EAST
A masterful blend of high technology and high sorcery; a world where magic rules—and science struggles to live again! "Ranks favorably with Tolkien. Exceptional in sheer unbridled zest and imaginative sweep!—*School Library Journal* "*Empire of the East* is one of the best science fiction fantasy epics—Saberhagen can be justly proud. Highly recommended."
—*Science Fiction Chronicle*

## THE BLACK THRONE with Roger Zelazny
Two masters of SF collaborate on a masterpiece of fantasy: As children they met and built sand castles on a beach out of space and time: Edgar Perry, little Annie, and Edgar Allan Poe. . . . Fifteen years later Edgar Perry has grown to manhood—and as the result of a trip through a maelstrom, he's leading a much more active life. Perry will learn to thrive in the dark, romantic world he's landed in, where lead can be transmuted to gold, ravens can speak, orangutans can commit murder, and beautiful women are easy to come by. But his alter ego, Edgar Allan, is stranded in a strange and unfriendly world where he can only write about the wonderful and mysterious reality he has lost forever. . . .

## THE GOLDEN PEOPLE
Genetically perfect, super-human children are created by a dedicated scientist for the betterment of Mankind. As the children mature, however, they begin to wonder if Man *should* survive. . . .

## LOVE CONQUERS ALL

In a future where childbirth is outlawed and promiscuity required, one woman dares fight the system for the right to bear children.

## OCTAGON

Players scattered across the continent are engaged in a game called "Starweb." Each player has certain attributes, and can ally with or attack any of the others. But one player seems to have confused the reality of the world: a player with the attributes of machinelike precision and mechanical ruthlessness. His name is Octagon, and he's out for blood.

---

# WINNER OF THE PROMETHEUS AWARD

**VERNOR VINGE**

## Technology's Prophet

*"Vinge brings new vitality to an old way of telling a science fiction story, showing the ability to create substantial works in the process."*
—Dan Chow, *Locus*

*"Every once in a while, a science fiction story appears with an idea that strikes close to the heart of a particular subject. It just feels right, like Arthur C. Clarke's weather satellites. Such a story is Vernor Vinge's short novel, TRUE NAMES."* —Commodore *Power/Play*

# JOHN DALMAS

## He's done it all!

*John Dalmas has just about done it all—parachute infantryman, army medic, stevedore, merchant seaman, logger, smokejumper, administrative forester, farm worker, creamery worker, technical writer, free-lance editor—and his experience is reflected in his writing. His marvelous sense of nature and wilderness combined with his high-tech world view involves the reader with his very real characters. For lovers of fast-paced action-adventures!*

### THE REGIMENT
The planet Tyss is so poor that it has only one resource: its fighting men. Each year three regiments are sent forth into the galaxy. And once a regiment is constituted, it never recruits again: as casualties mount the regiment becomes a battalion . . . a company . . . a platoon . . . a squad . . . and then there are none. But after the last man of *this* regiment has flung himself into battle, the Federation of Worlds will never be the same!

### THE WHITE REGIMENT
All the Confederation of Worlds wanted was a little peace. So they applied their personnel selection technology to war and picked the greatest potential warriors out of their planets-wide database of psych profiles. And they hired the finest mercenaries in the galaxy to train the first test regiment—they hired the legendary black warriors of Tyss to create the first ever White Regiment.

### THE KALIF'S WAR
The White Regiment had driven back the soldiers of the Kharganik empire, but the Kalif was certain that

he could succeed in bringing the true faith of the Prophet of Kargh to the Confederation—even if he had to bombard the infidels' planets with nuclear weapons to do it! But first he would have to thwart a conspiracy in his own ranks that was planning to replace him with a more tractable figurehead ...

## FANGLITH
Fanglith was a near-mythical world to which criminals and misfits had been exiled long ago. The planet becomes all too real to Larn and Deneen when they track their parents there, and find themselves in the middle of the Age of Chivalry on a world that will one day be known as Earth.

## RETURN TO FANGLITH
The oppressive Empire of Human Worlds, temporarily filed in *Fanglith*, has struck back and resubjugated its colony planets. Larn and Deneen must again flee their home. Their final object is to reach a rebel base—but the first stop is Fanglith!

## THE LIZARD WAR
A thousand years after World War III and Earth lies supine beneath the heel of a gang of alien sociopaths who like to torture whole populations for sport. But while the 16th century level of technology the aliens found was relatively easy to squelch, the mystic warrior sects that had evolved in the meantime weren't. . . .

## THE LANTERN OF GOD
They were pleasure droids, designed for maximum esthetic sensibility and appeal, abandoned on a deserted planet after catastrophic systems failure on their transport ship. After 2000 years undisturbed, "real" humans arrive on the scene—and 2000 thousand years of droid freedom is about to come to a sharp and bloody end.

## THE REALITY MATRIX

Is the existence we call life on Earth for real, or is it a game? Might Earth be an artificial construct designed by a group of higher beings? Is everything an illusion? Everything is—except the Reality Matrix. And what if self-appointed "Lords of Chaos" place a chaos generator in the matrix, just to see what will happen? Answer: The slow destruction of our world.

## THE GENERAL'S PRESIDENT

The stock market crash of 1994 makes Black Monday of 1929 look like a minor market adjustment—and the fabric of society is torn beyond repair. The Vice President resigns under a cloud of scandal—and when the military hints that they may let the lynch mobs through anyway, the President resigns as well. So the Generals get to pick a President. But the man they choose turns out to be more of a leader than they bargained for. . . .